# The
# CABLE DENNING MYSTERY SERIES

by
## James P. Alsphert

**James P. Alsphert**
**presents**

# The
# Black Widow
# Murders

## A
## Cable Denning
## Mystery

## BOOK
## 19

# CONTENTS

# PROLOGUE

The hot breath of the behemoth pursuing me was at my neck. I was desperate, running from it toward the sea. It lunged at me with unbridled ferocity, attempting to capture me in its giant jaws, but I always managed to stay just a few inches ahead of that fatal moment. I could feel my lungs all but burst as I lunged toward the edge of the cliff. I couldn't look behind to see the horror of my enemy without losing distance so I reached the edge without further thought and threw myself over to what I hoped was the roiling sea below, fraught with jagged rocks and giant waves thundering upon them. But then I found myself falling in slow motion and soothing angelic voices began to sing all around, filling my whole being...like angels comforting me.

Some things are so terrible that we separate them from anything else we hold in our consciousness. The voice I heard next was one of these. It was the deep, dark sound of *Cronus-Gor*. "Tell me, Denning...why do I keep you alive?"

"I dunno, Gor, why do you?" I was wiping my lip where one of his goons had hit me earlier while shoving me into a car for this audience. I didn't go peaceably, so I must've been conked out cold because I didn't recall how I got into the Great Hall of the *Oculus Pyramis Mandatum* headquarters.

"Perhaps it is because you are the last of your kind...and...and I wish to retain your...*services*...so I do not see you dying...anytime soon..."

"Ya don't eh? That's too bad. Sometimes I think it'd be worth getting off this planet just to know you wouldn't be breathing down my neck somewhere out there in that morass."

"By the way, Denning, Saturnalia and Cassiopeia send their regards." Saturnalia was Cronus-Gor's fetching goddess-wife with whom I had a very brief but satisfying affair some years before, which unfortunately didn't turn out well for her. And later on, her daughter Cassiopeia and I got together, despite my resistance—the result of that was stranger than fiction. They were from the planet Saturn originally, but ol' Gor boy had stolen Saturnalia away from her home kingdom, imprisoned her and eventually 'tamed ' her into marrying him and they had eight children, one of whom was Cassiopeia. Cronus-Gor's jealousy was such that he had consumed seven of those children—except for the last one—Cassiopeia. Eventually they were all disgorged from his belly and went on to live their lives as royal heirs. He continued. "I have a task for you to...to perform..."

No one ever saw Cronus-Gor. He was just a huge force that knew and saw everything. His voice quaked the building most of the time he spoke—and forget it when he was angered! I felt like an insignificant mortal dot looking up into an invisible face. Except I had chutzpah, so I faced the giant god with very little reticence. After all, if I considered my life over except for the last rites, what did I have to lose? Besides, he already said I wouldn't be dying any time soon. "A task for me to perform, eh? Who do you think I am—a trained seal?" I quaffed.

2

He laughed a giant laugh and the pillars in the great hall shook. "You dare to jest in my presence? But I do enjoy your 'moxie', as some might say. But...to business...I find it necessary to plant a few *seeds of destruction*—with your help, of course."

"Oh, yeah, ain't that nice? So what else do you do besides plant 'seeds', Gor—have Sunday picnics on some nice green grass at the zoo with your family?"

He ignored me. "I must create some mid-Eastern tension, or as they say in Arabia, an *al-nakba*—a catastrophe. You see, Israel is coming to life again—and I must crush it. It is run by our enemies—the *Edomites*—the descendants of Esau who now are part reptilian—they will wish to conquer and rule the earth. I must prevent this. *Only I will rule the earth!*" he bellowed and the hall shook again. Then his voice calmed. "These are the white races, Denning, from which you are descended. Some were pure before the *Alpha Draconians* invaded and mixed the genes so they would look like you. Some remain pure, but we know the difference, don't we, Denning?"

"Oh? Do wc? I'm not sure. It's been said that *I'm* a half-breed. So how do I know?"

"You are a mixture of early Edomite and *Sens Parafactor*, not reptilian. Haven't you wished to gain power, control humans and steal all the money from the ordinary human population?"

"Not lately...but it has occurred to me," I jested.

Again he ignored me. "I wish to destroy the new Draconians' phony country, Israel. I shall send Egypt, Lebanon, Syria, Iraq and Saudi Arabia against

3

them. But I must have Russia and China to do this with. Russia will dominate until I decide that the next century will belong to China—until it fails. If I do not do this, the Edomites in the United States will finance the state of Israel and they will be given power in the mid-East. This must not happen. I...must rule..."

"Well, as I see it, Gor, it's just one ambitious snake wanting to supplant another ambitious snake—what the hell's the difference?"

"*I...shall...rule...!!!*" he bellowed and the entire building vibrated. Then he calmed again. "No one shall have station above me, no one shall be greater than I am great...no lizard people have my know-how and history, my genius for ruling planets and populations!"

"Yeah? Well, you didn't do so hot with Hestia, your daughter!" Hestia was a warrior-god offspring of Gor's who waged war on him for quite a while out in the universe somewhere until he finally captured her and imprisoned her somewhere in some dimension. But that's another story.

"Silence!" he roared. "You *shall* assist me, Denning. And that is all to our conversation..."

"Just how shall I do this thing, your high asshole-ee-ness?"

He ignored my insult because for now he needed me. "You will detonate my newest super-weapon, the *Hydrogen bomb* and blow up that part of the mid-east."

"Won't that kill a lot of innocents? What about radiation, you know, atomic fallout and the like?"

"Some casualties cannot be helped...that...is war..."

"Well, get some other boy, Gor. I ain't gonna be responsible for blowing up tens of thousands of people because you wanna get rid of the Edomites and rule the world yourself—no siree, not this boy! Oh, and has anyone thought about the earth during this destructive period of yours? Why destroy the nest that nurtures?"

"You *will* do this, Denning. Else I shall kill your pretty little secretary, your son, your daughter and that strange woman who was tutored by the Tall Ones. Am I making myself...clear?"

I took a deep breath. I was defeated before I had begun. At that moment I loved Ida Latney and wanted her back, even if she was with some other bloke at the moment. "I will not...I repeat...will *not* pull the trigger to kill tens of thousands of people. Do I make *my*self clear, Gor?"

"You will be a compliant cog in the wheel. You shall act as my personal emissary to deliver what I consider to be essential diplomacy in carrying out my orders... go now, Denning, I am bored of you!"

I left with a heavy heart. How much of this pressure can a guy take? In the past Cronus-Gor was a mixed blessing. He'd helped me out and saved my butt a few times, and I was good to him in the ways I could be. I even helped myself to his voluptuous wife and charming, beautiful daughter when they became earthbound for a while some years back. I just wonder if immortals hold things like that against the perpetrator forever? After all, they have forever to think about it. So, I wouldn't be surprised if the son-of-a-bitch ordered up my execution one day. As long as he needed me, though—or thought he needed me, I suppose I was safe enough to get on with my life. I wondered in just what form my "essential diplomacy" would come? I knew what I would do and what I wouldn't. I think I made it clear to Gor—and to myself.

# Chapter 1

## THE MAGIC PHONOGRAPH

It was Wednesday, July 23, 1947. The afternoon was a muggy Los Angeles. I decided to walk over to Highland to buy today's paper from a newsboy named Tommy. Some days he delivered to my office after school, but not today. I liked Tommy. He was poor. He reminded me of me when I was his age. President Truman had signed the National Security Act. The Central Intelligence Administration was also set up. Buzz around town was that it was a highly secretive organization to keep its eye even on the F.B.I.! What in the hell was the world coming to!

Tommy's youthful voice brought me back to what was *real.* "Hiya, Mr. Denning, are you carrying your gun today?" Tommy asked me. He was about twelve, average in height. He had a mop of brownish red hair, thin lips and blue eyes.

"Nope...not today, Tommy—left it at the office."

"But what if you meet a robber or a gangster or something?"

"Well, remember now, Tommy, I'm not a cop anymore—just a pavement-pounding private eye."

"That's what I wanna be—I mean, when I'm bigger," he said, looking up at me admiringly. "Do you think I'll ever grow to be as tall as you? Nobody in my family's very tall." He had a metal coin changer on his belt and he handed out a couple of papers and gave change. "Heck, even my Dad isn't very tall."

"I don't even know your last name now, do I?" I inquired.

"*Knockers*—Tommy Knockers. Well, I wasn't born with that. I hate my first two names."

"And...what are they?"

"*Thomas Malcolm Knockers*—that was my grandfather's name."

I glanced at the headlines. "That ain't so bad—what did your grandfather do?"

"Oh, he was Irish, he was—a coal miner. My Mom told me that *Tommy Knockers* is the returned ghosts of dead coal miners—and you'd better be liked by them, 'cause they can cause ya a lotta trouble if they don't like ya."

"Did you know your grandpa?"

"He was really old—and he had no teeth, a little old shriveled man. Mom says my eyes look like his. But he died a long time ago. Working in the Northumberland mines in England, plumb wore him out, she said." He sold a few more papers as I stood at the corner of Franklin and Highland reading the headlines. "NINE UNIDENTIFIED DISCS IN THE SKY flying in formation, seemed to maneuver in unison and right themselves again at exactly the same instant..." It was a little filler article at the bottom right of the corner of the L.A. Times, that place where thumb and fingers cover it up nicely when you're turning the page. But it was interesting, nonetheless. "On or about June 27th of this year, a train engineer, one Charles Kastl of Joliet, Illinois, saw a display that made him feel incredulous that what he was looking at could possibly be real." The United Press article went on a little, but why read it? I *know* they're out there.

I handed Tommy a dollar. "I gotta go, kid, but remember, always do what is best for you—no matter what others say or do—got it?"

He eyed the dollar, took it and thanked me. "Yeah, but what if I'm unhappy and I want a different life?"

"Then do it," I insisted.

"You mean run away from home? But where would I live then?"

What the hell was I to say? I couldn't even communicate with my *own* son very well. "Well, ya can't be too hasty about things like that. Ya gotta think them through—you know, have an alternate plan or something."

"Al—alternate? What does that mean?"

"Something to back ya up if the original plan doesn't work, buddy."

"Oh...maybe I could come stay with you and you'd teach me how to be an undercover cop, huh? Rat-a-tat-tat!" he declaimed enthusiastically, shooting the air full of holes.

"Well, we can talk it about it another day, Tommy. Take care of yourself—and don't take any wooden nickels..."

"Oh, you! That's what you always say! I can sure tell a shiny silver nickel from a piece of wood—I'm not a dummy, Mr. Denning. Bye." He watched after me longingly as I walked away. I kind of felt sorry for the kid. Maybe he was a ship heading for a different port of call than most young boys his age. Who knows?

It was late afternoon and Ida and I were collaborating on a case when the phone rang. I let Ida get it when she was here because it sounded so much more professional when a very feminine voice answered. "Cable Denning's office," she purred. Ida seemed happy the past few days. Maybe it was the new boyfriend. Maybe it was because she'd spent a lot more time with me. Who knows what dames think? She told me a *Professor Theodore Gossman* was on the phone.

"Yeah, Cable Denning here."

"Mr. Denning, I'm Dr. Gossman, sir. I have heard of your extra-ordinary sleuthing abilities and I am in need of such a man, rather immediately, I fear."

"Pleased to meet you Mr. Gossman. Who referred me, if you don't mind? I always like to know my benefactors."

"I'm sorry to say I am not privy to extend that information to you, sir. But be assured it came from most reliable sources."

"I see. Okay...so what's your story, Mr. Gossman? Everyone has a story, ya know. Where are you located?"

"In San Francisco."

"Oh...well, I ordinarily don't travel that far on a case. Don't you have some local P.I.'s that'll do the job? What about Sam Spade? He comes from your neck of the woods..." Of course I was putting him on. Sam Spade was a fictional San Francisco detective created by a writer named Dashiell Hammett. Bogart made a classic movie of it in 1941 with Peter Lorre, Elisha Cook, Jr. and Sidney Greenstreet. I didn't care for the babe, Mary Astor—I thought she was kinda washed out...but maybe she was a good actress and that was her take on the character. Who knows?

"Sam who? I'm afraid I'm out of touch with local detectives, Mr. Denning. I will make it more than worth your while. I'm asking for one full day of your undivided attention, for which I will pay you $2500 plus expenses. That's for gas, food and lodging and transport here and back. The catch is you'll have to come this weekend...be at my institute no later than noon on Saturday the 26th. Would you be able to do that?"

"Just a minute, Dr. Gossman," I said, putting my hand over the mouthpiece. "Ida...would you be interested in a weekend trip with me to San Francisco, all expenses paid?" Her eyes brightened and she nodded her head up and down. "Yes, Mr. Gossman—with that agreed upon price in mind, I will arrive in San Francisco on Friday night and be at your door no later than noon on the 26th. How's that sound?"

"Delightful, Mr. Denning! But let me be more precise...no earlier nor later than 12:00 noon. I am thankful and most enthusiastic to meet you, sir! Oh—and one request—please tell no one where you are going or who you are going to meet—do you understand me? Or I will be forced to terminate our agreement."

"Not even my secretary? It might be necessary to let her know—"

"—no, sir...no one. I will see you on the 26th, noon, punctually. 2222 Broadway, San Francisco. Thank you, Mr. Denning." Then he hung up. That was odd, it almost sounded as if he were pissed at me for some unknown reason.

I checked out Ida. Those periwinkle eyes of her swelled with joy and I knew in that instant she still loved me a lot. "Uh...I know I asked you and you said yes, but, uh, but Gossman told me to tell no one—and what about your boyfriend? Are you gonna tell him where you're goin' and with whom?"

"Do you want me to go with you or not? I'm over twenty-one, or haven't you noticed lately?"

"Yeah, of course...otherwise I wouldn't have asked you."

"Then please don't ask me any more questions about my boyfriend, okay?"

"Okay...I guess. I just don't want him comin' back and sluggin' me in the face for taking you with me."

"Don't worry, he won't." She came closer to me and put down her steno pad. "Do you truly want me with you, Cable? Why did you ask me, really? I kind of have to know..."

"Because I've missed you, babe, and because I want you sitting next to me for a few hundred miles and I wanna hear your bubbly feminine voice and feel—feel—well, just have a good time with you."

"Feel what, Cable?" she egged me on.

"Well, you know...feel someone steady in my life, someone I care about and who's dependable. And...and I've missed some other things, too."

She smiled a naughty smile. "You have? Do you mind naming names or do I have to guess?" she tittered.

"Uh...well, I miss you—you *touching* me...and putting your nose at the nape of my neck...and then maybe kissing me a little..."

She goaded me on. "Anything else you can think of?"

"Yeah...when we're in the dark and you reach for me and I can barely see you pull your skirt down, and take off your blouse and then in nothing but your bra and panties come over and draw me to you, take your hand and grab my manhood—and tell me you want me...that...that's what 'anything else' could mean, I guess..."

She blushed, took a deep breath and brought her lips close to mine. "You mean...like this?" And she kissed me wet and deep. "Oh, Cable!" she cried out under her breath. "I've missed you so!" I took Ida Latney into my arms and held her tight as I reached between her legs. "Oh! Not now, Cable—I'm—I'm on the tail end of my monthly...I hope by Saturday I'll be...be okay to...be there for you," she amended.

I took a big breath. "Yeah—me, too, babe!" Well, that cooled that hot passion and the swelling in my pants! Hell, I was ready to take her into my bedroom and begin that ancient ritual that the two of us did so well. What was the turn-on with Ida? One thing was that no one would suspect a quiet, reserved young woman would be so sensual and transform into one of best babes I ever had between the sheets.

As I had imagined, Ida was the perfect traveling companion. We left Los Angeles early Friday morning and took Highway One along one of the most spectacular coast routes in the world, so I thought. After we left San Simeon and passed the old Piedra Blancas lighthouse—where once upon a time I had a harrowing adventure, the road began to ascend until we drove along the cliffs high above the Pacific Ocean. The view was spectacular as the fog cleared and then returned in bands of warm and cool. Almost no one else was on the road, so we traveled in relative peace and stopped off when we wanted to. Along the way we stopped at a magnificent bridge that crossed over a huge gorge. It was called the *Bixby Creek* bridge and Ida and I parked and walked out onto it. Over 300' ft. below the little creek trickled into the Pacific and fog swirled in and out below us, even though the sun lit up our faces. I felt free and happy with Ida on that Friday. I took her by the shoulders and kiddingly bent her over the precipice. She yelped and shuddered, but she trusted me. I hated heights, so we soon found a trail at the northern end of the bridge and walked down to the creek. Clumps of bushes and high brush covered the hillsides. A yucca plant stuck out of some rocks above us. We bent over and took a drink from the cool waters that bubbled by. I stretched out next to the creek looking up at the blue, clear sky. Ida bent down beside me. "Oh, Cable, I'm so happy today— being here, being with you—it's like nothing else ever existed before today."

I smiled into Ida's periwinkle eyes. "Yeah, babe, you're right. It's like it's a brand new beginning, eh?"

She kissed me gently on the lips and I sighed. "Cable...do you want to know something special—or at least special for me?"

"Yeah, what is it?"

"I'm not wearing a brassiere or any panties. Just my plain little ol' yellow dress." I took her into my arms and pressed her wonderful young body to mine. I lowered her to the grass. We rolled over until we were under this huge old bush. I reached my hand up Ida's dress and grabbed her wonderful, warm throbbing mound. She let out with a sigh and grabbed my manhood with her hand. Soon I'd lifted her dress and she sat on top of me as my male member slid into that swollen, wonderful wet womanhood of hers. We both climaxed within five minutes and collapsed into each other's arms. Damn but that felt great! Finally she spoke. "I—I don't want anyone else, Cable. I haven't even gone to bed with Ron because—because I would think of *you* whenever he began to kiss or touch me."

"I—I didn't know that, Ida," I whispered into her ear as I licked it. She got all excited again, so I put her on her back and spread her legs and licked her marvelous pussy until she came again from my tongue and fingers alone! Now, that was a woman after my own heart! And maybe that was the problem. Why did I resist? How complicated humans are that we should deny ourselves and someone else a potential happiness together. Without all the trappings of Los Angeles and the office and the shit of

15

everyday business, we were free together and brand new as lovers, as friends—as two people who simply enjoyed being together.

## The Mysterious World of Theodore Gossman

At five minutes to twelve on Saturday the 26th of July I stood at the huge arched door of the *School of the Sacred Heart*. It was a large old mansion located on Broadway near downtown San Francisco. One of the doors stood open and I walked in. I spotted a sign marked *Singing Arts Institute*. A svelte older butler-type approached me. I told him who I was and he led me to a massive room. I'd left Ida at our hotel to stroll around the nearby Union Square and go window-shopping for a couple of hours. My wait was brief in the large high-ceilinged room. I could hear operatic voices singing somewhere. I guess the place had been converted. Soon a rotund man in a wheelchair appeared from a corridor. "Built in 1912 after the earthquake by James Leary Flood for his wife Maud. She took their children and left San Francisco because of the earthquake and fire that took their previous home on Nob Hill. He promised that he would build her another that would be safe from harm...a mansion of marble on a hill of granite. This is that building. He was the son of a strike-it-rich tycoon and adventurer, one James Clair Flood. It took three years to build. When James L. died, his family lived there until the late 1930s, when his wife donated it to this order of the Catholic Church and it has since been School of the Sacred Heart. I have—

well, we have...an amicable agreement for me to use some of the rooms on the weekends for my institute...you saw the sign when you arrived." He gestured to the entrance as he approached me, wheeling his way until he extended his hand. "Welcome, Mr. Denning, and thank you for being punctual. I'm Theodore Gossman. I trust your journey was a safe one? We're off to a good start, I'd say." He had penetrating blue eyes and speckled grey hair that had peeled back on his forehead until he was all but bald except at the sides. I figured him to be in his mid-fifties or so.

"Good to meet you, Mr. Gossman—or is it doctor?"

"Either, either...my boy, but come, you must have a short lunch with me on the patio." He wheeled ahead and we went out onto a gorgeous plaza with lots of potted large plants and a table set for two. He negotiated himself into position and I sat opposite him.

"I enjoy the singing. You run a singing school here?"

"Yes, a mixed blessing I inherited from my family lineage. I am a professor of voice. I was a tenor many years ago. Who can live in this world and not be elevated by the likes of Caruso, Gigli, Bjoerling and that handful of the 'chosen', who have thrilled us through the years?"

"I wish I could share your sentiment, Mr. Gossman, but I don't know those guys—singers, I suppose. Of course, we've all heard of Caruso, but I never heard of the other two."

"A pity, Mr. Denning—like Rosa Ponselle in her prime, these men are divos of transcendental majesty." The butler-type came out and served us a marvelous soup with a small salad on the side. He was also pouring a wonderful Chardonnay. Not much of a wine drinker, I sampled it but preferred my English gin. "Now, we must get down to it, since we have only this hour, as we agreed." He fidgeted with his cloth napkin. "What...what do you know of women, Mr. Denning? You are a handsome man. I'm certain you have attracted many a fair damsel to enjoy your favors...am I right?"

"Oh, I guess you could say a few. But that doesn't answer your first question—what do I know about them? If ya ask me, I think they're mostly mysterious and elusive—except maybe once in a while, when the real thing happens along. Then you might say it's an even playing field."

He ruminated. "Hmmm...yes...even playing field. Well put, sir. You mentioned on the phone, everyone has a story. Well, here's my story. Quite a few years ago I became obsessed with a magnificently beautiful young woman. She was a dream come true for me. She had fine breeding, carried herself well, was intelligent—and even sang! Not opera, mind you, but the popular music of the day. Some of it I could tolerate before I met her. But the way she sang, she made an art form out of Tin Pan Alley music."

Sounded like a gal after my own heart. "I see...yeah, I'm a big fan of that music myself—and some of the babes who spread the good word with those lilting melodies."

"Yes, indeed. I forced myself upon the poor woman. I trained her and then married her. I was thirty-five, she was barely eighteen. I suppose I knew in my heart it was a dream, a fantasy, as my lust knew no bounds and I had to have her. She had movie star looks, was very bright and possessed a Champagne appetite. But it was doomed, as are so many marriages with such an age discrepancy. Ten years ago my angel took flight, flew the coop, as they say, took up with some tenor named Mario something or other. She cut off all communication with me. She never gave an explanation. She simply disappeared. She fled without divorcing me and has since become a bigamist. How many identities must she have that have illegally clouded her truth from society? Now I must legally undo what I have done, find her and sever all ties. I have cause to tell you she is in the Los Angeles area. But I also heard through my sources, that in the ten years she's been gone, she's sailed through *four husbands, all of whom have died* and she's working on her fifth as we speak!"

That sounded a bit odd to me. Who the hell was this woman—a female Bluebeard? "So, you want me to find her, serve her some papers and keep you advised—"

"—she's a *black widow*, Denning, don't you see?! She's become rich after mating with these gentlemen—and I suspect in some manner or other, disposed of them through—dare I say it?—a nefarious and murderous act of some kind!"

19

"Whoa Now! We don't know that, Mr. Gossman. How old were the deceased gentlemen in question?"

"Oh, of course I don't know for certain, but I was told they were considerably older than Evelyn. That's her game, I suspect. Her name was *Evelyn Nesbitt* before I married her. I hear she went through several aliases in her pursuit of singing in those dark, dingy nightclubs of Los Angeles. She liked the names of fictional literary characters, *Anne Shirley* from *Green Gables, Lucie Manette* from Dickens' *Tale of Two Cities*, and so on."

"So, if I may ask, Mr. Gossman, how old would you say the former Evelyn Gossman is in 1947?"

"Well, I'm fifty-six and seventeen years older than she is."

"So that'd make her around 40, then. Isn't that a bit late to be pursuing a singing career?"

"Oh, but you don't know Evelyn. She's forever young, you know the type. I'm sure most men have no idea of how old she is. My, it is hard to believe, is it not? She was just eighteen...never been kissed..."

"Except by you..."

He seemed entranced. "Yes...except by me..." Then he snapped out of it. "So you see your task, Mr. Denning. I would appreciate it if you gave this case top priority, as I wish to wrap up my affairs promptly and get on with my life here at the institute. I am willing to pay for that exclusive privilege. Name your price, sir..."

I thought for a minute. Things were a bit slow since Ida and I were rebuilding our client base as a result of my being gone so long the first half of 1947.

"You're paying me handsomely already, Mr. Gossman. I'd say another $2500 should—should, uh, wrap up the case."

"Done! Splendid! I enjoy a man of action." He took out an envelope from his breast pocket and put it on the table. "Here's your first half. I will deliver the rest when Evelyn has been served the papers—and oh, one other thing. I must be reassured that she did not commit a crime regarding the deaths of four husbands within the past ten years and that I in no way shall be regarded without impunity."

"How can I guarantee that? Are you afraid for your own skin? Is that it? Hell, Gossman, it could take months to track all that information down, especially if your ex-wife is the killer you suggest she might be."

"Did I intimate that?" His face paled. "Oh, dear, just the thought of it brings chills up and down my spine—like someone walking over your grave, as my mother used to say. To think that lovely woman could possibly be a murderess—"

"—we don't know that, Mr. Gossman. Suppose I find that out. But it might take me longer and cost you more."

"Money is no subject of concern, Mr. Denning. Please, I ask you—just do it and free my tortured soul of this—this terrible tangled web I've created for myself. Oh, our early lusts...how they pursue us!"

"Yes...so it seems, Mr. Gossman." I finished my soup and salad quietly as Gossman drank a special beverage of some kind. He was a bit melodramatic.

But then again, maybe he had a reason to be. "I do have one question..."

"Yes...?"

"Your source for this information—can that source be trusted? And if they know all this, why is it they don't know where the current Evelyn Gossman lives?"

"A fine question, sir, but one I cannot presently answer."

"I see...well, that may take some time—you know, uncovering the skeletons of the past and finding them in the present?"

"I have prepared a list of clues for you there in your pay envelope. I'm afraid it's all I know."

"Well, that'll have to do, then," I asserted, extending my hand.

"Do you like music, Mr. Denning?" Gossman asked me.

"Oh, yeah, but not the kind you were talking about earlier—all that operatic melodrama."

"But most opera is based upon real people who lived real lives, very far above the ordinary. Great composers gave them a voice after the grave and set it to music. Come, if you will..." He led me back to the main entrance hall, then we walked across that to a black door. He reached into his pocket and produced a black key shaped like a music note. He opened the door and suddenly there was a bluish glow in a fairly dark room with no windows. Sitting in the middle of the room was a large phonograph turntable mounted on a large cherry wood stand. "This...will perhaps change your attitude about the sound of some singers, some music—this method by which I present them to you."

"Okay…I'm willing to try almost anything once," I said.

Carefully he placed a multicolored disc on the turntable. But it wasn't spinning very fast, hardly at all, as a matter of fact. Instead of lowering a tone arm onto the disc, he took an "L" shaped tubular thing, put the short end in a hole on the surface of the phonograph. Now the rest of the shiny gold tube sat over the disc. Then I heard this glorious male voice singing, but as the record played, a hologram of fantastic, colored images came up out of the grooves immediately above the phonograph! There were like a million shimmering rainbows interlacing with one another. Then I heard this man's voice do what seemed impossible. He hit a high note and not only held it, but expanded it until it seemed to go into some other dimension. "Those images are the frequencies and overtones created by the voice you hear."

I was awed. "Whose voice is that—I—I never heard anything like it!" I exclaimed.

"He's called the Swedish Caruso. But he's so much more. His name is Jussi Bjoerling—and he's a god in human form, only on earth for a while." The short operatic aria ended and I stood there, transfixed.

"Just out of curiosity, what was the name of that song?"

"That *aria*…more correctly. And it is called *Amor ti Vieta* from a little known opera, *Fedora* by a 19th century composer named *Giordano.* That high 'A' he hit transcended this dimension and went into another." Well, as we know, I was used to different dimensions and all, but sonic dimensions from a slowly spinning record took the cake!

"What do you call this contraption?"

"My *magic phonograph.* What else could I call it?"

I laughed. "Beats me! What—what do you use it for?"

"To teach the chosen what the human voice was originally intended to do—call home to the stars."

"I see. Well, thank you, Mr. Gossman—at the very least I am impressed. I feel privileged. Why me?"

"Because, Mr. Denning, I got the feeling earlier that you are no stranger to the invisible world or dimensions not of this earth..."

"Oh, I don't know about that, sir, but I don't think anything is really disconnected from anything else. I think that's the meaning of the word *uni*-verse—it's all one, somehow."

"Very perceptive," Gossman mused. "Perhaps you are right, Mr. Denning. Who knows?"

"Yep, that's right—who knows, really?"

He led me out of the special room where the 'magic phonograph' was now sleeping, shrouded in mystery. We concluded our business as he handed me the envelope and we shook hands. We were off and running!

When I got back to the *Hotel Empire* I kicked back and waited for Ida to return from her window-shopping spree. I opened the envelope Dr. Theodore Gossman had given me. Yep, twenty-five very crisp one hundred dollar bills plus a folded piece of letter size paper with Gossman's scribbling on it. I wondered how Gossman got his dough. Maybe he was born with it. I noticed the name '*Cathy Ames*' written in darkened pencil and circled. He also mentioned another name we hadn't discussed at lunch, a guy named *Eddie Grant.* Then Ida came in and my mind switched to the lovely vision facing me. She was smiling. She came right up and kissed me. "Hello, handsome, how was your lunch?" she asked me.

"Okay, actually. He's an odd bird. Teaches voice, his wife ran away ten years ago. He wants to fix up the mess before he moves on. That's about it. Oh, and that the disappeared wife, so he tells me, has had four husbands in ten years who happened to end up dead before their time."

Ida's eyes widened. "Oh? Docs she eat them as well? Maybe she's a black widow or something, huh?" she chuckled.

"That's exactly what Gossman said...and what I was thinking." I pulled her toward me. "Ya know, you're beginning to sound more and more like me every day, Ida. Why do ya think that is?"

She put her arms around my neck. "Oh, being around you too long, maybe...maybe I absorb your words, just as I absorb your—ummm...your wonderful essences inside me when we make love. Are you interested in hearing more?"

"You bet," I said. "I'll tell ya what—let's go out to a damn fine early dinner and we'll take a cab and walk out on the Golden Gate Bridge, eh?"

"That'd be wonderful, Cable. Thank you for asking me along. I'm having such a fine time." Then she began to unbutton her blouse. "But first there's something else I would like to do with you, Mr. Denning. Do you have any idea what that might be?"

I snickered and then guffawed. "Damn, ya got me, Ida! What?"

"This," she murmured as she put her lips onto mine. I peeled her blouse off and helped her with her skirt. Soon she was dangling over me and I had one of her breasts in my mouth. That always drove her nuts. Before long we were naked together on top of our bed as the traffic four stories below honked and chugged and clanged its way through the afternoon.

About an hour before dusk we began walking out on the great engineering feat of Joseph Strauss. But it was Charles Alton Ellis who did the main math and designing of the *Golden Gate Bridge*. I saw that dirty deal in the paper when the bridge was being built. Strauss fired Ellis because he felt Ellis was taking too much time in his designs. But I noticed the bridge got built and it's strong as hell. The longest, highest single span and it had to be designed to withstand the power of the tidal forces.

The famous San Francisco fog bank had begun wending its way over the bridge as Ida and I reached about midway. A very cold chill filled the air and it was very windy—Ida cuddled closer to me. Cars passed like lighted ghosts and swished by us. I leaned over the railing and felt nausea almost immediately. Me and great heights just didn't mix. We couldn't see much anymore, so we walked back and found our taxi patiently waiting down below in the parking lot by the bridge. We got back into our room about 8:30 p.m. and the minute I opened the door, we saw that the whole room had been ransacked. But it dawned on me the thing the perpetrator was probably looking for was on me, tucked away inside my trench coat pocket. I told Ida this and she shivered, knowing that someone wanted something I had and that old story might be starting up again. We were heading back to L.A. early in the morning.

But suddenly I had this urge to dash out of our room, down the hall, into the dilapidated elevator, down into the lobby and out into the street, leaving Ida just standing there. "I'll be right back," I told her as I ran out. The fog was thick and barely moving. I could see very little and the sounds of the city had become subdued. But I sensed shadows. And I could feel a shadow watching me, fearful, but cautiously watching nonetheless. I walked past a few buildings and peered down an alleyway. Nothing. But someone was watching.

# The World of Eddie Grant

Ida and I had no idea who Eddie Grant might be. I suspected that *'Cathy Ames'* was a fictional character Gossman's wife had adopted to maintain the subterfuge of her identity. I sent Ida to the library to look up references to famous fictional characters. All she found on that name was it was a cold-hearted, psychotic, murderous female character that John Steinbeck was building for a future novel. Now *that* was telling!

A week later on a late Sunday morning, I was flipping through the newspaper when I came to the entertainment section and was delightfully surprised to find the name of Eddie Grant featured as the male singer at—the *Cocoanut Grove* no less—*and* with Bernie Hershfeld as the star and Eddie Grant the romantic crooner! How was that for luck?! I called Bernie and told him and Auina how much I missed them. I asked them about Eddie Grant and Bernie told me he didn't know too much about him, but he was talented and seemed a pretty nice guy.

August 1, 1947 was a warm Friday night. I decided to take Ida with me to catch Bernie's show and check out this Eddie Grant character. I'd never seen Ida happier than she was this night. She glowed and her blonde hair with those periwinkle eyes, turned lots of attention in her direction. Of course Ida was shapely and had improved her figure with age, filling out her cleavage and dressed with suave charm and a hint of sex tossed in for good measure. Of course,

Bernie's wit had made him a household name by now and Auina, his lovely South Sea Islander wife sat at our table.

The band played a fanfare and out came the plucky Bernie Hershfeld. There was huge applause.

"Thank you...thank you ladies and germs!
Men think too much about sex. The best way to get a man to think about other things is to kill him! But then again, that might spoil things at home!
A blonde and a brunette are standing on a corner. The blonde asks, 'What does IDK stand for?' The brunette says, 'I don't know.' The blonde looks alarmed. 'What? That's what everybody says! OMG, *nobody* knows!'
A family is at the dinner table. The son asks, 'Dad, how many kinds of boobs are there?' The father, surprised, smiles and says, 'Well, son, a woman goes through three phases. In her teens and twenties, a woman's breasts are like melons, round and firm. In her 30's and 40's they're still nice, but like pears, they hang a bit. But after 50 they're like onions. 'Onions?' the son asks. 'Yes, son, you see them and they make you cry.' Well, the mother and daughter are incensed at this. 'How many kinds of willies are there, Mom?' the daughter asks. The mother smiles and says, 'Well, dear, in his 20's, a man's willy is like an oak tree, mighty and hard. In his 30's and 40's it's like a birch, but still dependable. After his fifties, it's like a Christmas tree.' 'Christmas tree?' the daughter asks, puzzled. 'Yes, dear, dead from the root up and

the balls are just for decoration.'" The audience loved that one.

"A wife is looking at her husband. 'Honey, how would you describe me?' she asks. He smiles at her, 'Well, ABCDEFGHIJK,' the husband rattles off. 'What does that mean?' she asks. 'Oh, adorable, beautiful, cute, delightful, elegant, fashionable, gorgeous and hot.' 'But what about IJK?' 'I'm just kidding!'

A big Pollock is talking to another Pollock: 'My momma is so fat we took a picture last Christmas and it's still developing! In fact, my momma is so fat that when she got on a scale, the little ticket said, 'I needed your weight, not your phone number!'

A teacher is teaching a class and sees that Johnny isn't paying any attention. 'Johnny, if there are three ducks sitting on a fence and you shoot one, how many are left?' Johnny answers, 'None.' The teacher is confounded. "And why is that?' 'Because the shot scared them all off.' 'No, there are two ducks left, but I like your thinking.' So then Johnny asks the teacher. 'If you see three women walking out of an ice cream parlor, and one is sucking her ice cream, one is biting it, and one is licking it. Which woman is married?' The teacher responds, 'The one sucking her ice cream cone.' 'No, the one with the wedding ring, but I like your thinking!'" The crowd was in stitches.

"What happens to a frog's car when it breaks down? It gets toad away! One guy says to the other, 'Your momma is so fat and old when God said 'Let there be light,' he asked her to move out of the way.'

Two blondes fall down a hole. One says, 'It sure is dark in here, isn't it?' The other blonde says, 'Oh, I don't know—I can't see!'

At the doctor's office, Tom was getting a checkup. "I have good news...and I have bad news—vhat do ya vant first? 'Well, I guess the good news', the man says. 'Vell, you have 24 hours to live.' 'That's the good news? What's the bad?' 'I should have told you yesterday!'" The folks roared.

"A female duck is being groomed. The makeup artist says, how do you want your lipstick? 'Just put it in on my bill,' she said.

A blonde, a brunette and a redhead were all lost in the desert. They find a magic lamp and rub it. The genie says he'll grant one wish apiece. The brunette says, 'I want to be home in my cozy little apartment.' It is done. The redhead asks to be with her family, and so it is done. The blonde looks around and says, 'Ah, geees...I wish my two friends were here!'

A Mother Superior tells two nuns they have to paint their room without getting any paint on their clothes and suggests they go naked. So the girls disrobe and while they're painting there's a knock at the door. 'Yes? Who is it?' asks one nun. 'Blind man,' the male voice answers. They look at each other and agree to let the blind man in, what could it hurt? They let him in. He looks at 'em and says, 'Nice tits—where do you want me to hang the blinds?'" Well, Bernie Hershfeld owned that audience.

"What did God say when he made the first black person? 'Damn, I burned one!'

Why was six scared of seven? Because seven 'ate' nine.

Last week I told my psychiatrist, I've been thinking about suicide. He said I'd have to pay in advance from now on!

When I was a kid my family hated me—like the time I got kidnapped. The kidnappers sent my folks a note: 'Pay five thousand bucks or we'll send your kid home again!'

One night I came home. I figured, hell, let my wife come on—I'm ready for her—I'll let her make the first move. So she went to Florida.

And I was an ugly kid. My mother had morning sickness—after I was born!

When I was a teenager, I made love to a girl so ugly she was called a 'two-bagger'—that meant we both put bags over our heads in case hers broke!

I came from a real tough neighborhood. In the library the sign read, "SHUT UP OR ELSE!'

My male cousin is homosexual—I can always tell him on our family tree... he's in the fruit section."

People were doubling up in the audience. "What a kid I got—I told him about the birds and the bees—and he told me about the butcher and my wife!

Ya know, I came from a real tough neighborhood. Every time I shut my window at night I hurt somebody's fingers!

I can't win for losing. The way my life is running, if I became a politician I'd be honest!

So, folks, in closing I wanna say something very sincere to you: always look out for number one—and be careful not to step in number two! Love ya, guys!"

The audience rose to its feet and applauded this man who I had come to know and love. "This...lady...over here...sitting next to the beautiful blonde and the schmuck next to her—I ask you, who wears a fedora and a trench coat indoors and to an entertainment event unless he's got nuthin' under it?" That got a good laugh. "But really folks, this lady has an inside line to me—this is the lady who keeps me running—Auina Hershfeld!" People applauded as Auina bashfully stood and smiled at the man who adored her. "Now...ladies and gentlemen, a treat...originally from New York, this great entertainer has come to like us out here in Hollywoodland—so let's like him back—he hasn't got a bad front, either!—let's hear it for the one and only, *Eddie Grant!*"

The combo started up and a good-looking fellow about 5' 10" ran onto the stage, grabbed a microphone and began singing. Boy, and could this fellow sing! He opened the show with *I've Heard That Song Before*, the 1942 Harry James/Helen Forrest hit. Eddie Grant could hold his own against any male vocalist in my book. Hell, you had charmers like Crosby, Rudy Vallee, Perry Como, Vaughn Monroe—but Grant had a way about him. I couldn't tell whether he was a tenor or high baritone, but it didn't matter. He looked great in a tuxedo and everyone enjoyed him and not just the women. His second song was new to me. It was titled *Blue Gardenia,* a song about love lost. Ida took my hand firmly and led me out onto the dance floor. "Do you like that singer up there?" I asked her.

"Yes, but he's not you, Cable. And I wonder if he's got what you've got that most women want...?"

"Oh, yeah? What's that?" I whispered in her ear.

"Sex...appeal..." She whispered that into my ear. "And I want some later."

"What have I told you about that, Ida?" I kidded her.

"Be quiet and just dance with me." She danced close to me and cuddled her lovely lithe body into mine.

Auina had gone back stage to be with Bernie. It was my nature as a detective to sniff around. Everything looked normal except for one table. Seated alone at the very back of the Grove sat a lovely older blonde woman in a tight black suit. She kept to the shadows—it got my attention. But Ida and I were spinning slowly around the room and as soon as Eddie Grant finished *Blue Gardenia*, the big band began a fun version of *Life Is Just a Bowl of Cherries.* Next time I looked, the table was empty. I think the lady had flown the coop.

I needed to talk to this Eddie Grant privately. But first Ida and I went backstage to say hello and give Auina and Bernie a big hug. "I need to talk to this new singer of yours, Bernie. How do I get a hold of him?"

"You should be so lucky! Even I can't get a hold of him. He's dependable, but no one knows where he lives. He says he likes to keep a private 'private life', if ya know what I mean."

"Well, I guess I'd better get him before he leaves the Grove, eh?"

"Okay, Cable," Bernie said. "Ya know, my parents never liked me. One Halloween they dressed me up like a fire hydrant and then put me in the dog pound! I didn't tell my wife, but some babe calls me up the other night. She says, 'Come to my house—there's nobody home'. So I went over—she was right, nobody was home!"

We all laughed and I left Ida talking to them as I sought out Eddie Grant's dressing room. I knocked. "Mr. Grant?" I asked.

"Yeah? Who is it and whatta ya want? I got a second act coming up."

"My name is Cable Denning—I really enjoyed your show. I'm a private eye and I need to ask you a few questions."

"I don't know anything and I'm not in trouble with the law, Denning. Go away. I've got nothing to say."

"Well, you might if I mention a good looking blonde babe by the ex-name of Evelyn Nesbitt who became Evelyn Gossman who happens to be in your racket—singing—or perhaps I should say, entertainment?"

The door opened and Eddie Grant ushered me in and then closed the door behind me. He sat at his dressing table, touching up his makeup. "So...? Yeah, I met Evelyn a few years ago. We had a thing going for a while. But she kept marrying men and then losing 'em—to dying. I didn't wanna be one of 'em."

"You do know she was or still is married to one Theodore Gossman—a professor of voice and sometimes inventor in San Francisco?"

"Yeah, she mentioned him. She left him because she got bored. But she didn't want him to find her, so she changed her singing names—"

"—to Anne Shirely, Lucie Mannette and maybe some other babe."

"*Cathy Ames.* That might be who she is now. And she's working on husband number four or five—I can't keep track." He was nervous. He got out a cigarette and lit it. "So whatta ya want—as you can see, I'm a busy man."

"Well, for starters, perhaps you can tell me if you were the informer who squealed to Dr. Gossman in Frisco about his wife's bigamy and fictitious names? But if you did so, why...I ask myself?"

"Well, you can put that one to rest. I care for the dame. We've got some mileage together. As far as Gossman...? I don't even know the guy."

"So who do you think keeps Gossman informed—yet keeps her whereabouts a secret?"

"How the hell should I know, Denning! You're a private investigator—that's what you do, right? Maybe Gossman's playing his own game, ever think of that?"

"Okay, fair enough. So...do you think she's killed her four husbands? I haven't done the research yet, but did they die 'natural' deaths in your opinion?"

"No, not in my opinion. I think they were slipped some poison. But toxicologists couldn't find anything, so the coroner's report had to read their hearts stopped natural like. But Evelyn did not kill those men. Someone else did to make it look like she did."

"Now, who would wanna do that—Gossman himself out of jealous rage, revenge?"

"I don't know," Eddie Grant said, taking a big drag on his cigarette. "I just know Evelyn didn't do it. She's a lotta things, mister, but she's not a killer. Maybe Gossman—a lotta men are capable of murdering because of someone they still love. But he's in a wheelchair, I hear, so he don't get around much anymore."

"Ain't that the name of a song?"

"Yeah, Duke Ellington. Did ya really dig my act?"

"Yeah, I think your pipes are good. How come you're not a star?"

"I started too late. During the big band era I got messed up with the Jewish mafia and Rothstein. I made great money, so I didn't have to sing except to babes' ears in the bedroom—a new one every night! Then after the war, the big bands dried up, the jukebox industry went south and so did I—to Mexico."

"Oh?"

"Yeah, that's where I first met Evelyn Gossman, who was then Anne Shirley. It was in Mexico City and we had a hot affair. We both sang at a fine nightclub for rich Mexicans, Central and South Americans. But Evelyn wanted money. I didn't have much. So she dumped me for some Mexican creep named Alfonso Derita. She married him and he died three months later. And so you'll find out the rest of the stories have a similar m.o.—love 'em and watch 'em die, collect their fortunes and tuck it away for a rainy day."

"Except you believe she didn't kill 'em. Someone else did."

"Yeah, I already told ya that."

I rubbed my chin. "Ha! I guess you're lucky you didn't have any dough—otherwise you'd be pushin' up daisies now. So where is Evelyn now—I mean, who does she live with?"

"I don't know. She's very private. Keeps things like that out of bounds to anyone she knows."

"I think she was in the audience tonight watching you."

"She was? I didn't see her."

"She left early." I took out a cigarette and he lit it for me. "Thanks...you know—some things just don't make sense, Eddie Grant. For instance, if Evelyn is after money, she's gettin' it in big chunks from not so big hunks. Wouldn't that be enough motivation for murder?"

"Yeah, ordinarily. But there's got to be more to it. Personally, I don't know anything else, Denning. Now, as I said, I'm a busy man—and I'd appreciate it if you didn't bother me anymore about this, okay?"

"Yeah, sure, Eddie—thanks for the info. I'll check things out. But I might have to check back with you—or if this thing finally breaks wide open, you may have to appear in court as a witness for the defense."

I found Ida, said goodnight to Bernie and Auina and we filed quietly out of the Cocoanut Grove to the tune of Eddie Grant singing *I Don't Know Enough*

*About You*—which is exactly how I felt about Evelyn Gossman, alias Cathy Ames...or whoever she is now.

By August 6th I was no further along than the night I'd talked to Eddie Grant. I figured I had two ways to go. I could go see Eddie again and hope the dame would come in—or I could check the female singers in town and see if any of them looked like or came close to the name of Cathy Ames. I had no luck at the Grove and thought I'd check out a few clubs on the lower, dirtier part of town. I thought of a good place to start even though I had bitter memories about the joint because of the death of Lorena Downes and Jimmy Dunn. But ya know, hunches sometimes pay off. This Wednesday night found the place jumpin' with a lot of poor white trash who came to hear the poor black trash, much like the rich in New York used to go to Harlem to hear the great negro musicians like Count Basie, Duke Ellington, Billy Strayhorn, Dizzy Gillespie, Earl Father Hines, Fats Domino and others. But the club also featured white singers. I was hoping that Evelyn with some pseudonym would show up. Here she could enjoy what she loved doing and keep fairly undetected. But I had a surprise coming. Up on the stage, filled with smoke, a piano, bass, drums and a large mirror behind it, stood none other than *Eddie Grant* singing his little heart out with an Irving Berlin song entitled *Cheek To Cheek*—a song that Fred Astaire made famous singing to Ginger Rogers in the 1930's. And what was even more revealing—half way through the song, some beautiful middle-aged blonde comes up and starts dancing with Eddie! Only her name wasn't Cathy anything!—but *Beth Bennett,* I heard someone say. I kept to the shadows and watched the two interact. If indeed the lady in question had dumped Eddie Grant for a string of rich old fossils, why were they together and exceedingly friendly? Then they began to sing together and reprised *Cheek To Cheek* with some pretty hot sparks between them. I think they really meant it when they sang, "and my heart beats so that I can hardly speak"— and they were a hell of a lot more than casual acquaintances or even ex-lovers!

The tune ended and the two of them took a few bows and left the stage, darting out the back of the joint. I tried to follow but they must've had a car waiting out in the alley. I found no one.

## Librarians Can Surprise You

So the next day I wanted to find all I could about a *'Beth Bennet'* at the Hollywood library on Ivar. Fortunately I found a marvelously knowledgeable library assistant. Her name was Maggie Loggins and we hit it off right away. She wore glasses and looked like a bookworm. "Yes, sir, I know of no characters with the name of Beth Bennet who might've come from classical literature." Then she thought for a minute. "Except maybe—what if the first name was an abbreviation?"

"Whatta ya mean?"

"I mean...what if *Beth* is short for *Elizabeth*? One of Jane Austin's most famous novels was called *Pride and Prejudice*, and the main protagonist's name is *Elizabeth Bennett*."

"Damn!" I exclaimed. "That's it!"

She put her finger to her lips. "Shhhh…! Please, sir, not so loud. After all, this is a library."

"Sorry…so what if you have dinner with me and tell me everything you know about this Elizabeth Bennet?"

"Sir, I don't even know who you are?"

"My treat!"

"Sir! You cannot buy a woman—or anyone else you—you don't know!" she flustered.

"Well, how do people get to know each other if they don't socialize? It'll be a public place." I got out my P.I. card and showed her. "You see, I'd be using you anyway, Miss Loggins, so what's the difference? You get a mysterious private dick and a free meal!"

She took me by the hand and led me outside, giggling. She was about twenty-five or maybe a bit older, with lovely, long tapered fingers and thin lips with dirty blonde hair and blue eyes. She had a so-so figure, a bit on the thin side. But she had spunk, and I liked that. "Oh…you are so forward, Mr. Denning. That is right, isn't it—Denning?"

"Yep—so how about it? This is Thursday. Where can two people in love go on a Thursday night to dine?"

She eyed me queerly. "What are you talking about? In love? I don't even know you, and you know nothing about me. How do you know I don't have a boyfriend or I'm not married?"

41

"Well, 'cause you're a spinster type, Miss Loggins, if you don't mind my saying. You may have had a boyfriend, but he jilted you because you were—oh, maybe too thin, not enough on the upper deck there—or you weren't good in bed or—"

"—Mr. Denning! That's quite enough. If you wish me to inform you about the literary lady in question, you will have to stop being so rude! I am not cheap, I don't date, I don't smoke or drink alcohol and very forward men like you—"

"—are either dangerously tempting to you—or disgusting—which is it, Maggie Loggins?"

She smiled at me. Then she drew sad. "I'm just a lowly librarian. That's probably all I'll ever be. I'm a nobody—your life is probably exciting and you have lots of ladies at your beck and call—"

"—I'm a simple private dick, trying to make an honest living in a dishonest world—"

"—you said that before..."

"Said what?"

"Private *dick*...I know what it means, you know."

"What do you think it means?"

"It's an American slang word for 'detective', Mr. Denning. Probably evolved from dime novels in the early part of our century."

I chuckled. "You know, you're the first woman who either didn't know what it meant or didn't take offense at what it could mean."

"I'm a reader, Mr. Denning, and a librarian. The male appendage is not that interesting. I'm *supposed* to know these things."

"Great—so how about supper—you name the place, the time and I'll either pick you up at your place or meet you there. Whatever you like."

She looked me over and took a deep breath. "I know my mamma would've said no, but you can pick me up about seven tonight at *Edgemont Manor Apartments, 1716 North Edgemont Avenue Apt. 42.* It's just north of Hollywood Blvd. Have I said too much?"

"Nope...I'll be there, Miss Loggins. Thanks..."

I wasn't sure whether she was dressing to impress me or not, but the inimitable Miss Loggins dressed very nicely as I picked her up that evening. She had a medium-grey tight skirt on with a white blouse that revealed a little more bust than I'd previously thought she'd possessed. We walked down to Hollywood Blvd. and found a small coffee shop. We walked in, found a table and sat. "I just love their French Dip. Perhaps you'll have one?"

"One what, Miss Loggins?"

"A French Dip sandwich. With a coke—a complete meal!" she replied.

"Oh...let me see the menu..." I ended up ordering an old-fashioned hamburger with all the trimmings. We sat opposite one another. "So, now, if you don't mind, I'd like to pump you a little more, Miss Loggins."

"Maggie's alright. May I call you by your first name?"

"Sure, Cable... So, as I was saying earlier, fill me in on this Jane Austin's *Elizabeth Bennet.*"

"Well, first of all they called her Eliza, and she wants to marry for love and not for station or economic gain. She's beautiful and charming, falls in love with a man named Darcy, but is prejudiced against him for several reasons and refuses to marry him. But in the end she is wrong."

"So give me the plot and all the detail you can think of."

"Well, truthfully, there's not much. Elizabeth, Eliza, is pretty proper. She encounters this handsome, objectionable man. The whole plot is really about five sisters finding suitable partners. Eliza ultimately settles for Darcy and that's that," Maggie Loggins said, tossing the whole thing off her shoulder. "It's all about manners. After all, it's England in 1814. Women were to be seen and not heard."

"That's it? No intrigue—no mystery, no murder? No sex? It's basically a book for women, right?" I asked.

"I didn't say there wasn't sex. Those days things were kept under wraps pretty tightly, Cable. Frankly, I'm shocked about how mores have changed since the end of the war. Women seem to be much—uh, much more bold."

Our meal came and we dug in. We drifted into silence. I liked this sparkling young woman with the librarian's brain. "I have written a mystery myself, you know..." she said with her mouth half-full.

"You have?"

"Yep...*The Counterfeit Murder*. It's about a woman who sacrifices herself to protect her daughter. In the dark, the murderer has come to kill the daughter, but he can't tell it's the mother and murders her instead. And the rest of the book is unraveling the plot. Kind of like an American Sherlock Holmes story. Do you like Arthur Conan Doyle?"

"I—I know of him. I think *Hound of the Baskervilles* is the only one I actually read, though. So you like to write, eh? How good are ya?"

"Okay, I guess. I just do it because I love to take surreptitious adventures—you know, a way to get out of my boring life."

"Yeah, I know what you mean. I've never known a female writer personally, I mean, in depth. I once loved a poetess, though."

"I've written some poetry. But I'm not very good. What was the lady's name?"

"Maria Voldt. She's dead now. Would you like to hear something I memorized she wrote?"

Her blue eyes sparkled. "Yes...I'd like that... "

"This is about Maria's sadness, the fact that she never fit, but saw herself in a cosmos in which she belonged nonetheless. '*It's April. I am caused to think of you, my breast heaves, my groin aches and I know not why, I am usually shy, but feel your presence press on my chest and take the best of me. Your kiss, a princely gift stolen whilst I slept by the brook, awakened me, my love, opened the portals to my heart and soul, made me whole as I walk this earthly trail, strewn with heartache—travail—and unfulfilled dreams. Yet you are the beacon for me, that keeps me alive when I strive to do myself in, pull the pin on the grenade that stayed so long within my craw—now this spring, it's April, it will thaw...and I will bloom again within the arms of your love.'"* I checked out Maggie's face. Her eyes were tearing.

"Oh...my...I could never be...be that good, Cable. She was—was a master of words, don't you think?"

"Yeah, I think. Maria Voldt was the most beautiful little soul I think I've ever known."

"How did she die, if you don't mind my asking?" she inquired, sipping on her coke.

"Because of me, some son-of-a-bitch poisoned her—just to spite me. I've—I've had some rough moments over that, as you can guess."

"Oh dear! I'm sorry, I didn't know. Of course it must've hurt you. Were the two of you in love?"

"In love? Perhaps not in the common sense of the definition, Maggie, but, yes, we lived in a state of love. But I never received her poetry book until after her death. So, I guess you could say in a way she's continued to speak to me and love me throughout these years."

Maggie was staring at me, transfixed. "Yes...I like the way you talk, Cable."

"Thanks." She took off her glasses and rubbed her eyes. She was actually pretty good looking under the glass peepers.

"So, now, perhaps you can tell me about your case and why you came to the library looking for women of literary history. I'm intrigued."

I chuckled. "Okay, mystery writer, here it is, blow by blow. I get a phone call from a singing professor in San Francisco. He says he needs to hire me. So I go. He tells me he married a woman much younger than himself. Her name at the time of their marriage was Evelyn Nesbitt, and she became Evelyn Gossman. After a few years, she got tired of him and flew the coop...but no divorce. She becomes a bigamist in L.A. by marrying four different men during a 10-year period—but wedding them under a fictitious name each time, I'd assume. The husband gave me three of the names. Anne Shirley, Lucie Manette, Cathy Ames and maybe one other."

Maggie's mind was spinning fast. "Hmmm...let me see...Anne Shirley from *Anne of Green Gables*—*'The sorrows God brought us had comfort and strength in them, while the sorrows we brought on ourselves, through folly or wickedness, were the hardest to bear'.* Lucy Maud Montgomery was the author and the book was published in 1908."

"I'm impressed. Why the quotes?"

"Because I attended a girls' school and we had to memorize passages."

"I see. So what about Lucie Manette?"

"Dickens...1858...this is where *'it was the best of times, it was the worst of times'* comes from, *A Tale of Two Cities.* That's the French Revolution. Lucie Manette is essentially good, and has a daughter with the same first name."

"Wow! You know your stuff, kid. So who is Cathy Ames?"

"Well, she's a new character creation of Steinbeck's that he may build a future novel around. I've heard she's evil personified... unredeemable. That's about all I know."

"Yeah, that's all I found out too...and now *Elizabeth Bennett?* What do you think?"

"Could be a ruse, to throw someone off. Maybe it's a name she'd use only in certain circumstances. Or maybe not..."

I mused for a minute. "What do you make of her so far? Why would a woman choose those three first characters?"

"Maybe that depends on the fourth character she chooses, if indeed *not* Elizabeth Bennett. Who else is involved in her life that you know of?"

"Ummm...well, a singer I just met. Evelyn is also a singer. His name is Eddie Grant. Pretty good crooner, at that."

"What does he know?"

"Hey, now, you're sounding like a detective!"

She giggled a girl's giggle. "Yes...! I'm enjoying myself. Please, indulge me, Cable. My life is pretty boring."

"Eddie Grant knows Evelyn, they had a love affair some years back—and by what I saw the other night watching them from the shadows in a dump of a nightclub, they've still got something going."

"Then they share a secret."

"They what?"

"Share a secret. They both know something most people don't. That's what I get from what you just described."

"What if they simply enjoy each other and make love now and then since Evelyn married much older men until they kicked off, one by one? She's working on number four now, I understand."

"How did the husbands die?"

"The crooner thinks poison...but *clever* poison—no forensic doc could prove it as murder. So he labeled all the toe tags, 'from natural causes'."

"As suspicious as it looks, Evelyn Nesbitt Gossman may not have killed her husbands. She may have profited from their demise. But I suspect two things."

"Yeah, what?"

"One—someone else has got it out for Evelyn and two—there's something else going on in San Francisco—something hidden."

"You mean besides the *magic phonograph*?"

"The magic phonograph?"

"Yep, I saw it, I heard it. When a record is played, it creates a multi-colored hologram. It's quite amazing. You should see it."

"What's a hologram?" Maggie asked.

"Well, it's kind of a new thing—a three-dimensional light image produced by sound, in this case."

"Will you take me to see and hear it?"

"Hey, you're a librarian, not a female detective. Whatta ya talking about?" Besides, it's all in San Francisco. How can we do that without getting caught and raising suspicions—or you getting hurt? And this Gossman guy might get wise to us.

"Don't you read, Cable? There are a lot of clever ways to break and enter, access and escape," she laughed. "C'mon, where's your sense of adventure?"

"At my age? Stowed away pretty safe somewhere in my office, thanks. I've had enough adventure for a dozen lifetimes, lady."

She checked out my eyes. "Please? We could leave on a Friday after work, spend Saturday and Sunday investigating."

I was hesitant. "I don't know...it could be very dangerous." I couldn't help thinking about my lousy track record when dames get too close to my cases.

"I'd love it! Whatta ya say, Cable?"

I smiled as I surveyed the young miss. "How old are you, Maggie?"

"I'll be 30 in December. Funny, too, I always wanted to be a December bride—but no one was ever interested."

"But San Francisco?"

"Because there's a major part of the puzzle missing and I believe it lies somewhere with the husband, what's-his-name."

"Yeah, Theodore Gossman—*doctor* Theodore Gossman."

"What is he a doctor of?"

"Music, I guess..."

"Maybe not. We need to know. I'll look him up in the library when we get to San Francisco."

"I'll have to tell Ida we're going. I know she'll wanna come."

"Ida? Is that your sweetheart, wife—what?"

"My secretary of several years. I took her when I went the first time. I never did that before. I must be I' soft."

Maggie drew quiet for a minute. "Are you...are you lovers?"

"Well, I don't like to mix business with pleasure, it can have some pretty awful side-effects, ya know."

"You didn't answer me, Cable...do you mind?"

"Once in a while we—we, uh, kinda slip into an intimate escape or so. But that's about it, I told Ida I don't wanna have women around my neck. But truth is, I don't want anyone getting hurt...as in permanently."

She ignored my concerns. "When can we go, Cable? I am really jazzed!"

"The sooner the better, I guess. Gossman is paying me pretty good for this. I'd better come up with something soon—"

"—even if it's him, huh?" Maggie laughed.

"Yeah...even if it's him...that'd be ironic now, wouldn't it?"

## Books, Trains and Lovers

Maggie Loggins and I boarded the Southern Pacific Owl on that Friday night. We left town without telling Ida that I was taking someone else—especially a young woman. I didn't wanna hurt her. I just told her Gossman called and wanted to see me again. We traveled all night and around 8:00 a.m. Saturday morning we pulled into San Francisco. Maggie's head was resting on my shoulder. She was fast asleep. "Hey, sleepy head," I muttered, prodding her gently. She started and then looked up at me.

"Oh! Where—where are we?" she said sleepily.

"San Francisco S.P. train station, toots. You about ready to face the day? It's about 8:20 a.m. Saturday morning."

"Oh. Yes, of course," she answered. Then she looked at my shoulder. "Did I...did I fall asleep on you there?"

"Yep, and I'm gonna charge you rent, too," I quipped.

She smiled and we made our way to our luggage. We stopped off at the restrooms inside the depot and soon we were off looking for a cup of coffee to wake us up. After our first cup of java, Maggie's brain went into gear and she began musing. "So, Cable, the first thing we must do is find a way to enter without being noticed."

"You like snooping into other people's stuff, hoping to find the answer to some grand mystery, don't you?" I asked, grinning at the slim librarian with the wire-rimmed glasses.

"Yes, don't you? Especially if we find something juicy."

"Yeah, I guess that's what we came for, eh?"

"Yes, Cable, and you may have solved this case so you can get on with the next one. I believe in efficiency."

"I see. Yeah, me, too. So how do you propose we enter the joint?"

"I don't know. Here's what I think. If you'll take me by the old house, I'll get my first ideas. Then we need to find a couple of rooms for the night, maybe have a late lunch and after dark, do our prowling and see if we can't enter the building undetected."

"Okay, sounds like a plan." We continued walking down Market Street and found the *Hotel Whitcomb*, at Market and Eighth Streets. The sights and smells were different for both of us. San Francisco had a charm that L.A. did not possess. It was three bucks for one room or six for two separate rooms. I thought Maggie didn't mind if we spent the three extra bucks left over on that *late lunch* at Fisherman's Wharf. She wanted to zip by the old Flood Mansion first. It was too far to walk, so we grabbed a trolley car up to Broadway and walked a couple of blocks over to the mansion. She took a careful look at the architecture from the street and memorized where she thought certain accessible rooms might be. But she was smarter than that. She asked me to remain outside while she went in to "inquire about violin lessons", as she put it. Twenty minutes later she found me meandering down the street and we walked back over to Broadway and Van Ness streets to continue up to Fisherman's Wharf. I asked her what she'd discovered and she told me they don't teach instruments—just the human singing voice. It was a Saturday and a lot of people crowded the wax museum across the street and we went upstairs to a joint called Fisherman's Grotto and ordered a big bowl of clam chowder, with lemon buttered French bread and two glasses of wine.

I could tell Maggie felt freed up from her usual routine in L.A. She even loosened up a bit. "My mother is a prude. My Dad's an accountant who married his business, essentially. I have a brother who's a drunkard and my cat got run over last year. That's about the extent of my life, Cable," she said taking a big sip of wine.

"Yeah, well, that doesn't sound too encouraging."

"What about you? Your profession, your social time—what do you do, may I ask?"

"Well, my favorite thing is going down into a nightclub late at night to listen to some pretty babe out there in front of the band singing Irving Berlin, or Cole Porter or Harold Arlen or the likes. I look at a few skirts and walk the streets when I can't sleep. My job keeps me busy most of the rest of the time."

"Oh...and girlfriends? A handsome man like you must have girlfriends—I mean, lots of them, right?"

"Not at my age, Maggie. Besides, my line of business is kinda dangerous and someone could get hurt hangin' around me. It ain't safe territory."

"*Isn't*...safe territory..."

"Yeah, well, I came from the ghetto by the river and '*ain't*' was the preferred lingo. American slang, lady, or don't you accept slang as part of the American language world?"

"Yes, one has to. But one can still speak properly, you know."

"Well, 'ain't' sounds proper to me."

"Okay, Cable...just commenting. After all, I'm a librarian and I—"

"—yeah, I know—you're supposed to know those things."

"Yes." She took a big, deep breath and let it out. "So...would you like to take a walk?"

"Yeah, that sounds swell." We got up and I paid the bill. Maggie thanked me for the meal and we walked north toward the Golden Gate Bridge along the wharf area. Finally we sat on a cement sea wall watching fishing boats come and go. The fog had peeled away and hovered a few miles out to sea. The day was pleasant and breezy. "So...you never been engaged or gone steady with a guy?" I asked the slim young woman.

"Nope. Not me. I just don't appeal to men. I read this article about how some people are naturally charismatic—like you, Cable—and maybe, just maybe there are chemicals released by the body that attract or repel others. Maybe some people 'smell' other people. I don't know."

"*Pheromones*—that's what they're called. Different people detect some genetic make-ups more easily than others. It's kind of a coding system, I think. Like people attract each other, maybe."

She looked at me, puzzled. "'*Pheromones*—now what kind of a word is that? You must have made it up, right?"

"No, it's just that society or the general public doesn't know about it yet. Probably won't for some years."

"So, smarty pants, how come you know about such things? I thought you were a private detective, not a biological scientist."

"Let's just say I've been privy to certain things in my life, Maggie—and leave it at that."

"You do know there's no such word—at least it's not in the dictionary—and besides, nobody knows why some people are attracted to other people."

I sighed. "Have it your way, Maggie. We'd better go take a nap if we're gonna be up all night exploring the Singing Arts Institute."

"Take a nap? I haven't napped since I was six. Besides, the way I have it planned, we'll be in and out within a half-hour or so."

"We will, eh? Well, then *I'll* take a nap and you— well, you can go for a walk, a streetcar ride—or watch me sleep."

"Watch you sleep? I thought we had separate rooms."

"Well, we just spent the difference for lunch. I saved us two bucks—but don't worry, I don't bite and you have a separate twin bed."

She scowled. "And you didn't ask me? I'm a woman, Cable, you're a strange man—I don't even know you—"

"—yeah, yeah—how many times do you have to say that? I get it, okay?" I took out a Lucky Strike and lit it. "If ya want a separate room, I guess I can spring for it. Damn, why are you so—so obstinate?"

"Obstinate, is it now? I would simply like my privacy."

"What, for one night when you won't even be in your bed?"

"Well, I won't be in *your* bed, if that's what you mean…"

"No, I didn't say that—we'll be working!" I raised my voice, getting a little impatient with my librarian acquaintance.

"Okay…I guess it's just for a night. But you keep your distance, mister. Do you snore?"

"Yeah, probably. Why?"

"It keeps me awake."

"Stuff your ears with toilet paper or somethin'."

We fell silent as we looked out into the bay. "Have you ever thought what you'd be like if your life had turned out differently?" she asked me, day-dreaming.

"Yeah, as a matter of fact I have. We can dream, but who can know that? I guess we all turn left when we could've gone right or whatever. But then, life makes us what we become, based on our breeding, environment, the people we meet, where we live, how much culture we've absorbed and reflect back to our world—"

"—Karl Marx said *'society does not consist of individuals, but expresses the sums of inter-relations, the relations within which these individuals stand'.* We're just a cog in a wheel. You know, sort of like honey bees, co-operating out of necessity for survival—"

"—yeah, until an Einstein, Beethoven or FDR come along. Then where do you 'cubby-hole' those who stand out?"

"Simple...faster brains, higher I.Q. Their work, what they leave behind them, you know, some kind of legacy?"

"So you got it all figured out, eh?"

"I don't know about that, Cable, but most people live rather simply, I'd say. I'm just a cog in that wheel. I really have no individual identity..."

I sat down on the grass near the sea wall. "Blah, blah, blah—come here you..." I said as I opened my arms. Hesitantly Maggie approached me. I lay down on my back, she bent down and came into my arms and I brought my face to hers and kissed her.

"Oh! What was that for?!" she questioned me, her eyes open wide.

"Oh...just for the hell of it—to see what you'd do..."

"Cable...you can't play with people's emotions like that! What if I really felt something?"

"Well, did you?"

"Even if I did, I wouldn't tell you. I'm—I'm not used to that—that kind of thing...you know smooching and all."

"Too bad, ya don't know what you're missing." She got up and went back over to the sea wall. I followed. "How about just the natural expression of your female self, Maggie? Or has she gone to sleep?"

"None of your business, Mr. Denning," she cautioned me. "I'm not attracted to your overtures because I know what you want at the other end."

"You do, eh?"

"Yes. And I don't want it—or you."

"Alright. Then you sleep alone," I kidded her.

She became incensed. "I planned to anyhow! What gives you the right to assume anything about me, mister?"

"Okay, okay...I'm just giving you a bad time—I'm sorry, okay?"

"You'd better be. Now...you go get your rest, Mr. Older Man. I will be about exploring San Francisco's library system."

That night the fog blanketed the city...low and sinister...fingering its way through the streets. About midnight we had arrived back at 2222 Broadway and sneaked around to the side. There was a small panel truck parked by the back door. Maggie told me she'd already unlocked a studio window when she was waiting for someone to see her in regard to taking music lessons. No one  had locked it since. I opened the window, boosted her small butt through it and she helped me climb over the edge. We were in like porch-climbers! We checked the floor level story and found nothing unusual except the door behind which sat the magic phonograph.

To the rear of the building, just before the kitchen, we found another door that led downstairs. There was a dim light at the bottom. Stealthily we made our way down the old wooden steps. We walked toward the light. It came from a room that smelled of some kind of chemical. The odor was a kind of ammonia smell, but layered with other unfamiliar odors as well. I drew my gun. I led the way into the large anti-room. It was a printing press room! The small overhead light, however, revealed no ordinary product was being printed—but fresh new greenbacks! "Jesus," I whispered to Maggie, "the guy's a counterfeiter!"

"I forgot to mention to you, Cable—at the library, I found out what kind of doctor Gossman is."

"And?"

"He's a chemical engineer and researcher. So was his father. Only he ended up in jail for printing phony money!"

"Good work, Maggie." Now it made sense. The music academy thing was a front. There were some twenty-dollar plates on the counter below the printing press. There was a drawer. I opened it. There were some smudged bills. I grabbed one for evidence. I wasn't sure what I was gonna do with this new twist. "I think that's enough for one night. We've got what we came for, right?"

"I'm not so sure," Maggie commented. "Uh...what about the magic holographic phonograph you told me about?"

"Yeah, if we can gain entrance. That door was locked with a special key when Gossman took me in. Obviously we can't play the damn thing without waking everyone up."

"Yes, but I'd like to see the room and the phonograph nevertheless," she continued to whisper.

We made our way upstairs until we found ourselves facing the mysterious black door. The lock opening was unorthodox and had a slight "hook" at the bottom of it. But that didn't deter Maggie. No sir, she took a bobby pin from the side of her hair and stuck it in the lock. She fished around for a minute and then we heard a loud click. She'd opened the damn door! I was impressed. "How'd you learn that?" I asked her.

"Remember...? I'm the one who reads, detective," she answered.

Then we stood before the magic phonograph. Maggie eyed it curiously. "Hmmm...a regular 78 r.p.m. turntable and odd-looking tone arm." Then she looked at the rear of the tone arm. "But the output wires go—go nowhere! That means it won't play records. What did you say it played?"

"Holographic discs—from a drawer—somewhere over there," I whispered. I went over and opened a drawer. There were several platters. I took one and showed it to her. "This went on the turntable like an ordinary record—like this," I said, placing the record on the turntable. But that was a mistake. As soon as I did, something triggered the damn thing to start playing and I was listening to that Jussi Bjoerling guy again singing some fantastic operatic aria! The room began to light up with those incredible rainbow colored, undulating images again. But I couldn't tell where the light source was. How could the disc itself have created both the sound and the projected image?

Just then a bright light switched on. "I'm glad you enjoy my music so much, Mr. Denning," the voice of Theodore Gossman spoke as he wheeled himself into the room. "But it is rather late, don't you think? And really, you should have called for an appointment. I would be only too happy to show you my invention once again."

Maggie and I stood frozen. "Oh, doc, I'm—I'm glad you dropped by. Sorry about the intrusion. Oh, and this is Maggie Loggins, a librarian friend of mine from the Hollywood library."

"Oh?" He came forward and greeted Maggie. "Delighted to meet you, Miss Loggins. But you must know I'm surely unprepared for this visit—and you *are* breaking in, you must realize. Shall I call the police?" He went over and turned off the magic phonograph. Then he swung around his wheel chair and faced us. "So what else might have you two discovered whilst prowling around, may I ask?"

"Oh, not much. Just a printing press that cranks out nice crisp twenty-dollar bills. That's about it," I said, tongue-in-cheek.

"I see...and what do you plan to do about it? Perhaps I shan't call the police, in that case. So...shall you clamp me in irons—or what?"

"Actually, Gossman, *nothing*. You see, I'm a man of my word—remember, the truth guy? You didn't hire me to discover what illegal acts you might be perpetrating, but I'm supposed to solve the mystery of your wife Evelyn's strange and distorted life since she left you. Right?"

He checked out my face. "Right. By George, I *do* believe you are telling the truth. After all, a man has to make a living. And you'll find I am not a violent man, Mr. Denning. Nevertheless, I am relieved that you have chosen that particular pathway to follow." Then he looked at Maggie. "And you, Miss Loggins? Are you a moral purist or are you able to accept the modicum of 'live and let live'?"

Maggie grabbed my hand tight. "I'm with him, Dr. Gossman. I'm able to keep secrets very well. And as Cable says, after all, we're here to discover—discover—"

"—discover what, Miss Loggins?" Gossman said, his eyes purveying Maggie's face.

"Discover missing facts about your strange case. I read a lot. I know many bizarre plots people cook up to protect something or someone else—"

"—and you thought perhaps I was 'covering up' something about my ex-wife and her curious and maleficent ways? Yes, the haunted heart makes many untoward decisions, doesn't it?"

"Yes, sir, it does. But there's always something left out, a detail, some pertinent clue that links the crime or crimes..." She was right on.

"Oh, yes, to be sure, young woman. But Evelyn is a killer, a murderess of the first rank. How can we let that go unpunished?"

"Because I don't believe Evelyn Gossman, Elizabeth Bennet, Anne Shirley or Lucie Manette is a killer," Maggie asserted.

"You don't? How have you drawn such a conclusion?"

"That's why I asked Cable to bring me here."

"How about *Hester Prynne*? Could she be a murderess?" Gossman added.

"Hester Prynne? No, *The Scarlet Letter*—1850, by Nathaniel Hawthorne. She constantly is confronted with the battle between her chastity and her sexuality—but definitely not a killer, Mr. Gossman."

"Indeed? You *are* a well-read scholar, my dear. Where does that lead us, then?"

"I'm not sure yet, but I will tell you I do not believe your wife committed those crimes. She may have benefitted financially from her husbands' demise, but I think that's the extent of it. That's my stance unless I find further proof of Mrs. Gossman's involvement in more clandestine activities leading to the murder of those four men. But why Hester Prynne, if I may ask?"

"However selected, Hester Prynne is the number four identity—preparing for number five husband...also old and decrepit—and like so many other older men, a victim of his own age, falling for some damsel young enough to be his daughter. What sexual fixations we create, eh?" Then he looked at me. "So...Mr. Denning...what led you to discover my little operation downstairs?"

"My nose. Oh, Maggie suspected something—and I smelled some kind of ammonia or the like. So we followed our noses, so to speak."

"Very good. Yes, *ammonium zirconium carbonate*—an advanced chemical the Federal boys haven't come up with yet. It's a polymer, meaning a derivation from coal tar, a kind of *flexible plastic*, if you will. No one will detect the genuine from the counterfeit. I am that good, sir."

"I see," I said. "Well, I think we found out what we needed. So, you don't have to worry about either your money-printing operation or your magic phonograph. The world isn't ready for *that*—yet," I commented.

Gossman seemed surprised. "You astonish me, Mr. Denning. A gumshoe with an intellect? Ah, you see, I did choose the right man for the job! Yet...what guarantee do I have?"

"We all walk a thin line, Gossman. There are no guarantees, written or implied in this life. Plus, it ain't over yet. And you do know about Eddie Grant, right? We didn't discuss him on our first meeting, but his name was on your list. I found him. In fact, I thought I saw your busy little wife at the Cocoanut

Grove on a recent night Grant was singing there. Fairly tall, slim, blonde, wears black a lot, sits in dark corners?"

"Yes, that does sound like Evelyn."

"You did know that Eddie Grant and she had, shall we say, a passing affair some years back?"

He looked surprised. "No... I didn't know that. I wouldn't have suspected. I only know they sang together in the past."

"And why weren't you threatened, Gossman?"

"I was led to believe he was homosexual and not interested in the fairer sex. Maybe they just liked each other."

"Wrong, at least from where I sat watching him. He had a lotta sex appeal and the gals seemed to like him just fine. Ya see, I thought Eddie might be your informer. But I have my doubts now. Maybe someone else is pulling the strings. How do you get this mysterious information that keeps you sort of on the track of your beloved Evelyn?"

"Always a typewritten note. And it's always mailed from a different city. Santa Rosa, Santa Fe, Portland, San Diego."

"So there's a mole somewhere in the works, eh? You'd better start thinkin' who that might be, Gossman. I also have one more question. If four husbands are dead in ten years and she's working on number five—where is the *fifth* name? So far, correct me if I'm wrong, I have *Anne Shirley, Elizabeth Bennet, Lucie Manette* and now *Hester Prynne.* Isn't there a name missing somewhere?"

Gossman took a deep breath. "I have wondered that, too, sir. But Mexico has no record of any of those names...including Evelyn's. She may have used a Mexican name to marry that one." He looked up at me. "You want to know something curious?"

"What, Gossman?"

"I still love her—I'd do anything to have her back—even if she's used goods. Isn't that stupid? How can intelligent men think with such narrowness of mind, driven by their passions?"

"It happens all the time, mister. Look around you...men flail themselves onto the rocks of lust and desire all the time."

"I suppose...but you must accelerate your hunt in Los Angeles, Mr. Denning. I cannot bear this suspended life I'm leading—I must either have Evelyn—or be free of her. Remember, your job is to find her, where she lives—"

I glanced at Maggie. Her eyes were wide with amazement. "—yeah, I remember! Well, so long, Gossman. Maggie and I will be returning to L.A. tomorrow—and don't worry, both of your secrets are safe with us."

"Somehow I believe you, Mr. Denning—and for both your sakes, I hope this is true." He led Maggie and me to the front door and wished us a pleasant trip back to L.A., reminding me of my obligation to locate the former Mrs. Evelyn Gossman so he could serve the proper legal papers to her. I still believed he felt she had killed her husbands. But what if she hadn't? Where did that leave the case? And why in the hell would he want her back after ten years? People change...or maybe they don't.

Maggie and I started back for our hotel. When we were about half way down Hayes Street when out of nowhere a speeding little green car came bearing down on us just as we crossed the street. I grabbed Maggie to the sidewalk and we hit the pavement. It missed us by inches! "Gees, Cable—what was *that*?!" she shrieked.

"Oh, off hand I'd say it was someone trying to kill us." We remained lying on the sidewalk.

We smiled at each other. "Gees! she declared. "Your life really *is* dangerous! But you know, I think I like you better now, than I did at noon today."

"Oh? Maybe it's that fight inside you between chastity and your sexuality."

She didn't fight it this time. "Maybe...maybe you're right, Cable. I have been feeling things for you. And I'm not so afraid tonight."

"Maybe you come out after dark, eh?" I kidded her.

She tapped me on the shoulder. "I think I have never come out. I don't think I even know *how* to come out. Lame, isn't it?"

I got up and pulled her with me. "Well, regardless of that, we've got a killer trying to do us in—but who?"

"It's the informer—you know what I think?"

"No, what do you think?"

"I think the killer and the informer are the same person."

"But why would a killer want an ex-husband to know about all the affairs and pseudo-names of Evelyn the singer, the philandering wife, the mysterious woman in black?"

"To torture him. To punish him for something maybe he did. Someone knows something no one else knows, Cable. My instincts are usually right on."

"So, you don't think it was Gossman trying to cover up what we discovered tonight by running us over?"

"No, I don't. I think he's running frightened inside, too." We began to walk, keeping to the dark of the sidewalk. We reached the Hotel Whitcomb and went directly to our room. As soon as we got in, Maggie told me she was gonna take a bath and for me not to disturb her. I said I was going to sleep, and that was that. She also asked me not to smoke in the room. That would be harder than peeking through the keyhole to see her naked little body! I decided I'd check to see if anyone followed us. I lifted the shade a bit to peer outside. The streets were still enshrouded in fog. I checked under the streetlamps. No one.

I must've drowsed a bit, for when I awakened, my little roommate was in her slip, sitting on the edge of her bed, looking at me. I knew instantly what she was thinking. "Can't make up your mind, eh?" I mumbled as I yawned.

"I was just watching you...wondering what it'd be like...if—if—"

"—let me do it for you, kid. We're in different leagues. I'm sorry I made that pass at you after

68

lunch. I had no right. Now, go to sleep like a good girl and have merry dreams of one day meeting Mr. Right—and forget me, except as your crime associate, okay?"

She puckered her lips. "What if I just discovered I liked the kiss—and I might want more?"

"It ain't me, Maggie—now go to sleep. We've gotta be at the train station by seven-thirty."

"Well, it's already three a.m. Why even go to sleep? Will you talk to me? Even if you don't want my—my feminine favors…at least will you do that?"

"Talk about what, lady? I don't like small talk. You're wondering if you should take your slip off and come into my bed naked and let the chips fall where they might, right? Well, let me short-cut it for you. I don't wanna hurt you, Maggie, or give you bittersweet memories of one night of lovemaking—when there can be no more."

She tilted her head. "And why is that? "

"Because you're a quality gal, and one who deserves her first time to be with someone she truly loves—and maybe he might just love her back—the kind that lasts."

"How do you know it'd be my first time?"

"Trust me…I know a virgin when I'm talking to one, babe."

"I like that."

"Like what?"

"The way you say 'babe' to me. I think it's romantic."

I guess I'll never know how to figure a dame. "Go to sleep, Maggie. I gotta catch some shut-eye, okay?"

"Okay…" she said begrudgingly. " But you still don't know if I'm a virgin or not—or if I even want you! So *there*, Mr. Bigshot!"

# Chapter 2

## A MALFORMED SOUL

It was Wednesday, the 13th. Maggie and I got back to L.A. the previous Monday and I suppose life went back to normal. At least for a while. I dug into my work, Maggie went back to her library and Ida and I continued to work on the usual cases of tracing down errant husbands, wives, lovers and miscellaneous people who had trespassed against a moral society that forbade stepping over certain boundaries, although it was done a thousand times a day behind closed doors. It was my job to locate and then find evidence to present to the interested parties, including the lawyers who profited from the 'sins' of the offenders. Usually a few Kodak photos showing the offending couple was all it took to cinch it in court. *Money* was still the name of the game, for the most part.

Ida seemed a bit antsy this day. She also seemed clumsy and uncoordinated. "I've known you a long time, Ida—but I've never seen you drop so damn many things as this morning."

"I'm sorry, Cable. I think I'm coming round to my cycle—and Gary proposed to me last night."

I sat there, trying to examine my thoughts. How would I respond? My elegant, lovely blonde with the periwinkle eyes, my Ida, getting married? "That's swell, Ida—how many years have I told you—"

"—I haven't said yes—yet. I'm thinking it over carefully. It means a lifetime of commitment, you know. A husband, hopefully children and a little house somewhere in Glendale. He owns his own home there."

"I see. Well, indeed, it's a big step, Ida. Do you love him?"

"Do you mean do I love him as I love you? The answer's no. Gary's practical, not a romantic bone in his body. But he's steady—which is more than I can say for you, lover man," she chided me lightly. "You're like a summer storm—you come and go, and go and come..."

"Yeah, I guess we did a lot of that, huh?"

"But it's funny with you—as wildly as I wanted you, I always felt like I was still a virgin afterward. Isn't that weird?"

"Ha! And that's just how you'll stay—a virgin. Tell your Gary he's getting first-hand merchandise. That's how we'll consider you from here on out, Ida. You're a virgin, pure as the driven snow, and twice as nice!"

She frowned. "Maybe I will marry him. I was hoping—"

"—hoping what, Ida? That at 47 I'd still be panting at your door when you know I'm a chain-smoking alcoholic with a price on my head? When I can't remember who I am when I wake up in the morning—or who's the next client I gotta go to court for? Without you I wouldn't even have clean clothes because you remind me there's a laundry down the block, or shop for food once in a while because sometimes eating is *good*, and maybe you'll be there when I come home at night? Is that what you hope for, lady? Forget it, I'm through, washed up, a marginal has-been with dark shadows still haunting me after twenty years. Start new, Ida, begin a fresh life with a guy who's gonna be there for you. So what if ya don't love him in a passionate, sensual way. Hell, what did it ever get you except some good moments and at least two pregnancies?"

"Three…" Her eyes were wet and she sat down opposite me. "You left one thing out, Cable. I loved you with a forever note in it. And I'm not going to stop loving you just because I might marry someone else. There's love—and then there's *practical.* And you were right about one thing. If I'm going to have babies they must have regular lives, an organized home with two parents who care about them, a nice house with a playground nearby and a nice school to attend." She got up and paced. "And my heart? Well, that'll have to go on vacation, indefinitely. I guess the six years or so I've known you have taught me a lot. I'm now a skilled secretary and—and I know what it feels like to be in—in a union with someone. You brought chills to my body when we made love— and you still do! It's hard for a woman to forget that. I told my Mom about you one day, you know…"

"No, I didn't know. What did she say?"

"She was appalled that we'd been intimate outside of marriage and that I'd better get hitched very soon! I told her it was my choice and I fell in love with you, but she couldn't understand that. A lot of people don't know what love feels like, Cable, did you know that?"

"I—I guess I never thought too much about it, Ida."

"She thought you were too old for me and in the wrong profession, and that I might end up supporting you *and* our children if we got married and had kids."

"Not to worry, Ida, that ain't gonna happen. Okay, so from now on, it's friendly, but *business* between us, okay? And no hanky-panky. Think of San Francisco as our farewell liaison, okay?"

She didn't say anything more, but went back to her desk and put her glasses on and continued typing. What was she thinking? One thing for sure—ya never know about a dame!

I was feeling low because the times were changing and so many wonderful nightclubs had run their courses and were closing up. There was still the *Cocoanut Grove, Neon Flamingo, Mindy's, Blue Gardenia,* and the *Florentine Gardens,* but I suspected many were suffering from lack of business. In the old days, people drank, ate, smoked, flirted, danced and cavorted to the tune of some singer up there on the bandstand until the wee hours of the morning. After the war, all that changed. The old breeds of men and women had either drifted off into oblivion, alcoholism, marriage or simply changed their life styles. And I suppose many of them just plain died. That was the way with humans, ya know.

But this one night I decided to walk the streets and ended up at *Mindy's*. I liked the joint because it still had that old-fashioned atmosphere of class and good crowds. The streets of L.A. were like flat ant-hills, everyone going to that mysterious place called nowhere, but seeming to have importance, purpose. And maybe to them, the task or the walk or the ride was important. That's how I perceived humans— busy little ants going nowhere, really, but about some task that served the queen, whose bloated and undulating body was helpless without the workers. It reminded me of government, military leaders, politicians—how hopelessly impotent they were without the taxpayer, the soldier, the tailor, the carpenter, the tank driver—well, you get the picture. And one day, if someone pulled the right trigger at the wrong time and blew us all to kingdom come, the world would become a *City of Bones*, like the secrets held in the bowels of Nicaragua's highlands.

How surprised I was to see Scarlett O'Hara's picture on a post board in the lobby of *Mindy's*. Last time I saw the lady she was a guest at the *Florentine Gardens*, a place of many memories for me. Now she was headlining a joint by comparison. Of course *Mindy's* was a lot more intimate, but it had the right atmosphere, reminding me that some of the old clubs had kept their clientele and good music, booze, cigarettes, food and fast women were still in vogue somewhere. As I recalled, Miss O'Hara had a fine voice and mannerisms that were familiar, but I couldn't put my finger on who she reminded me of. She was singing a song I'd never heard before. It was called *The Facts of Life*. '*You've got to face the facts of life, he really never loved you,*' she sang. I wondered. Had anyone? She had an appealing aloofness about her. Those green eyes contrasted with that dark, almost black, short hair was siren-like and her voice was breathy and sexy. "She's pretty good, huh?" a man's voice said next to me as I stood at the bar sipping my hot honeyed whiskey. "She dresses as well as she sings, too."

I turned to look at a handsome young man about my height with warm intense brown eyes. "Yeah, it's my second time seeing her," I said.

"Oh? I thought this was her first engagement," he responded.

"Well, I happened to catch her as a guest singer one night at the *Florentine Gardens*. Glad to see she's got her own club now."

He extended his hand. "*Johnny Splendid*," he said. I shook his hand. "I know I've seen you somewhere. No doubt you've seen me?"

I checked him out. "Nope, can't say that I have. Under what circumstances do you think…?"

He looked disappointed. "Oh, I guess you don't frequent the movies much."

"Hardly at all. I see a hard-boiled Bogey flick now and then. But not too much else. Why, what do you do?"

"Well, three years ago I was the gallant *Captain America,* Republic Pictures' most expensive serial at $223,000. And that was in wartime 1944 bucks. I was handsome! Incredible! Stupendous! It was a great action serial. One of these days they'll release it as a movie in one piece. It's about four hours long. I figure they can do it in two two-hour segments with a long intermission, you know, give the audience a chance to breathe." He heaved his chest out. "Yep, I was great, I even resented my stuntman. Hell, I could've done it all!"

"I'm sorry I missed it. I'm not much into movies. My own life has all the drama and mystery I need."

"Oh? Whatta ya do, Mr.—Mr.—?"

"—Denning, Cable Denning, private eye."

"I should have known, you know—the fedora, trench coat. Are you packing under that coat?"

"Could be," I answered, lighting up a Lucky Strike.

"Is your life dangerous?"

"Yeah, sometimes...and has been known to put me at risk." I said that underplaying the tightrope walk of my life. "So, what are you involved in now? Are you still doing movies?"

"Are you kidding? I'm better than ever, Denning. In fact, we're filming right now. I think they'll release it to theatres sometime before Thanksgiving."

"Oh, good for you, Johnny Splendid."

"Don't you just love that name? I think it has charm, power, charisma—sort of like I am in real life, you know the power to influence people, win over women..."

"Is that so?" I chuckled, realizing how this guy put himself up there on some majestic pedestal. "Do you have a non-stage name?"

"Oh yeah, but that's not exciting. Especially to women."

"What is it, if I may ask?"

"Bruce Froppenheiser—now, isn't that a winner...huh?"

I chuckled. "I see what you mean. Exciting, action, titillating the female psyche and all that stuff—is that what ya like?"

"Yep! That's it. My new serial movie is called *The Black Widow*—kinda crazy plot, some babe is an import and disguised as a fortuneteller, does some pretty evil shit. I play Steve Colt, an amateur criminologist who breaks the case open. Pretty scary at times, though. Nothing more dangerous than a poisonous female, I say," he laughed.

But I didn't laugh. I was thinking that maybe Evelyn Gossman was that "poisonous female" and they just hadn't caught her yet. "So exactly what did this 'black widow' babe do?"

"Well, when Sombra the villainess wants someone eliminated, she'd take poisonous black widow spiders from a jar, agitate them and command them to bite the victims. But damn it, I had an affair with my movie secretary, Virginia Lindley, and her husband almost stopped production because of it."

For whatever reasons, my brain zeroed in on the method of killing people by black widow spiders. "So, how do you, as the hero, find her out?"

"Eh...it's Hollywood schlock—you know, following someone until you find incriminating evidence and of course near the end I get a whole jar of spiders tossed at me when Sombra is pissed. But I'm the hero—and heroes always win, don't they?"

"I don't know—do they?" I responded with a question.

"Well, we have to keep the kiddies believing it anyhow, huh?" he laughed and we toasted one another. We both glanced up at the stage as Scarlett O'Hara launched into 1933's Nacio Herb Brown and Arthur Freed's *Temptation*. '*You came, I was alone, I should have known, you were temptation,*' she breathed as the band played a sexy Latin beat in the background. The first time I saw her she was dressed in green. Tonight she was dressed in shiny black with white gloves. She looked great. She seemed almost too good to be true. Beautiful young woman, composed, talented—maybe even intelligent—who knows? I was curious about how she chose the name *Scarlett O'Hara.* It's doubtful that she was born with that name. Maybe it'd give me a hint as to how Evelyn Gossman chose famous literary names for her phony identifications. I decided to meet the attractive young singer. So I excused myself from the presence of one Johnny Splendid and went up and introduced myself. "I like your singing style, Miss O'Hara," I complemented her. "I don't think I ever heard a female singer do *Temptation* before."

"No, I guess it's just Bing, Perry and me, Mr.—Mr.—"

"—Denning, Cable Denning." I didn't extend my hand but half-bowed. She checked me out carefully, those intense green eyes surveying me from top to bottom.

"You look like a cop—are you?" she asked. I noticed a tinge of apprehension.

"Not a cop, just a private investigator. But that's not why I'm here. I needed to get out and walk—and I invariably end up in a club somewhere listening to some fine young singer like you."

"Well, thank you, Mr. Denning. I enjoy singing."

"Scarlett O'Hara—is that your real name or—"

"—no, but you wouldn't want to know my real name."

"No? Okay...but why did you choose such a powerful literary figure for a stage name, if you don't mind my asking?"

"Oh, I don't know—I guess it just appealed to me. I saw Scarlett O'Hara as a heroine, someone to look up to, I guess. Are you being a private detective now, Mr. Denning?" She started to move back onto the stage. "I—I, uh, have to go back up for my next number. To answer your question, I just liked the name. I'm not even Irish."

I laughed. "Yeah, I guess it's my instinct, to be nosy, sorry. Well, thanks, Miss O'Hara—my gentleman drinking companion and I think you're swell, for what it's worth."

"Thank you—enjoy yourself," she said and walked away.

I got back to the bar. "Struck out, didn't you?" Johnny Splendid commented with a cigarette between his lips.

"Oh, I wasn't really trying to make points. I just like good singers and great music—I thought I'd let her know how appreciated she is."

"Maybe, but I'll bet you'd still like to have some of the luscious stuff under her dress now, wouldn't you?"

"I'll tell it to ya straight, Johnny Splendid—there was a time I loved chasin' skirts. But these days I ain't in such a hurry. Like good aging wine, I take a little more time...to enjoy..."

"Not me. Hell, I'd take her to bed in a heartbeat! She's classy and elusive—I like that. I've tried a couple of times. But...no luck. She's really very private. No one seems to know where she goes after hours. Maybe home to bed—alone, or maybe she prefers her own sex—damn, these days ya never know—know what I mean?" He licked his chops. "Yeah, all that good woman going to waste..."

"Yep. I used to think like that."

"And now, Denning?"

"Well, let's just say I *savor* the fairer sex."

"Not me, hell, I'd jump into that lady with both feet!"

"Good for you, Johnny Splendid." I checked my watch. It was 12:30 a.m. Scarlett O'IIara had begun to sing *All or Nothing at All* in a steamy Latin style and I was wondering how many young guys got bulges in their pants listening to the gal warble *that* version of the song. But I had other plans. I drank and small talked with Johnny Splendid a little longer, then told him I was going home. But what I really wanted to do was see where this young dark-haired beauty went after hours.

I said good night and waited in the shadows across the street from the front of *Mindy's*. About

81

2:00 a.m. or so I saw her come out—with Johnny Splendid in tow! He was doing his best to talk her into the nearest bedroom. But dear Scarlett seemed to take offense and hauled off and slapped the dude across that pretty face of his, hard. She walked away and stood at the curb as Johnny slinked away toward his own car and sped off into the Hollywood night. Soon a little dark green Dodge coupe pulled up and Scarlett O'Hara got in. I jumped into my car and followed. They drove off on Sunset toward downtown. Soon the Dodge left Scarlett off at 138 North Grand, near the corner of West Temple. It was an old building with a small dump of a club with sputtering neon lights down in a basement level. I didn't know anything about this club. I parked and waited a few minutes and lit up a cigarette. Why would this classy babe go down into a seedy joint like that at 2:30 in the morning—when it was supposed to be closed? She was admitted and disappeared. I was tired. It was probably all I could do for this night, so I packed it up and went home to bed. At least I knew where she hung out—or lived.

## The Thermo-nuclear Horror

It was Thursday, August 14, 1947. The rest I hoped for was not to be. Before dawn that fateful morning I heard a hard pounding on my door. I grabbed my gun and staggered up to face the interloper. "Yeah? It's five o'clock in the morning! Who the hell is it? Friend or foe?"

"It is neither, Mr. Denning—but kindly let us in..."

"Let *us* in? And who are you? And where do you come from?"

"If you open the door, Mr. Denning, we will inform you immediately."

I kept my .38 trained on the door and opened it. In walked an unlikely pair of men. One was a squat Chinaman while the other had a certain tall Russian look about him. The squat man did most of the speaking. "Okay...so what's this about—I just got to bed!"

"Yes, we know, you have been followed this night."

"Oh? So you'd better start explaining before I start firing away at your sorry asses, boys!" The Russian stepped forward aggressively. The Chinaman was more diplomatic and held the big guy back.

"It is our understanding you have been spoken to by a certain party regarding your next assignment. *We* are included in your next assignment." I'd all but forgotten about Cronus-Gor's last threat, to put me in charge of some diplomatic bullshit about the newest invention on how to destroy the world—a thing called the *hydrogen bomb,* so Gor called it. And he wanted me to stir up some shit in the mid-East with the help of the Russians and the Chinese. But why? And *how?* I'm an everyday American Joe, not a saboteur! Russia was fast turning against us—as were the Chinese. Hell, I was still thinkin' *American!* Jo Stafford hit number one on the song charts with a comedic version of *Temptation*, my hero Joe Louis k.o.'d Mauriello and was still the champ, but Russia, called the '*Soviet Union*', refused to participate in the Marshall Plan. India was about to get rid of Britain as its dominator, some flying saucers were spotted hanging around Mt. Rainier in Washington State, President Truman signed an executive order...the 'Loyalty Order' which generated new investigations by the House Un-American Activities, and the rest of the world was being cut up and sliced to accommodate the powers that be. And now Cronus-Gor wanted to toss me into the middle of some nefarious scheme to rattle the sabers of war? How many layers of secrets were kept under wraps? And hell, I didn't even speak Chinese, Russian—*or* Yiddish. Nope, come hell or high water, I just wouldn't do it. Period.

"Well, tell your certain party I'm not interested in his offer. And  I'm not particularly fond of his henchmen, either. So go away and don't bother me anymore."

The Chinaman was trying to be adamant and persuasive. "But surely, Mr. Denning, you know they will terminate you should you not do their bidding. No, sir, I think you should reconsider and come with us—they will kill you for certain otherwise."

I looked at both of them. "Then good riddance. I'm not all that happy here, are you? And the planet's getting too crowded anyway."

The two men looked at each other. The Russian spoke in a deep, dark accented voice. "You not afraid to die?"

"Nope, are you? It's always just a step away, you know. You'd better make friends with that ol' Grim

Reaper, gentlemen—nothing's worse than being caught with your pants down the moment you die!" I said that with my tongue-in-cheek for shock value. "Now I suggest you go back to Papa and tell him what I said."

The two men looked at each other. Still at gunpoint, I led them to my office door. They said nothing and left.

I went back to bed and was still sleeping when Ida peeped into my bedroom. Then some huge hand moved her aside and as Ida screamed and flailed helplessly against the intruder, he literally picked up my bed and shook me out of it! Then he started pounding on my naked body. It hurt like hell. Finally after we punched and wrestled for a couple of minutes, I found a near-empty gin bottle and conked him hard over the head with it. He went down like a sea lion. He must've been 6' 5" with a sixty-inch chest and a shaved head. Ida was both terrified and repulsed all at once and as soon as she saw I was okay, went into the office to call the police. I told her not to. This guy was probably not even traceable. But I knew who had sent him. Then the Chinese man appeared in the doorway as I was wiping my own blood off with a towel. "Oh...so sorry—Icknas can be a little rough...are you badly hurt?"

"Oh, no more than usual. What the hell are you guys up to? Leave me alone, goddamnit, or I'll shoot you myself."

"You know *who* wants to see you."

I played dumb. "Uh...*who*?"

"Please, Mr. Denning, come peaceably. It would be better for all concerned."

"It would? Ya can't prove it by me, buster!"

"It is Mr. *Lo*—if you don't mind." He drew his gun. "One more time—I am asking you to follow me down and into a parked car without incident."

I didn't say any more. I got dressed and told Ida I'd be back and not to worry. But she did. She loved me. What else would I expect?

## Into the Jaws of Uncertainty

An hour later I was facing an empty stage at *Oculus Pyramis Mandatum* headquarters, hidden somewhere within the bowels of the city. Cronus-Gor liked things big. The reception room was more like a basketball gymnasium and eerie lights made the space glow like we were inside a spaceship. And maybe we were. Soon I heard the imposing voice of Gor fill the room and address me.

"Denning...I am told you have refused our original agreement....that saddens me, for now I have to hasten your demise. You are an entertaining, human curio to me—a pity."

"I said yes to get you out of my hair, Gor—I reasoned I don't even speak those goddamned languages you'd be sending me in to—Russian, Chinese—and of course Yiddish or whatever the Jews are speaking these days. How about Edomite?"

"Silence!" he boomed. Then there was a silence. "I will give you one more chance to—to 'redeem' yourself, Denning. Unfortunately, you have gotten under my skin—you have seduced my wife, one of my daughters and caused me untold difficulty—perhaps even an insurgence among the ranks. If you will do this one thing as penitence, perhaps I shall dismiss your refusal as a stupid, human whim—and you did not realize the—the *consequences*."

"I ain't that stupid, Gor—your so-called 'consequences' are always bullying, threats and fear! That's how you control us little 'curios' called humans. But I told you before and I'm sayin' it again, I'm not afraid of you, Gor—torture, maim, think of a devilish plan to do me in—I've seen too much, buddy—and death would be a relief!"

Again there was a silence. "Hmmm...you are indeed incorrigible, Denning. Nevertheless, you *will do my next assignment!* It is simple, straight-forward, without complication."

"Oh? Pray tell, what could it be—what diabolical horror are you cooking up now besides setting the world at war once again?"

"Ha! I have always liked your wit, Denning—however, your sense of humor engages at the most precarious moments, for *you*—like this one. I am puzzled as to how you manage not to fear me as do others."

"One can always tell a phony from a distance, Gor. Maybe you forget, but I learned a lot about you through your daughter and your wife. Lord knows why they love you, but I know at least Saturnalia does. Count her as among your loyal champions, mister."

He was quiet for a few seconds. "So...now to the deed at hand. I wish you to kill someone for me. His name is *Dr. Vaclav Mendel*, a geneticist. He is worthless now, but he knows too much—more or less like you, Denning. In a way, this will be a rehearsal for *your* elimination."

"And just where will I find this Dr. Mendel?" I asked. Of course I had no intention of killing someone for the satisfaction of a monster madman creep who wasn't even an earthling!

"In Prague, Czechoslovakia, hidden away in a secret laboratory."

"Shit, Gor, I'm really not in the mood to travel— how about someone else?"

"*Silence!*" he bellowed, shaking the huge room. Then as usual, he calmed down after the outburst. "You will go under the auspices of Mr. Lo and he has orders to kill you if you do not obey *my* orders. Is that clear?"

"Oh, yeah, nothing like traveling with someone who's willing to kill you at the drop of a hat. Makes for a comfortable passage, don't you think?"

"Very funny, Denning...but do not laugh—it might be your last..."

"What about the *Fen de Fuqín* and the marvelous knowledge I have stored up here in my noggin?"

"I have thought of that..." He said, mulling things over. "Perhaps I shall not have Mr. Lo kill you— maybe just *maim* you, so you might live long enough to have me extract the valuable information you have stored up there in that primitive little brain of yours."

"Have you ever thought of suicide, Gor?" I kidded him.

"Quiet, you puffed up philanderer! Besides, I am immortal—I cannot die..."

"That's too bad. The universe could do with a lot less creatures like you. Might even be a more harmonious place."

He ignored my last statement and sent for Mr. Lo to escort me out and back to my office—blindfolded, of course. Ida was still there when Mr. Lo and I entered. "Cable...are you alright?" she asked as Lo removed my blindfold. "Why would you use a blindfold in the middle of the day?" she inquired of the Chinaman. "Isn't it rather obvious—"

"—please lady to shut-up. Lady may be seen, but not heard. Chinese way. So should also be way of Americans."

"Well, I'll second that," I teased Ida. "So long Lo—it was definitely *not* a pleasure meeting you."

"We shall meet again, I assure you, Mr. Denning...and soon." With that he bowed slowly and left.

"Damn, he's got some nerve! Oh, Cable—don't tell me, Gor has you up to no good again."

"Yeah, but it's better than starting World War Three. I'm just supposed to kill some genetic doctor in Czechoslovakia, that's all."

She looked at me incredulously. "What?! You mean, you'd be an assassin for that horrible creature thing—"

"—put yourself in my place. Rubbing out one old mad scientist to preserve the likes of a tall, handsome, charismatic music loving son-of-a-gun like me? C'mon now, Ida—how can I resist the urge to keep living—at least for a little while longer." She knew I was being sarcastic.

"It's not funny, Cable. I've gone through thick and thin with you and the prospect of you being a killer, frankly makes me ill."

"Well, I've killed people since I was twenty-six. I think that was my first homicide. A young cop with little sense, a ghetto rat with kill-or-be-killed etched on his brain. How's that sound, lady?"

"Horrible. I can't believe you'd just do premeditated murder like that—I mean, not even self-defense!"

"Ah, leave it up to the feminine wiles to say something like that. Wind yourself around my psyche, Ida, remind yourself how warped and twisted I am and how I'd do almost anything to finish out my stay here on planet earth. At least until the real time comes."

"I can't believe you're saying that."

I used my forefinger to beckon her to me. "C'mon, Ida, you know I couldn't do cold blooded murder. But they've gotta believe I would."

"So what are you going to do, Cable?"

"I dunno. I don't even know when I'm leaving."

The rest of the day went okay and Ida went home around 5:30 p.m. I sat at my desk and took out a bottle of gin. Hmmm...a brand new bottle. I don't even remember buying it. Maybe I was really becoming an unconscious alcoholic with less and less recognition of my life and its surroundings. I opened the bottle and poured a generous amount of English gin into my old bathroom glass. Noticing it was sparkling clean for a change...Ida...I took a big swig. Then the phone rang.

"Yeah, Cable Denning here..."

"Cable, it's me, Maggie. Boy, Mr. Detective, have I got some new ideas for *you*! When can we meet?"

"New ideas or facts, Maggie—we can't arrest a killer on ideas, ya know."

"Well, a little bit of both. It's about 7:30—can we meet at some place to have a drink?"

"I thought you didn't drink."

"Maybe when I'm with you, Cable. I trust you. You didn't want me anyhow, remember?"

"Yeah...okay, so how about..." I went leafing through the newspaper on my desk. "How about the *Mocambo*, 8588 Sunset Boulevard? One hour? Dinah Shore's appearing there. I like her. Want me to pick you up?"

"No, thanks, I'll meet you. Okay, one hour, Cable..."

I left my bottle on top of my desk and got myself changed and by the time I got into my car, it was already 8:15 p.m. I pulled away from the curb. So did another car. I was being followed. I tried to give 'em the slip, but whoever it was knew their way around Hollywood and I couldn't shake 'em. The *Mocambo* opened in 1941 just in time for WWII and flourished ever since. Big headliners were what brought in the people. Add to that the sexy Latin décor and the atmosphere for dining and dancing 'til dawn. I almost couldn't believe how great Maggie looked as I greeted her at the entrance to the club. She was dressed in a light-blue pleated skirt, a cream-colored blouse, fairly low cut and patent leather shoes to match. The only thing that did her in were those glasses with the thick frames. We hugged and we went to the bar for drinks. It was too early for Dinah Shore to sing yet, so a little combo was playing up there on the stage. The stage, enhanced with a large black grand piano, was floor level with a little podium for a singer, I guessed. The bar wasn't that big either and had a huge overhang making it feel a little more intimate. We ordered and I paid.

"So...? What's the good news, kid?"

"I'm not a kid, Cable, I'm a grown woman with—well, with lots going for her. Plus, I *read*—a lot. How much do you read?"

"Oh, try me out?"

"What fields—fiction or fact, biography or—"

"—how about science fiction? That's always fun."

"Okay, name the top three science fiction writers in the past ten years, smarty."

"Okay...*Siodmak, Campbell, Bradbury, Asimov, Arthur C. Clark, Heinlein*—for starters."

Maggie looked surprised. "Why, I apologize—I never guessed—"

"—that ghetto-raised gumshoes could read? It's okay, Maggie, don't sweat it."

We drank two drinks before Maggie began to open up. "Well, back to the case of Evelyn Gossman. Here's what I've discovered to be fact. There's an older blonde woman who is currently singing at the *Newport Harbor Yacht Club* on the Balboa Peninsula.

She uses the name *Marla Felíx*. I discovered she's also the fiancée of one of the private club's richest men. Interested?"

"Yeah! Go on! But isn't Marla Felíx a Mexican movie star and still alive somewhere in mid-career?"

"Yes, Cable, that's why this fifth name is intriguing. *That* lady's first name is *Maria*—not Marla, but close enough to make it interesting...don't you think? It gets better. *Maria's* first husband...Enrique Alvarez Alatorre worked for *Max Factor* in Mexico. One of *Max Factor's* sons is *Sidney B. Factor,* born in 1916 and is currently...*now listen to this*!...none other than the fiancé of the phony Maria—or *Marla* Felíx."

"Hmmm...good work, Maggie! But this Factor guy's only 31 years old—isn't she robbing from the cradle? Not exactly been her pattern."

"I don't think so. I think it's intentional. He's one of the richest men around. She's still very good looking and appears a lot younger than her early 40's. I think Evelyn wants to rake in the biggest haul of all time. The wedding is set for September. Wanna go?"

"Oh, yeah...so how do we catch her?"

"I don't think she killed the other husbands, Cable, as I said, and I don't think she'll kill this one. She's maybe ten years older than her future husband. They seemed to be in love. I watched them one night from fairly close up."

"How'd you do that?"

"I've got a friend whose husband is rich and a member of the yacht club. I told him I was doing research on the long history of the club. He took me there. I had a good time, too."

"Did he propose to you?"

"No, silly man, I'm waiting for *you* to do that! Do you—do you want to dance?"

I said no more and took Maggie's hand and led her to the dance floor. The band was playing a slow version of *Blue Moon* and my little female companion snuggled in close to me. I enjoyed this peppy little gal more and more. "So...where'd ya learn to dance so well?"

"Lessons...at *Arthur Murray's Dance Studio* on Wilshire Blvd. How am I doing?"

"Great."

The music was smooth, romantic. We drifted over to an uncrowded corner of the dance floor. "Now for the conjecture, Cable. Here's what I think. Someone wants to frame Evelyn Gossman, wants to pin these murders on her. But...and this is a big *but*...I am assuming for the moment that the murderer is going to take this last haul of money and quit doing what he's doing. But before he does that, he has to make sure there's enough evidence against Evelyn to arrest her on one hand, and access the Factor fortune on the other."

"So, it's the ol' 'take-the-money-and-run' scheme and he'll dash Evelyn's dreams of happily-ever-after by killing the new fiancé, eh?"

"Looks that way to me."

"What evidence do you have—and of course, who's the killer, Maggie? Without that, we're back to square one, capisce?"

"I don't know. Some *mal-formed soul* no doubt. That's the piece that's missing." Then she lowered her voice and spoke into my ear. "But I know one thing that's not missing."

"Yeah? And what's that?"

"Feeling as I do toward you. It hasn't been easy going without seeing you since we got back from Frisco."

I pushed her back from me to look into her eyes. "You ain't kidding, are ya?"

Her eyes misted a little. "No, Cable, no—I'm not. I think for the first time in my life I'm in love. And wouldn't ya know it?"

"Know what?"

"The least available of all men I could have chosen to fall in love with. It's like a jillion books I've read. Why do women go for a guy who's on a different planet?"

"I don't know, why do they?" Dinah Shore came on the stage as the place filled to capacity. Talk about pretty blondes!

Maggie drew me closer to her and said no more, but nuzzled her face onto my shoulder. Then she asked me if I could take her home.

As we pulled out into traffic, I noticed that same dark little coupe was following us. I pulled up in front of the Edgemont Manor Apartments and parked. It was late. "I know I'm crazy, but would you like to come in?"

I glanced at my watch. "Hell, it *was* Thursday, Maggie—now it's Friday and you have get up and go to work."

"So? It's a short bus ride to Ivar."

"We're being followed by the bad guys. I don't want you involved, lady. Just get out and go into your apartment building, pronto!"

"I'm not afraid, Cable. A couple of drinks with you and I can face anything. You have to stop running someday, Mr. Detective."

"Well, it's not tonight, kid. Now, go!"

"No. Somehow we're not through for tonight. Or at least, I'm not through. Don't you feel something—something else?"

"Yeah, *danger.*"

"I repeat, would you like to come in for a while?"

I knew in my heart she was grabbing at straws. "Why, Maggie? Do you enjoy torturing yourself? We've been down this path before. Why would you want an old, washed up gumshoe in your bed?"

"Because I'm irredeemably stupid...because I'm a girl without a history with a man—because I'm a woman in love—*you* pick one, Cable—but that's just the way it is. Are you coming up—or not?"

"Not, Maggie. I'm sorry. I told you before, it's just not me you're lookin' for, babe."

"How are you so damned sure—how do you know who's inside me here? I'm impossibly itinerant in my soul, Cable—are you man enough to discover that!?" She undid her hair and let it fall to her shoulders. "I live a double life, Cable—one prim and proper and educated and morally upstanding on the outside...but wanton, restless and carnal on the inside, mister—wanna try your odds!?"

I was shocked at Maggie's sudden confession. "*Impossibly itinerant?* C'mon, Maggie, you've seen too many movies. Aren't those awful big words to be tossin' at a bum who lives on Franklin and—"

She didn't let me finish. She plunged herself at me and forced her lips onto mine. Her arms reached around my neck and kept me there so tight that my hat fell off. "If I have to take my dress off right here in your car and show you what you're missing—"

"—you just sealed your own fate, lady!" I declared. I grabbed the keys out of my little coupe and got out, went around to the rider's side and pulled Maggie out of the car and shut the door. She took the lead and we went into her apartment building and we climbed the stairs to the third floor. She lived in #42, the last door on the right. Neither of us spoke. She locked the door after us and had me pull down the wall bed. She pushed me onto the bed, turned the lights off and began to undress in front of me. Only the light from a tall building across the street shone through the window. She peeled off her blouse and let her light-blue skirt fall to the floor. Then she stood there as she slowly lifted her slip up over her head. White panties and white brassiere were all that remained. Then she got on her knees and took off my shoes, socks and undid my belt buckle. Slowly she peeled my britches down. Quickly she tossed them aside and came creeping up my legs to my boxers and placed a hand inside to draw out my half-mast penis. Gently she licked my male member to attention and then put as much as she could into her mouth and sucked gently, then harder and harder. It was difficult to believe this was her first go at it. She straddled me and took my hands to quietly slip her panties off and undo her bra. I was quite surprised how much bosom Maggie Loggins had. They were still young and firm, and if not beauty contest winners, they were fetching, not to mention inviting.

She slid her naked body like a snake up to my face and put her lips slowly onto mine. She was shaking. "This is your last chance...I'm asking one more time, Maggie...are you sure you want this?"

"Yes!" she whispered enthusiastically in the darkness. "You are the *one*, Cable..." Before I knew it, her straddling posture brought her lubricated womanhood down onto me. I had penetrated her unknown territory, broken the hymen, conquered her full, almost over-blossomed womanhood and she went wild with pleasure and excitement. I just hoped her neighbors were heavy sleepers!

We lay naked in bed together. Maggie was on her side, wrapped around me, the dull glow from the light across the street lighting parts of her face, her eyes. "Now I'll be a legend...at least to myself...a legend in my own time. Isn't that something? Do you realize I'm no longer a virgin, my beautiful man? I...I knew...I could only give myself to someone I loved. I'm sore, but I'm happy. I didn't realize the first time would *really* hurt!" She tilted her head up to look at me. "I love you, Cable. Plain and simple. But I know one thing that will break my heart..."

"Break your heart? We've barely gotten together, Mag."

"I just have this feeling—I'll hear the closing of that door over there a lot of times, times when you leave me after—well, after we've made love. And I know you'll smile, you'll be sincere and you'll just walk away, maybe not even saying good-bye."

"I hate good-byes, kid. I've known too many of 'em."

"Maybe that's why I—I might feel selfish, wanting you more and more—and wanting you to stay."

"Some things remain hidden, Maggie—maybe they're behind forbidden doors—I never promised you anything—including tonight. *You* took the initiative here, not me."

"You're right, I did. And I might even get pregnant because we didn't use anything." She toyed with my hair. "But I wouldn't mind...having your baby...I know that wouldn't be a reason why you'd stick around. You're not that kind of man."

"No, and I don't want you to cry when it's over." I lifted her chin to look at her in the semi-dark. "And one day it *will* end, doll."

"I don't want to think about that now. And maybe like a book, someday you'll turn a page inside your head and find me. And maybe one day you'll take one more look and see my love won't bind you. Can you understand that much, at least?"

"Understand what—that someday you won't hear the closing of that door you talk about—and that I won't get up and roam the midnight streets of L.A., or I won't still be searching for myself in the heap of noise and pollution and music and pain and heartache out there? C'mon, kid, I'm only a winner when I hold someone like you in my arms, Maggie. The rest of the time I'm an uncertain, struggling loser whose lights are about to be put out—permanently!" I raised my voice.

"No! That's wrong, Cable—people have choices! You can decide not to have that experience—have me—*us*—instead, and I'll read to you every night!" she vowed in the darkness.

I chuckled to myself. "I think Maria Voldt answered that best."

"Oh, you mean your poet girlfriend? She was in love, too."

"Maybe, but she had a wisdom beyond sex and romantic love and frail human emotions and the shit humans have become."

"Oh? Was she above it?"

"No, but she *saw it from the top of the hill*. That's what the difference was."

"So...what'd she say?"

"Are you sure you wanna hear it?"

"Of course, if it was meaningful to you..."

"Okay. '*Robins sing on another plane of existence; we hear, copy their song and their fear—of us—for we are the pus that corrupts them if they let themselves change their grey claws for feet of clay. Another day I would tell you this, but the hell with this—you are a reckless lover! You leave me before you come fully to my bed—instead you copulate with strangers named with dangerous names on the wicked streets of Gomorrah—all the while your sweets remains in her bed, legs spread, longing, her voice, songing through the night like the orange-breasted Robin. Lucky for you, you plucky you! her song is short and her breath will dim before she thinks, links with him...again...the day comes soon, but I, my love, await on the waning moon for you..."*

There was a silence. Then Maggie rolled off of me and sat up on the edge of the bed. "I've got to go to the bathroom. I'm not sure what she was saying, but she was in love with you—and somehow you dashed her hopes, didn't you?"

"People dash their own hopes, Maggie." I got up and went to my shirt and took out a pack of Lucky Strikes. I lit up. Maggie came back out of the bathroom. "I've been bleeding, Cable...do you think it's natural?"

"Yep, I'd say so for your first time. You know, the penetration, the friction—it'll get better."

"Better? It was pretty spectacular just the way it was." She glanced at the cigarette in my mouth. "Oh, do you have to smoke in here? It lingers for days. I would rather not have that kind of reminder of you...please, if you don't mind."

"No, I'm sorry." I got up and went into the bathroom, took a pee and tossed the cigarette in the toilet bowel and flushed. I came back out and Maggie was in a short little yellow robe. "Well, I'd better get going. I've a couple of court appearances this afternoon."

"More people getting torn up on the rocks of unholy matrimony while escaping into the arms of someone else?"

"Yeah, something like that, I guess. Every case is a bit different."

"What about our case, Cable—will it be different, too?"

"Whatta ya mean?"

"Will it have the same Cable Denning ending? You know, girl falls in love, she sleeps with him, he gets tired of her and he leaves her? Now she has a war-wound, a scar that won't go away, maybe ever..."

"Ya gotta remember, Maggie, you and me started out investigating a murder case. Remember how topsy-turvy this whole thing became? You were cold. I was cold. I was warm, you were still cold. Tonight you were warm and look where we ended up! And we still haven't solved the damn case!"

She reflected a moment. "Well, then maybe I'm a fool, Cable. In the *Great Gatsby*, Daisy Buchanan says, '*I hope she'll be a fool. The best thing a girl can be in this world, a beautiful little fool.*' Is that me, Cable?"

I went over to her and kissed her gently. "Today you're beautiful, Maggie." I put on my overcoat, fedora, smiled back at her and exited.

# Chapter 3

## JOURNEY TO JIRNY

I left Maggie Loggins just before dawn that Friday and drove home in the smoggy cool of an L.A. morning. I watched as the same little black coupe pulled out behind me and followed me back to Franklin. I had this feeling they were about to pounce. But when?

Tomorrow evening I would check out one Marla Felix at the Newport Harbor Yacht Club. I'd see for myself. But how would I get in? I got to my desk. I needed a drink. I lit up a Lucky Strike and settled back with a nice double shot of gin. Ha! Maggie Loggins turned out to be quite a dish. She had not only brains but was filled with wildness and innocence in the bedroom! I took a big swig of gin. I had this niggling in my brain. I got a pencil and wrote on my scratch pad: *"Dear Ida, If you get this then they've taken me. I'll be out of town for a while. Please take over—and don't worry—they need me! Cuble.'* I tore off the page and placed it on top of Ida's desk. I never made it back to my desk. Someone must've spiked my gin and I felt woozy as I collapsed to the floor. Soon I was out cold but dreaming of something wonderful. Maybe I'd died and Heaven *was* beyond fantastic, and peaceful. Skies were perfect, the temperature grand, I could breathe freely as I'd never breathed before and my head was cleared of all heavy thought.

## The Journey

It was Wednesday, August 20, 1947. Only I didn't know it. Somehow I'd been doped up for days and gotten aboard a private that landed in Prague, Czechoslovakia. Hitler's war hadn't damaged the city all that much. The big Russian and the Chinaman had disappeared. In their places were a couple of European goons and a smartly dressed conman by the name of *Harry Jelinek*. Oh, yeah, I was wild about Harry right from the start. He'd speak kindly for a few seconds, and then suddenly he'd hit ya in the stomach pretty hard and then continue talking as if nothing had happened. I tried to be prepared by bracing my gut but you never knew when it was going to happen...and a guy's gotta breathe sometimes. He was nuts. But then again, so was I. Otherwise I wouldn't have gotten myself on this insane journey to an unknown European location to kill some guy I'd never met! Harry had me tied in a pilot's chair and had taken off his cabbie's hat to talk to me. I was sweating from the dope they'd kept me half-asleep with. He spoke rather softly and without an accent. He took his forefinger and wiped it across my forehead. "Now, Mr. Denning, I have a problem with humans. You see, they are not true mammals—perhaps more like a disease carrying vermin." Then he smelled his finger. "Like a virus, they come into a territory, use it up and then—well, then they simply move on to the next territory, consuming it and then –well, need I paint a picture? Humans are wasteful and a scourge upon the planet. Personally, I would rather see them gone from the face of the earth—but then again, I am not in charge of that decision." Out of nowhere he punched me in the gut. I responded with a heavy grunt. "So you see," he continued gentle-voiced, "nothing would make me happier than to terminate you and all humans. But that is not my current task. Let me fill you in, Mr. Denning. I am to deliver you to an estate in a small town about forty-five minutes from here called *Jirny.* Once there you will be greeted by another Harry—you may call him *Harry Two.* He will introduce you to one *Dr. Vaclav Mendel.* You will have papers on your person. These papers will introduce you as a secret agent for the United States Government. You will inform Dr. Mendel you have come to remove him from danger by taking him back to the United States for asylum." Again, he hit me hard in the stomach. I winced in pain. "That will put him at ease. Certain parties have been harassing Dr. Mendel lately. We can't have that. Nevertheless, I am perplexed as to what to do with humans. Personally, I am decided, but other parties would rather play with your species a while longer. Strange, isn't it?"

"What's that, you crazy son-of-a-bitch?" I mumbled.

"That creatures such as you exist. I think things got twisted long ago and you were a created abomination." He hit me again, hard. "But now you must rest, for tonight you will be left off to do your dirty deed on a fellow creature." He hit me again. This time I was ready. "Make certain, Mr. Denning, that

you...you do the job...else there shall be consequences..."

## Of Love and Allegra Blossom

We drove for about an hour. Near a large, run-
down estate near the edge of a small town called
*Jirny*, I was let off on a dirty road called *Tovarni*. In
fact, I was told the original owner of the estate was
one Frederick Tovarni and since he died, the house
has allegedly been empty. But not really. No one accompanied me. I was given a luger, a beat up photo
of Dr. Mendel and instructions as to what door to
enter by. That was it.

It was dark with a cool settling mist hanging
about. I forgot to ask about dogs, but I heard none so
assumed it was safe enough to proceed. Near the far
side of the huge building I found the servants' entrance door I was instructed to enter and quietly did
so. I guess I was to meet up with *Harry Two*, another
one of the henchmen-mugs Cronus-Gor was famous
for hiring. Why? Because they were expendable if
something went wrong. And believe me, something
must've gone wrong. There lying across a large
chopping block in the kitchen lay a prostrate figure
of a man in his mid-years somewhere. He had a note
across his chest. *"First Mistake..."* it read. I drew my
luger and looked around. Then I heard a rather authoritative female voice coming from out of the
shadows. "He was rather obstinate, you know.
Please drop your gun, sir," the voice purred. She
stepped out of the shadows. She was about thirty-

five, fairly tall with lovely red hair that flowed to the nape of her neck. She had a great face with blue eyes and a pair of bazooms on her that would make a burlesque queen blush. She was wearing black pants and a black shirt and held a .38 in her hand—pointed at me, naturally.

I put up my hands and my gun dropped to the floor with a clunk. "That, uh, that must be Harry Two, eh?" I observed.

"Oh, an American! I didn't know who they'd send." Her voice was fairly low and sensual. "But I do know why you came Mr.—Mr.—"

"—Denning, Cable Denning, Los Angeles, U.S.A."

"A long way from home to be killing someone, don't you think, Mr. Denning?" She moved toward me slowly, like a cat. "My name is *Allegra Blossom.* You see, my father was a musician and my mother a Cockney flower vendor from London's East end—so there you have it."

"I see. Why is it you don't speak with a Cockney accent?" I commented.

Then she launched into one. "Okay, Gov'ner, I've been ashamed o' bein' one o' them poor 'ard-workin' bastards ever since I left Chelsea, ya see. I hain't 'arkenin' to no Cockney in *me* business—them lowers strike the iron outta me, they do! Nonetheless, I was born in Bow, could 'ear the bells of St. Mary-le-bow until the Nazis destroyed them during the war." Then she checked me out. "Yer quite the 'andsome bloke—what is it ya do 'ceptin' 'ire out to do people in?"

I chuckled. "Very good! I love British dialects. So, what do you speak in nowadays—middle-class or upper-class? If ya don't mind... before you kill me, I'd like to know."

She then launched into the perfect tea-time English accent. Aloof, sophisticated. "Oh, my dear, that hat is scrumptiously awful—you mustn't be seen in public with it, you know. Courtney was wearing that god-*awful* perfume the other afternoon—dreadful! It's called *Tondoleo* or some such nonsense. I simply cannot bear to be near her when she wears it. Would you pass the milk, dear?"

I laughed. "You should've been an actress or a comedian! I think I might like you under different circumstances." Then I bent over to pick up my gun. "But somehow I don't think you'll kill me just yet. So, if you don't mind, I'll just tuck this in my pocket until I have to do my—my assignment."

Then she went into a tamer British accent. "But you realize, darling, I simply *had* to kill Harry Two here. That was the trouble with Harry, you know—very pushy!"

"I see. Well, I ain't pushy, but I'm in sort of a dilemma. Maybe you can help me out."

"Help you out? Are you not in control of your life?"

"Do you know anyone who is?"

"*I am*. I decide what, when and where and how much for my life, thank you." She must've trusted me a bit because she put her gun away, too. "Would you care for a cup of tea?"

I chuckled inside. "Cup of tea? Honey, I'm seldom interested unless it's at least eighteen proof and it curls my toes! I'm a gin drinker—actually *English* gin, to be precise. I don't even drink *water* if I can at all help it!"

She went to the stove and put on a kettle to boil some water. She leaned against the stove and looked me over again. "You don't look like a killer...hmmm...more like a bobby—a policeman..."

"Well, when I was young I was a cop, as a matter of fact. Then I got fed up with the corruption downtown and became a private dick."

"Oh, yes, one of those. So tell me your story, Mr. Denning. If I buy it...well, we'll just see..."

"Okay. Long story short—years ago I saw something I wasn't supposed to. A huge invisible alien named Cronus-Gor is head of an octopus of an organization called the *Oculus.*" I slowly reached into my pocket and took out a pack of cigarettes. I offered her one. She took it. Soon we were both puffing and I kept talking. "So this Cronus-Gor wanted what I knew. I was 27 at the time. I'm 47 now. But he's an immortal—he's got lots of time. I don't. First of all, during my current relationship with Gor, he mandated that I assist in stirring things up in the mid-East by getting Russia and China together to blow up Israel—just being formed. Seems they resent the Jews slicing out a piece of land for themselves. About half the Palestinians have lost their homes and property. Gor wants to destroy the new Jewish state before the projected 1948 completion date. So he wants me to 'diplomatically' tell the Chinese and Russians he'll provide a thermo-nuclear device called the *Hydrogen Bomb* to destroy that goddamned sand trap in the desert. Problem is, the bomb is so big it'll probably kill everyone around Israel, including about 100,000 Palestinians."

"Goodness!" Allegra Blossom exclaimed. "And you—you refused to do this dastardly deed, right?"

"Yeah...as a matter of fact, I did. And since Gor wants what he thinks I have in my head, he won't kill me—just yet. So he forced another assignment on me, to assassinate one Dr. Vaclav Mendel, whom I assume resides within the bowels of this dilapidated estate."

"Yes, Dr. Mendel is a geneticist—has done many wondrous things, Mr. Denning. Why is this Gor character wanting to kill him?"

"Because Gor tells me Mendel knows too much and is now useless to him. So that translates as '*expendable*' in the language of the *Oculus*. It usually means Gor learned all he could from the good doctor and doesn't want the secrets to leak out among the human population."

She drew silent for a minute. The tea water was boiling and she turned her back to me, tossed some loose tealeaves into a large cup and poured the hot water. "I believe you, Mr. Denning..."

"Just call me Cable—I hate formality..."

"Okay...Cable...you may call me Allegra. So I guess we're not on opposite sides, after all. We're more or less comrades in arms, so to speak, wouldn't you say?"

"Yeah, I guess you could say that..."

"You may have killed some people in your lifetime, but I do not see you as a cold-blooded killer, as they say in America. I take it you do not wish to implement this sordid deed on poor Dr. Mendel."

"No, that's right. I don't wanna kill anyone." I checked out her eyes as she sipped her tea and looked at me. I was thinking this lady could be pretty damn sexy under the sheets. "Just...just, uh, how do you fit into all of this?"

She turned with her tea cup in hand and asked me to follow her, leaving Harry Two's body still draped over the butcher block. We meandered down some hallways until we descended some stairs and found ourselves in a basement laboratory. No one else was around. "*Genetics*...the road map of our genus and composition, our behavioral systems, the 'quality and predisposition of the product', so to say. Undoubtedly you have wondered why some people have the finest qualities, whilst others are terribly remiss, having no redeemable traits making them worthy of the term 'human'."

"Oh, I've thought about that a lot. But so has Gor..."

"As has Dr. Mendel. He has conquered how to create wonderful and ideal human beings by genetic mutation and select breeding. You see, mutations can involve duplication of large sections of the DNA and RNA within our genome make-ups."

"I'm not sure—what do 'DNA' and 'RNA' and 'genome' mean?"

"Oh, I'm sorry—I'm a trained technologist. DNA is a molecule that designates genetic instructions, it

111

and RNA encode the 'substance' of your body's makeup via *genomes*, the genetic material of an organism. When one dies of cancer, mutations occur that disrupt the natural sequencing of the DNA and the signal map begins to fall apart. Suffice it to say, beyond that it gets pretty technical."

"Yeah, I guess. Okay, so you're also a geneticist?"

"I'm sorry, I can say no more, Cable."

"Fair enough. So you still didn't say how you fit into this whole scheme of things—I mean, the doctor, knowing I was coming to assassinate him and so on."

"Let's just say I work for a *third* party. I'm here to protect Dr. Mendel, kill you if necessary, then return to my home base."

"Which is?"

She came up to me and touched my nose with her finger. "Wouldn't you like to know, Detective?" She smiled at me. "I think I like you, mister." I reached for her. She drew away. "Uh-uh, no hanky-panky during work hours, Mr. Denning."

"When are work hours over?"

"When the job is done."

"And what is that—after I'm dead and you've completed your task?"

She laughed. "That's funny, honey! I have no intent to kill you, Cable, unless absolutely necessary. You see, I've already grown fond of you—and we've barely met! No, but my instructions are to take Dr. Mendel to a safe location, eliminate you, dispose of Harry Two's body—then burn the entire estate to the ground."

"Oh. Then you return to headquarters, eh?"

"Yes, indubitably, so it goes—duty first."

"So how am I gonna get out of not killing your Dr. Mendel?"

"I've an idea. It's far-fetched, but it might work."

"And what might that be?" She led me around the laboratory. It was unusual inasmuch as several large modern looking machines stood against a wall with blinking lights and all. The rest was the usual Bunsen burners with flasks, test tubes and colored liquid substances. I'd never seen anything like those mammoth machines, though. She stood in front of one of them. "This advanced *Transgenitor* may do the trick. Here's how I suggest it might work. We extract a blood sample from Dr. Mendel, we inject that into Harry Two's body, if it isn't too set with rigor mortis yet—place the body on the tongue of this machine and hope Harry Two's body transforms into that of a reasonable facsimile of Dr. Mendel. Then you take your gun, shoot a hole in Harry's head, and you're off the hook. You get to go home having accomplished what this Gor character wanted of you—and I get to go home for a small vacation in Switzerland."

"You think you can pull all that off?"

"Why not? No imagination, no accomplishment in this world, Cable. How many situations have you been in where you had to creatively think your way out?"

"A lot."

"I rest my case, detective." Then Allegra Blossom led me upstairs. It was a musty old place and I smelled wood burning from a chimney. We knocked and entered a room with a large hearth. Seated on an over-stuffed chair sat a little man with lots of curly white hair sound asleep. She gently roused the man. "Dr. Mendel—sir, I need to extract some blood from you, if that's alright..."

The little scientist blinked his eyes open and looked at both of us. "Uh...who...who is dis, Miss Blossom?" he remarked with a thick accent.

"His name is Cable Denning. He's an operative for an evil organization in the U.S.A. He's come to shoot you."

The little man looked astonished. "Vell, den, vhy don't you defend me by shooting him first?!" he exclaimed.

"You see, Dr. Mendel," I offered, "I really *don't want to kill you.* I never did. I was forced into it. But Miss Blossom here has a suggestion that may save all of us."

She helped the older man to his feet and he went to the fire, put his hands behind his back and faced us. "I see. In dat case, I am pleased to meet you. Are you an undercover agent, or a double—"

"—no, sir, I'm a simple private detective in Los Angeles, California."

"Ya...vell, vhat is your idea, Miss Blossom?"

"Well, doctor...I felt if I could extract a little blood from you, inject it into Harry Two, the man I killed downstairs and then place his body in the *Transgenitor*, he might turn into a decent facsimile of you. Then Cable here will be freed of his obligation, you will come with me to Latvia, all your enemies will think you dead and we'll burn the house down and what traces are found will resemble you sufficiently that those meddlesome bastards will think you deceased and write you off. What say you?"

"I like ze idea, Miss Blossom," the older man said, scratching his head. Then he yawned. "So, take your blood. I am exhausted und must sleep. But I do have a question."

"Yes, doctor, by all means…" Allegra smiled at the man.

"How do ve get de Transgenitor und my valuable research equipment und papers out before you burn de place down?"

"As soon as I have finished with the Transgenitor, my organization will begin moving everything into a van and take it safely over the border."

"What if you're bein' watched?" I asked. "Lest we forget, I was motored here by some pretty unsavory characters with an eye out to make sure I follow through with killing the ol' doc here."

"Our people will eliminate them before they can act, believe me," Allegra answered.

She fetched a kit and soon had extracted a vile of blood from Dr. Mendel. Then together Allegra and I went down into the kitchen and took Harry Two's body and dragged it into the laboratory. She injected the corpse with Mendel's fresh blood, we placed the body on the lip of the Transgenitor and stepped back. It was an incredible sight. What might have taken thousands or millions of years was taking place before our eyes. We watched as Harry Two slowly began to look more and more like Dr. Mendel.

Even his body shrunk to accommodate the smaller man's appearance. In fifteen minutes the transformation was complete. Allegra turned off the machine and we took the newly formed dead guy and placed 'him' in a chair by a lab table. Almost immediately five men came into the laboratory, dressed in black, wearing masks. They ignored us and began packing things up.

Upstairs Dr. Mendel had fallen asleep once again in his comfy chair. Allegra asked me to gingerly pick up the old man and take him down the hall to his bedroom. When he was tucked away, we went back to sit by the fireplace. Allegra Blossom was easy to be with. Somehow she felt familiar. There was a small table radio on a nearby coffee table. "Do you dance, Cable?" she asked me.

"Oh, I guess I'm better than two left-feet, but you might be sorry."

"Why is that?"

"Because there's something so attractive about you that I—I wanna do things to you that you might not be all that receptive to."

She did a naughty smile. "Oh? Why don't you try me, big boy?" she said in very sexy low voice.

"Well, maybe it's not just pure animal desire I feel for you, either. It's a kind of professional camaraderie—a kinship of sorts."

"You mean like two guys liking the same things?" She slipped off her light jacket and her breasts stood out like circus balloons.

"No, I—I, uh, didn't mean it quite like that. You see—"

"—make up your mind, Cable, either I'm a desirable woman to you or one of the boys—which is it?"

The song *The Very Thought of You* came on the little radio. "Wow, that's old—don't the Czechs have modern songs—at least early 40's?"

"What's *time*, Cable, when it comes to music? Will you dance with me? This is probably our last night—I'd say forever, darling. I suggest you make the best of it."

I embraced her body and we moved slowly around the clear space before the fireplace. Allegra knew how to hold a man and sidled her whole body against mine and we moved like two dolphins in the water or two birds in the air, exactly together. She sure felt wonderful and comfortable for someone I'd just met. "Can you feel it?" I asked.

"Of course, we're the same kind, you and I..."

"Same kind?"

"C'mon, Cable—let's not fool one another. We're both *Sens Parafactors,* both of us only half here. Why do you think I put my gun away down in the kitchen and turned my back on you to fetch the tea water? I knew then." She snuggled her nose into my ear. "I know who you are, my star-wanderer."

The music came to that place that said, "*I'm living in a kind of daydream, I'm happy as a king, and foolish as it may seem, to me that's everything...*" I brought her body even closer into mine. I brought my lips to hers and in the firelight we kissed. Soft and shallow at first, but then deeper and deeper un-

117

til our mouths consumed us with passion and we sank to the floor, entangled, roiling, rolling, sighing, out of breath. "You're the third one," I breathed.

"The third one is the charm, darling," she replied, kissing me all over my face. "Do you want me? If you do, I have to tell you something."

"Yeah, of course I want you."

"I'm—I'm beyond the human old animal way of intercourse. I have trained in the ways of the Parafactors."

"Yeah? what's that?"

"This," she responded by putting her index finger up into the air. Instinctively I did the same until our fingers touched. The second they did, sparks flew between us like gods in an electric chair! Our bodies surged to new highs I'd never experienced before and we both reached an orgasm at the exact same time. I could feel the warm wetness in my shorts and then we collapsed alongside one another. For a long time not one word was spoken. Then she kissed me gently on the lips. "You're delicious, Denning," she announced quietly.

"So are you, lady," I whispered. "I wish I could take you home for a few weeks or so. I could get used to your way of—of *doing it.*"

She chuckled. "Me, too. I've never had just—just an extended time of lovemaking. I was bred and born to *perform, do*—not trained for a personal life. Non-native life forms experience this as a harsh, unrelenting existence, don't you think? Has it been the same for you?"

"More or less...maybe I just escaped with human babes to rub the edge off of thinking that I might be dead the next day or month or year. *That's* been most of my adult life."

"I didn't even have that. Some pleasure along the way, but mostly helping the higher humans gear themselves up—or else they won't survive."

"Why is it important that they survive? I've never been nuts about humans anyway."

"Everything in the cosmos has its own sense of 'random balance', as I've observed. Humans are a lower form of evolving five-sensed creature. But one day from them, there is the potential that a great seed within them shall burst forth with a new bloom. That basic goodness will signal, one by one, the beginning of a wonderful new species."

"Well, ya can't prove it by me. But who knows?"

After about an hour, someone was coming down the hall looking for my new lover. She got up, dusted herself off and went to the door. One of the men in black masks muttered something to her and she quickly became her business-like serious self again. "Cable...it's time...I have to go now...so do you. We're going to gather up the doctor and burn the place."

I got up and extended my arms. "And us? Is that it? You just forget us? I've had tantric sex with a Chinese Princess of the Lotus but never did I touch fingers and spark off the heavens!" I explained to her.

"Perhaps one day I shall seek you out. Our lives here on this plane are brief, though, Cable. I have a sister in Los Angeles. Her name is *Sonata*. In fact,

119

we're twins. I'll tell her of you. Perhaps *she'll* seek you out. You'll be hard-pressed to tell the difference, I'd wager." She drew serious. "You'd better get out, now. Go out onto the road as soon as the fire begins sufficiently that your captors can see the smoke and fire."

"Okay, Allegra Blossom—thank you!" I said. She hugged me briefly and was gone. I stood by the fire for a few minutes while the radio played another oldie but goodie tune from the 1930's. It was the old Irving Berlin song, *Let's Face the Music and Dance*. I still remembered Fred Astaire and Ginger Rogers gliding to that number aboard one of the most fantastic sets I'd even seen, supposedly aboard ship. It was music and dancing like that which gave me the feeling that the highest expression of sensuality could never be experienced while in the flesh. It was an ideal, a thing dreamed of, aspired toward and in not reaching it, one became a better being for having had the experience.

# Chapter 4

## LOVE LOOK AWAY

The bad guys led by the now-deceased Harry Two must have been satisfied that Dr. Mendel was dead and I'd killed him because I was back in the good ol' U.S. by September 2nd, the day after Labor Day. Ida had been worried sick by my absence, and happy to see I still existed. Maggie had no clue of my journey to Czechoslovakia and thus assumed I had simply deserted her. Ida suspected something when Maggie kept calling the office. But she didn't call me on it. So I kept my mouth shut. Maggie also seemed a little put off. But when I told her the situation, she still complained but understood. Dr. Theodore Gossman was a little harder to appease but I told him I'd had an emergency in another country and wasn't able to contact him. If I told these people I was kidnapped, who would believe? I assured him I was on the job and recited the few new clues I had. He admonished me for taking so much time in locating Evelyn Gossman, his errant wife.

Ida was always something else to deal with. On one hand she was worried at my absence. I left her the note. But you know women, they worry until 'Lassie comes home'. The other part of Ida Latney was frustration, wanting to be with me but having to keep her place and hope that I'd continue romantic advances toward her when the spirit struck me to do so. I felt awful about that. It wasn't that I kept her from living her life the way she wanted it—but *I* was the way she wanted it—and as long as we continued to make love on sporadic occasions, she would stay locked into loving me, no matter how seldom we had social time together. We did however, get together on my birthday, September the 13th. But we didn't make love. I told her she was off limits to me, much to her consternation. We still had a good time. And for Ida, young women around me close to her age made her jealous, whether she admitted it or not. I guess she thought I was sleeping with them. She was right about some of them. I guessed I was still a slowing sexaholic, alcoholic and tobacco addict. Not bad for one lifetime, eh? Life catches up with you, sooner or later.

It was Tuesday, September the 17th. Cronus-Gor had summoned me *can* and once again I stood before the rumblings of his low voice. "You see, you do my bidding, Denning," Gor said in a satisfied voice. "I am encouraged." He summoned a deeply produced, slow laugh. "Tell me, was it easy?"

"Not as easy as you slicing off Jane Slaughter's hands and putting them under the lid of a hot tray for my viewing pleasure. What did you think the shock value of that would be for me, Gor? At least an eight on a scale of one to ten?"

He chuckled. "Lessons....are taught in different ways...one does not cross an immortal—and I...I am an immortal—all knowing—all powerful, and all foreboding to those who do not obey me."

"I don't easily forget things like that—especially when you do things like that to my friends."

"I'm warning you, Denning!" he roared.

"Yeah, yeah, yeah—and you're full of bullshit! All powerful? How about *'all loving'*—wouldn't that work better? How close are you to your wife? Your daughters? Your sons? Is it filial love they bear for you, Gor, or do they just hang around for the goodies you bestow upon them when you are so disposed? You don't fool me, mister—and after you've destroyed me someday, I'm gonna haunt you in your head, Mr. 'Immortal', because no matter how long you live, if you don't get your own lessons, then you've missed the point of the journey."

"It is not a friendly universe, Denning—look at your own earth here—filled with depravity, starvation, disease, warfare, sectarianism and corruption in all departments of human activity. Ha! That's the part of the so-called 'journey' I get. So you can see how easy it is to manipulate and dominate a stupid breed of being such as humans."

"Despite all that, there are still *miracles* taking place all the time. Healing, a smile from a dying person, bequeathing gifts to those you care about, a sunrise, a rainstorm, the sea in the tropics at sunset—falling in love, being in love—"

"—bah! You're a sentimentalist! I bore easily with your gibberish, Denning! Just be thankful you have a few more days to breathe while in physical form. You are right...one day I shall have you killed...I will pull out of my magic hat one of those 'miracles' you speak of—whoever shall kill you may be unsuspected...ha! ha! How're them for apples, little detective!?"

"Indigestible, Gor. But I gotta hand it to ya. You're the cruelest bastard without a conscience I've probably ever encountered. Yet there's something I like about you. Talk about being perverse."

His voice quieted. "And I am fond of you, Cable Denning. What you perceive as cruel, I perceive as governance—being a king over his subjects requires certain traits and disciplines. I have...those..."

"Yeah, and in spades! So whatta ya want this time?"

"Nothing...at the moment. I simply wished to...to congratulate you for carrying out my—my mandate. I would still like to have you for the Israel problem—"

"—forget it, Gor! Wasn't it enough to have me kill a man I never met until the night I killed him?! Leave me alone for a while, Cronus—let me sulk in the monsters of my own creation—you're another case altogether."

"Very well, Denning—go now and be at peace. You have served me. In that I am pleased. Until the day I extract the knowledge of the *Fen de Fuqín* from your head, I shall spare you. But I also forewarn you—the day I obtain that information, I shall have to dispose of you. Do you understand that?"

I hesitated. "I don't know, Gor. Maybe, maybe not. I ain't you. You think like the monster you are. I think like a human, more or less. So long , chump, don't call me—I'll call you."

I saluted the empty air in front of me and left.

## The Twisted Life of Evelyn Gossman

On Friday September the 19th I decided to venture into the private world of Evelyn Gossman , aka Elizabeth Bennett, Anne Shirley , Lucie Mannette, Hester Prynne and now Marla Felix. No telling what one might find. The Yacht Club was fancy to begin with. I called an old acquaintance of mine, one Jamie Lambert, who worked for an old rich salt named Henri Addinsell. Henri had a cousin in England named Richard who was a movie songwriter. His claim to fame was the wonderful music from a movie called *Dangerous Moonlight.* The theme song was the *Warsaw Concerto.* Anyway, as guest of Henri Addinsell, I gained entrance that Friday night. As soon as I mentioned my 'sponsor', I was led to a table to sit. It was early, about 8:30, and the featured singer of the evening didn't come on until 9:00 p.m. But looking at most of the aging members, I thought it was well past their bedtimes.

I was transfixed looking at the piano player moving his hands deftly across the keys when I heard a voice above me. "I don't know you, do I, chap?" a very British sounding voice spoke to me. He was a pleasant looking gentleman with a pale face and a lot of whiskers. He wore a captain's cap and was fairly slim. "I'm Henri Addinsell, sir. And your name is?"

I stood up. "Denning, Cable Denning. Frankly, I didn't expect you, sir. When I talked to Jamie he simply said to use your name to gain entrance."

"What Jamie didn't tell you, Mr. Denning, is that the host himself must be present to verify who you are–and why you came." He checked me over. He saw my fedora and the trench coat draped over the chair next to me. "May I?" he asked as he sat down across from me. "Now, suppose you tell me what you're doing here, Mr. Denning."

"Of course, Mr. Addinsell. I'm a private investigator tracing down someone whom I believe to be here tonight."

He raised his eyebrows. "Oh? And under what circumstances might you be looking for such a person, if I may inquire?"

"Murder, Mr. Addinsell. And for the sake of discretion, naturally I can't divulge the person's name or location in the room."

"Of course, sir, I understand." Then his eyes lit up. "Oh, but would it be sporting for me to look around nonetheless? I love murder mysteries! See if I can guess..."

"Be my guest, sir." He bought me a drink of fine English gin and we spoke small talk for a while.

"I fell in love whilst I was in the West Indies, I did. I was twenty-four then and ruled the world at the helm of my trusty yacht, *The Sea Maiden.* The boat was a she, you know."

"Yeah, most of 'em are," I replied.

He looked at me intensely. "Hmmm...male or female? Murder, you say...most murders are committed by males...but...what if it were a careless damsel who might've killed her husband for—for *money?*

That's usually the reason...maybe that and another lover in the picture somewhere, eh?"

"Could be," I said, taking a sip and lighting up another Lucky Strike. I was thinking of Evelyn Gossman and Eddie Grant.

"My South Seas lady was dark-skinned. She wanted to be with me for the rest of my life—and I with her. But those days, I wouldn't dare come back with a negro peasant woman sharing my bed—at least openly, you know."

I took a big drag on my cigarette. "No, I guess not..."

Just then a slim blonde in a nice tight-fitting black dress and a profile like Lana Turner came in as the piano player did a fanfare. He stood up. "Ladies and Gentlemen, may I present *Miss Marla Felix*!" There was light applause and the babe launched into her first song of the evening. The voice was deep and warm, somewhat sensual. The 1935 song the lady chose to sing was *Red Sails In the Sunset* and I thought it appropriate that it had a marine theme, considering our surroundings. There was another thing I noticed. When Marla Felix sang *"we marry tomorrow, and he goes sailing no more,"* I watched her glance at some smiling bloke at a front table. Yep, she was sharp as a razor and twice as cunning. Sidney B. Factor was about fifty, maybe ten years or less her senior. But he was stinking rich. And that...was the lure, even if he was skinny and unattractive.

When Marla finished, she offered her hand to her fiancé who came up and took it. "I have the honor to announce our official engagement tonight, ladies and gentlemen—to my future husband, Sidney!"

The crowd did a fairly enthusiastic applause thing, but I wondered how many were curious as to just why a "commoner" without social station like Marla Felix would choose a sort of nothing guy like the wealthy and perhaps stupid Sidney B. Factor. But I knew.

The newly elected fiancé sat down while Marla sang a sexy up tempo version of *Beyond the Sea.* She immediately followed that by sitting down next to the pianist and crooning a version of *Slow Boat to China.* Yep, the gal could play footsy with an audience okay, I thought. And she sang well. She finished up and soon I was rising to put on my coat and hat. "You didn't leave your coat and hat at the hatcheck, Mr. Denning," my host mentioned.

"Well, it's rather awkward, Mr. Addinsell. You see, I'm—I'm carrying a concealed weapon—and well, that I would not like to see get into the wrong hands, if ya know what I mean."

"Oh, indeed!" I shook the man's hand. "Well...did you?"

"Did I what?"

"Find the killer?"

"I'm not sure, Mr. Addinsell, but thank you for the drink—and the hospitality."

"In a way I envy you, chap."

"How so?"

"Well, you get to live the exciting existence—you know, the kind where you're rather on needles and pins all the time, I'd imagine. Your friend and my employee, Jamie Lambert, told me very little. Are you a famous private detective, Mr. Denning?"

"Nope, just a simple aging self-employed guy who lives in a hole-in-the-wall on Franklin in Hollywood in back of his office."

He seemed dismayed. "Oh...well, anyway, chap, good meeting you." Then he walked away. I went outside and wandered along the dock for a few minutes. The sea was calm, the weather balmy. I didn't see what else I could do this night when a warm female voice spoke to me from behind. I turned to face Marla Felix! She was still delicately beautiful. She had that clean blonde movie star look. Immaculate white skin, dark eyes, great little figure and she carried herself like she knew what she was doing. Yet there was a vulnerability to her as well, I sensed.

"You're new, aren't you—why aren't you with someone, if you don't mind my asking?" she inquired of me.

"Why aren't you with your new fiancé?" I smartly answered back.

"Because maybe I—uh, I needed some fresh air."

"I enjoyed your singing, Miss Felix."

"Thank you—and I enjoyed looking at *you*, Mr.—Mr—"

"—Lovejoy—Carl Lovejoy," I said, covering my tracks.

"Funny...you don't look like a 'Carl Lovejoy', sir. Seems your name should be more *daring,* sensual—you know, like *Cable Denning* or something?"

That floored me—she knew! "Oh...yeah, I guess that'd be more daring alright."

"Eddie has a big mouth. He told me about your visit in his dressing room the night I was there at the *Mocambo*. I also know Theodore hired you to find me. But there's only one thing I want you to know, not that it will stop you—but *I didn't kill anyone!*"

"Sorry, but so far the evidence points in that direction, doll. All those husbands...all that money. My, my, my—I've seen gold diggers before—"

"—and that's *all* you can accuse me of , Mr. Denning. What's wrong with a girl providing for her future? What I've done is not illegal."

"No, but it stinks nonetheless, lady. Look, your husband hired me to find out where you lived so he can be legally free of you—that  includes your address so you can be served papers to begin the proceedings. He believes you're the murderess, and understandably doesn't want to be implicated when the authorities finally do come for you to haul you to the hoosegow. Your dear and loving hubby wants that address!" I stated firmly.

"Well, he won't get it. Neither will you," she replied belligerently. "Even my fiancé doesn't know where I live."

"He doesn't take you home?"

"I drive my own car."

"You know, I have a friend downtown. His name is Lt. Lester Keith and he's chief inspector of homicide. I don't think ya wanna get involved with him. You stand there expecting me to believe you had nothing to do with the so-called 'natural' deaths of

your previous husbands that weren't so natural—
but you're talkin' to a guy who's had a little experience dealing with broads who like to leave out details. Women like you are the *black widows* of the
world, Evelyn Nesbitt—your husband's words, not
mine. You live in a twisted world full of misery and
heartache, confusion and unfulfillment. You sing because it lets you be somebody else, kicks your blues
out for a while, lets you breathe as a real woman
without all the trappings of your sick, diabolical
plans to eliminate people who conveniently fit into
your life for the moment—but you attracted them
because money was at the other end of your true desires—"

"—yes, yes! So what? What did men ever give
me?! What I want from a man I can *buy*, mister!" She
was upset. I must've pushed a button.

"Sure, with someone else's ill-begotten dough!
You know as well as I do that it was poison that was
given your dearly deceased ex's, but it was so expertly concocted that even the coroner couldn't detect it. Who's helping you? Now, if you don't tell me
where you live you know I'll follow you home—"

"—oh no you won't!" a man's voice spoke up behind me. It was a mug that looked and sounded like
Dan Duryea and he was holding a gun. "Mrs. Prynne,
would you kindly leave us now?" The lady said no
more and left. My captor had me look out toward the
ocean so I couldn't see what car Evelyn would get
into and drive away with. "Too bad, copper, she's
going, going—gone! Nice night, isn't it?"

"Yeah, if you don't mind dying for it," I answered.

"Whatta ya mean, buddy?" Just then a few people came out of the club above us. I used it as a cue to be on my way and so I just walked, leaving the man with the gun standing there under a harbor light.

The next day I called Dr. Theodore Gossman in San Francisco and told him how close I'd come to accomplishing my task. He wasn't surprised that a "killer like Evelyn would have hired help", as he put it. He was disappointed and said he'd send me an extra five-hundred bucks if I cornered the widow in her web within the next five days. I told him I'd do my best.

## Love in the Afternoon

It had been a while since I'd seen Tommy Knockers, my little newspaper boy down on Highland and Franklin. He'd been delivering the paper to my office when he could and Ida paid him as I'd been pretty busy lately. But this day he came by with a paper for me. He looked sad, depressed, wilted. "Hey, there, Tommy—long time, eh?" I said in a rather condescending tone of voice.

"Hello, Mr. Denning. Here's today's paper for you." He handed me the newspaper and I gave him a quarter.

"Thanks. So, how goes things for you these days, Tommy?"

"Not so hot. I'm gonna run away. I wanna go see the world. But I haven't saved enough money."

"How old are you, Tommy?"

"I'll be thirteen next April—that's pretty big, isn't it?"

"Yeah, that's pretty big, but maybe not big enough to be out on your own. It's a pretty big world out there. And it can be dangerous—even scary sometimes."

"I'm not afraid—heck, I could lick most of the guys on my block anytime."

"Yeah, while that's nice, it ain't always about bein' tough, kid. Sometimes it's about bein' smart and keeping your fists in your pockets. If the other guy swings at you—well, that's a different story."

"Yeah? How? My Dad always tol' me to hit the other guy before he hits me—so I wouldn't get hurt or somethin'."

"I can understand that—I was raised in the Ghetto over in Boyle Heights—and I got beat up a lot on my way to school. Trouble is, Tommy, people gang up on you. Sometimes three guys were waiting for me and pounced on me before I could defend myself. So I had to learn how to be tough very early in life—but I never laid the first punch."

"Didn't you get hurt?"

"Oh, yeah, a lotta times. But after a while I got pretty good at fightin' and the bullies started leavin' me alone."

"Yeah! that's what I'd do—punch 'em hard, huh?"

"You see, buddy, the world's full of bullies. They're not too tough when they're alone, but they like to gang up and do what they can to agitate you and make your life miserable. I don't like bullies."

"We've got a really bad bully in our neighborhood—Stan Ledder—and he's really mean. He's two years older than I am and he's beat me up three times already. And he always has three other bums with him. Now he makes me pay a penny each time he sees me or he says he'll do it again—beat me up."

"Extortion—that's how criminals start out in life, Tommy. I'd avoid him if I were you. Or beat the shit out of him yourself."

"How could I do that? He's a lot bigger than me..."

"The bigger they are the harder they fall, me boy. Next time you see Stan Ledder, call his bluff. Tell him you're not gonna pay him anymore and to get lost."

"Gees, you think I could do that?"

"I don't know, do *you* think you could do that? Are you scared?"

"Yep, I guess I am, a little. After all, there are four guys to one."

"Tell him he's a coward for having three idiots to help him beat up a much smaller boy. That'll get his goat. Maybe he'll take you up on it."

"I'm still scared—what if they really beat me up bad?"

"Then that's life, kid. Roll with the punches. Do your best. Sometimes a guy's best *is* the best."

"I don't understand, but thanks anyway. I gotta go now. Lots of papers to sell today."

"Think twice before you run away, Tommy. Nothin's worse than takin' in the world when you're not ready. Let me know your decision so I can buy my newspapers elsewhere."

"Oh...well, I'll still sell papers for a while. I haven't really decided yet. Good-bye, Mr. Denning." He left my office and I hoped he grow up a little more before he struck out on his own. I liked the kid. He had a sensitivity deep inside that no one had bothered to explore. Kids like that could grow up to be something special. Yeah, like me. Ha! Who am I kidding?

I'd given Ida the afternoon off and I felt like female company of the studious kind. So I drove down to the Hollywood Library about lunchtime. I found a studious Maggie Loggins pouring over some books. She looked up to see me smiling at her. "Cable!" she whispered loudly. "I have a lunch break coming up—can we—"

"—yeah, sure. Let's hop on over to Pink's...my treat." We drove over to Pink's Hot Dog stand near La Brea and Melrose. The owners had just graduated from a pushcart business to a small building and a couple of outside tables last year. Best chili dog around. It hadn't gotten busy yet...we sat at a table. "How are you, Maggie?"

"No thanks to you—*or* thanks to you—worrying about what happened to you, worrying about being pregnant, worrying about if our first time would be our last time—"

"—save it, kid. I don't wanna get into that right now. I saw Evelyn Gossman last night, where you said she'd be...at the Yacht Club. I was gonna follow her home, but some slick gob with a gun changed my mind and the bird flew the coop."

Maggie was a trooper. She changed her brain frame and began thinking with me. "I've done some research in previous cases that included a conniving female, several older male victims and a boyfriend who ended up being the killer. I still don't think Evelyn killed those men. How did you find Mr. Factor? Did you meet him?"

"No, but I'd guess he's rich and dull. But, as I said, it was the hireling with the gun that finally dissuaded me from pursuing the matter any further last night. He covered for Evelyn while she got into her car and drove away while I was forced to look out at the wonders of the sea."

"Gees, I wish I was there, Cable! So you didn't see the make of the car or where it went?" Maggie asked me.

"Right. So what'd you learn about women who *appeared* to be the killers but weren't?"

"Our erroneous justice system—it's haywire, I swear! A lot of people are in prison for crimes they didn't commit. That's just for starters. The world's a scary place, Cable."

"Tell me about it."

"I just did. But you know, I'm sure. You just never seem to be afraid." Then she scooted her chair closer to me and leaned toward my ear. "Would you consider coming home with me and—and, well, you know," she whispered as she blushed. "I could play hooky from the library..."

"In the middle of the afternoon?"

"What's the matter with love in the afternoon?" A quiet desperation came over her face. "I don't want to be an old spinster maid, Cable. '*She had a dour look upon her beautiful face. Had she wasted her life, had she whittled away the hours, months, years resolute no man would own her? Now she was old, inexperienced, unclaimed by love.*' Clayton Poole wrote that from his *Prometheus Punished*."

"Why was he punished?" I chuckled.

"Oh, he stole fire from Olympus to give to humans, without asking permission of Zeus. It ought to be a familiar story to you, Cable—Prometheus Denning fought Cronus Gor, as did the other Titans—and eventually won." She nestled her nose in my coat lapel. "I want to belong to someone, Cable—someone like *you.*"

I didn't know how to answer. The mildly attractive Maggie Loggins might very well spend the rest of her life looking for Mr. Right. I took her hand and we walked to my car. I drove her to her apartment complex and before long the door closed behind us and we were alone together in Room #42. It was quiet. Maggie went into the bathroom and undressed. I pulled down the Murphy bed and did the same. She came to me as I was sitting on the bed and eased her naked belly into my face. I kissed it. Before long she bent her face down to kiss my lips and soon after that we were wrestling on top of her bed, initiating that ancient ritual of the he and she world. She was a bit awkward and desperate, but she was in love and her anxious body yielded to my manhood.

Afterward we sat naked at her little breakfast nook and she served me a cup of coffee. Suddenly she was business-like. "So, women accused, judged and sentenced for crimes they didn't commit...how many layers of so-called evidence did you need to find before someone was granted a divorce in your bread-and-butter business?"

"Ha! Usually just a really good Kodak photo," I answered with a smile, thinking that's how I'd trapped her—or him.

"Any judge or jury can see a photo and make a snap judgment, pardon the pun. But what about the layers?"

"For example?"

"Okay...It all starts in 1922...called the *Lemonade Murders*. Helen Jefferies had three husbands, all of whom died within two years or less of one another. Autopsies found the only linking chemical in the bodies were traces of lemon, sugar and aspirin. Each of these husbands was considerably older. She gave them this drink three times a day and the aspirin was detected in the blood. But...he also found accumulated traces of *arsenic*. A hasty decision prompted the D.A. to accuse Helen of poisoning her three husbands via dermal absorption. She was brought to trial and solely by the admissibility of the coroner's dismal findings, Helen was found guilty and sentenced to life in prison. Oh, and a surgical needle and Trivalent arsenic were found hidden in her home. Evidence?

"Oh, yeah, I'd say so," I commented as I sipped my coffee.

"But one man, a dear friend of Helen's, didn't believe the findings. He went to bat for Helen. And what he found...was the *truth*, Cable. In the end, the real killer was brought to justice. Who was the real killer? How'd they do it? And why?"

I thought for a minute. "Some rejected boyfriend from the past, a banker who wanted the money she'd accumulated—a dear sweet auntie—even Theodore Gossman himself acting out a love-hate relationship. I don't know. Who?"

"Food for thought, Cable...food for thought. Who, indeed, would want to see Evelyn Gossman dead or in prison for life?"

"Okay, I give up—who?"

"In Helen Jefferies' case, it was a disfigured older step-brother who hated her. He'd disappeared for years, went to prison for stealing lethal drugs from a Chicago coroner's laboratory where he worked as a janitor."

"So how'd he do it—what method did he use and how?"

"Simple. All the husbands smoked tobacco. Two smoked cigars, one smoked cigarettes. The killer injected the trivalent arsenic into the tobacco. When inhaled, the victim would accumulate the arsenic by what is termed as *dermal absorption* and eventually die."

"Damn—that's smart! What did the stepbrother expect to get from the lady?"

"He'd blackmail her by threatening to tell of the hidden hypodermic needle and arsenic, which Helen Jefferies knew nothing about. In the end, Helen's friend traced down the stepbrother and heard him talking one night when he was dead drunk. That was enough to turn the tables and exonerate Helen Jefferies. The brother ultimately confessed."

"Hey! Good story, kid."

"I'm not a kid, I'm a grown woman, in case you haven't noticed."

"Oh, yeah, I've noticed, Maggie. But I—I, uh, don't wanna get hooked on having sex with you, as good as it is."

"And why not?" she said indignantly.

"I don't love you and you're too damn young. At first it was okay because you were so infatuated with me, so I obliged."

"Obliged?" she snapped back. "Does that have anything to do with 'obligatory'?"

"No...I...uh, I just thought satisfying that urge would put an end to it—you had the older guy, now find someone young and exciting." My comment didn't seem to go over so well.

She reached her hands across the table to me. "But I found *you* exciting, Cable—handsome, adventurous, ardent, dangerous—all the ingredients of a girl's fantasy."

"And you don't care if I don't love you?"

"Yes...and no. If we continue, I think eventually you will. Men are slow to some things. Women can change men, you know..."

"What book taught you that?" I said in a sour, frustrated voice. "I think that's mistake number one in a woman's lexicon."

"History is filled with love stories with unrequited ardor either frustrated or unfulfilled. *La Vita Nuova* by Dante, in love with a woman who's dead but he saw her only a few times whilst she lived and fell deeply in love. Charles Dickens, *Great Expectations,* Pip is in love with a cold-hearted beauty, *Middlemarch* by George Eliot—even the composer-pianist Chopin and Georges Sand—she came too late when he was so tubercular, their intimacy could not be consummated. See how lucky we are, Cable? Making love comes so easy to us."

I thought for a minute as I started to light up a cigarette, then stopped, knowing how the lady didn't want her apartment corrupted with the lingering smell of stale tobacco. "Maybe you're right, Maggie. Maybe for you the coin will come up heads on both sides. I don't know."

She sat there naked, her young breasts almost touching the tabletop. "Will you make love to me again—before you go?"

I cracked a half-smile. "I don't know...I'm more expensive after five o'clock and it's getting late."

She stood up and took my hand, then led me to her bed. "I'm wet and open for you, Cable. Doesn't that mean something to you? Doesn't that say I want you and I'm willing to give my body to you without expectation of tomorrow—although I can hope?"

I didn't reply, but took Maggie Loggins in my arms and lowered her to the bed. She got her way. I also got mine. I really *did* want her.

### Lover Girl

I got back to my office about 5:30. Ida had gone and left a note. Eddie Grant had called and wanted to talk to me. I dialed his number. "Eddie? Cable Denning here...what's up?"

"Oh, thanks for returning my call. I hear through the grapevine that you harassed Evelyn. Why? Why don't you leave her alone. Maybe she'll have a happy life now—"

"—your grapevine is pretty long, Eddie—what makes you think I'll give up chasing down a broad who possibly murdered four men—and maybe a fifth if Marla Felix has her way? Plus I'm being paid by Gossman to find out where she lives so he can serve papers—"

"—you came late to the movie, Cable—you don't know the whole story. Gossman isn't what he seems to be."

"Oh? Who is? And why should that deter me from finding Evelyn?"

"Because she didn't do it, that's why." I was leafing through the newspaper and saw that Scarlett O'Hara had changed venues and now sang at the old gangster-owned club, *Bella Notte*. Only it wasn't called that anymore. Its new name was *Roscoe's Hideaway*. "Did you hear me, Denning? I repeat— Evelyn Gossman did not kill those men."

"How can you be so sure, Eddie? Do you live with her, inside her, beside her, do you read her thoughts and intentions? No one knows what the human mind really thinks—including yours. What if she's two or three people? What if she's a real talent with a hidden bluff deep inside? What if she's sick mentally or emotionally?"

"You're a son-of-a-bitch to convince, Denning. I wanna help her. And I want you to help me help her. But I see it's pointless. You don't believe she's innocent. So, I guess we'll just leave it at that, eh?"

"Yeah, for now, let's leave it at that. In fact, I gotta go see a policeman about your ex-flame, Eddie. Sometimes a guy needs a hard pound on the head to have it driven home...have someone tell him he's crazy alright, but he ain't completely bonkers yet."

"Good luck, private dick. I'll do it alone if I have to, but one way or another I'll exonerate her from suspicion."

"Don't hold your breath, Eddie Grant, if the new bridegroom Mr. Factor happens to 'pass away' from natural causes, I'm sure the D.A. will come down on her like gangbusters, buster! Five times ain't no co-incidence! Don't count your chickens before they hatch. So long, Eddie," I said impatiently and hung up.

It was Tuesday, September 23rd. I woke up feeling like I'd gone ten rounds with Joe Palooka. My eyes were glued shut, my chest felt tight and I needed a drink and a cigarette. I sat naked at my desk searching for a match. I lit up and kicked back with some fine English gin. But there were red lights going on inside me. I was drinking earlier and earlier these days. Alcoholism had been defined as an addictive disease, so I'd read. Between tobacco and booze, I guess you could call me that. The constant din of the traffic outside, sirens, horns blowing, noisy trucks—reminded me that one day I'd wanna be free of it all, say good-bye to the city for good. But that day wasn't this one. I had to clean up and go see a man about a policeman.

Police Inspector Lt. Lester Keith of the Los Angeles Police Department downtown, was a tough, leathery man with a good heart. That heart had simply hardened through years of seeing what he'd seen and going through the hoops of corruption that haunted his line of work. Plus he was married to a woman I'd never met. One never knows how that stirs up the mix.

Keith looked at me with his usual scanning eyes and sour disposition. "So, you came to tell me this now? I've got three fresh murder cases, eight corpses deemed the result of foul play and look at this—my desk looks like the draft lineup for World War Two!"

"I need your opinion on a case, Lester. Maybe a fresh insight or two. Wanna get some lunch?"

"Yeah, sure...you treat, I eat." We went down to Clifton's Cafeteria on Broadway near 7th Street. Known by customers as the 'The Cafeteria of the Golden Rule' it was the second to open. It was said no one was ever turned away...not even Lt. Keith, who loved to chow down a little bit of everything, washed down with a cup of java.

He ate across from me in silence for a while. Keith had grown older—fast—in the last few years. The pressure of his job after the war had taken its toll. "So...what's the scoop, Denning? Don't bore me with details—just lay out the facts of the thing, okay?"

"Yeah, sure. Well, I get hired by this quasi-singing teacher in San Francisco to trace down his escaped younger wife here in town. He pays me well and so I—"

"—well enough to pay for this meal?" he jabbed at me.

"And then some. So, anyway, turns out she's had four much older husbands—all of them now dead, I might add. This doll has inherited quite a sum of dough from each, changes her name each time she decides to do it again—and she's about to do it again. This time it's one *Sidney B. Factor*, of the Max Factor clan."

"Impressive," Lt. Keith said while chewing on a turkey drumstick. "Now...there's money in that, alright. What did the coroner's report say about the other stiffs?"

"Death by natural causes. But I happen to know she's using a deviously elusive poison to do her dirty work."

"Using a what? Speak English, Denning. Where in the hell do you come up with those fancy pants words—you're not even educated! So why don't you give me a report and we'll bring her in?"

"I have to find it, prove it—not to mention finding where the reclusive *Marla Felix* lives. She's smart, Lester. She knows how to hide and even when she's seen, no one knows where she goes afterward."

"Oh?" he said, taking a toothpick to his teeth. The waitress came and filled our coffee cups. "And why is that, Denning?"

"She hires tough guys who carry iron and a lotta muscle, that's what I *know*. I ran into one the other night at a yacht club where the original Evelyn Nesbitt-Gossman—now known as Marla Felix...was singing. She went home without being seen, while I was stuck at the other end of a gun with a guy making me to look toward the sea while my suspect drove away into the mists of night."

Lt. Lester Keith wiped his mouth with his napkin. "I don't know about you, Denning. You get yourself embroiled in complicated cases that should be filed with the police department in the first place. Then you come to me--"

"—stop pretending, Lester! You know damn well that case would sit on that crowded desk of yours ad infinitum and gather dust."

"Ad *who*? Jesus Christ, there you go again with all the fancy words?!"

"I've been brushing up on my Latin recently," I said.

"Well, brush up on your English, buddy, and look for the *facts*. Number one, you suspect the lady is a husband killer. Number two, you can't find her. Number three, you have no case. Over and out, Denning. Thanks for the lunch." Lester Keith rose. I followed. We walked back through busy traffic, crowded sidewalks and streetcars clanging their way along the rails. "It's a shame, ya know. I hear the goddamn oil companies are tryin' to get rid of the streetcars in favor of buses. L.A. won't be the same without 'em."

We shook hands and I left. But Lester Keith had said one thing that stuck: *facts*—find the facts and maybe solve the case. He was also right about another thing. I had no case—as yet. All I had was a man who paid me money to try and find his wife. What other facts did I have? Four men were dead, I had no killer yet and Evelyn Nesbitt-Gossman's whereabouts was still unknown. The main fact was that I didn't know what the shit I was doing! Where were all my detective smarts?

I got to the office with my tail between my legs. Ida was hard at work as usual. I'd more or less neglected her lately. I also needed to pay her a little more. Hell, she'd gotten $2.50 a day since 1940! Her rent was $27 a month. Add food and expenses to that and she didn't have a lot for personal items. I needed to do something nice for my faithful secretary. "I'm giving you a little raise beginning next month, Ida. $15 a week—and maybe another boost later on…how's that sound?"

She looked up at me through her glasses. "Gee, Cable, that's swell. I could sure use it. A quart of milk is eighteen-cents this year, you know. Thank goodness, overall prices have finally come down after the war ended."

"Yeah, I know…I took Lt. Keith out to lunch. Cost me a fortune at Clifton's downtown."

"Yes? And…?"

"He says I don't have a case against Marla Felix."

"Do you?"

"No, I guess I don't."

She thanked me again for the forthcoming raise and went on with her business. Just then the door opened and in walked a gorgeous red-headed dish. She looked familiar. "Yes? How may we help you?" Ida asked from her desk.

"Oh, me? I'm—I'm looking for Cable Denning, Private Investigator." In fact, she was a dead-ringer for Allegra Blossom!

I stood up and greeted the looker. "I am said Cable Denning," I gestured, inviting her in to sit opposite me.

She sat down and plopped her purse on my desk and proceeded to search into it for something. Finally she found her cigarettes and soon was puffing away. "My name is Sonata—Sonata McCambridge, although, you may know me as Sonata Blossom—you see, Allegra is my twin sister. She wrote me and asked me to call upon you and thank you for—for—" She glanced at Ida. "—for your recent help in solving what Allegra said was, I quote, 'a current dilemma' in her life. You see, Allegra is always solving current dilemmas, Mr. Denning." She had a very slight Southern accent and for an English woman, that was quite a feat. But she was quite striking. She looked a hell of a lot like Allegra.

"I see. Well, pleased to meet you—identical or fraternal?" I asked. Ida was snickering quietly.

"I—I'm not certain to which you are referring, Mr. Denning—myself or my sister..."

I smiled. "Are you born exactly alike, or far apart enough as to not resemble each other identically?"

"Oh, me? I see, sir. Well, now that you mention it, I guess we all don't look quite exactly the same now, do we?" She glanced at her stupendous bust and wavy long hair. "I think I am more greatly endowed here than my sister and I have always worn my hair differently—Allegra was always the proper one. I am, what you might say, sir, a little less *stringent*." I actually thought Allegra's bust all as much as abundant as the sister sitting before me now.

I laughed. "I see. Yes, I—I can see where that may apply in your two separate cases. I've been told that the DNA is constantly adjusting to the exterior environment of a twin's life experiences—thus they may appear to look, act and turn out quite differently than at birth."

D—what?" Sonata queried me. "I'm afraid I'm not much into scientific discussion these days—"

"—oh, that's alright, Miss McCambridge, there's no link that DNA plays a major part in heredity—yet. Maybe someday..."

"I declare, Mr. Denning, you sound just like a science person! Was your pappy a scientist or the like?"

"No, ma'am, my 'pappy' was a world explorer."

"Sounds exhilaratin' to me, sir." She shifted in position on her chair. She was wearing a tight grey skirt with a fine white blouse. "Now, I do have an order of business to discuss with you." She glanced at Ida. "What I have to say is very private—perhaps only for the ears of a private investigator such as yourself?"

I looked over at Ida. "Ida...?"

Ida frowned, got up, went to the coat rack and got a sweater. "It's 4:30 now, Mr. Denning. I think I'll go home." She glanced at the saucy Miss McCambridge. "Good to meet you, Miss McCambridge."

"I don't think we were properly introduced. But all the same, I am delighted to meet you likewise—Ida? Is that what your name is?"

"Yes...Ida Latney..."

"Oh, I knew some Latney folks in Georgia—are y'all from there?"

"No ma'am, originally the Midwest."

"Oh...I see. Well, delighted to know you, Miss Latney."

"Thank you—and good night." She began to walk away, then she turned to face me. "Oh, thanks again for the raise, Mr. Denning."

"You're welcome, Ida, good night."

Ida left. "Sonata McCambridge, I'm all ears. Everyone has a story. What's your story?"

"Oh, I can rightly say it's a doozy, Mr. Denning. Why don't you simply call me Sonata? I am also quite musical, you know. I played the harpsichord in my younger years. Allegra is also very musical."

"Oh? What instrument did she play?"

"The cornet—a shortened instrument of brass, I declare—that noise drove the whole family plumb out of their minds—now when Allegra practiced, even the birds left the trees!" she laughed. It was a good laugh, positive and fun-like. Then she drew serious. "You see, sir, I have been violated...grossly and unfairly violated."

"Did you report it to the police? Do you mean rape or something like that?"

"—oh no, nothin' of that sort, Mr. Denning. I have been unfairly extricated from my place of happy residence by some rich hussy who simply prevailed upon the landlord to...to push me out so *she* could take possession. It is known the lady in question plans to be married soon and needed my deluxe apartments to accommodate her new husband."

"I see. Did you have a contract with the landlord?"

"No, sir, I did not. It was an honorable word-of-mouth transaction. But he violated his end of the bargain. Now I am all but thrown out into the streets of Los Angeles!" she cried.

I took a deep breath. "Without an agreement in writing, Sonata, I'm afraid it's the landlord's discretion as to who may reside on his property. He did give you at least a 30-day notice?"

"Yes, but that's not nearly enough time for me to exit his premises and re-locate to a fine house, the luxury of which I am accustomed to. I need at least another sixty days! What can I do?"

I thought a second. "Well, just because I like you and your sister, I'll go talk to the landlord and see what we can do, okay?"

"That would be mighty appreciated, sir. Maybe he'd allow me to remain even longer—"

"—that I doubt, Sonata. But I'll keep you posted." She gave me the information I needed and I walked her to the office door. "Good to meet you, and thanks for stopping by. I'll call you when I know more, okay?"

"Mighty fine of you, Mr. Denning. I thank you on my behalf and that of my sister's."

"Your sister's?"

"Well, truth be known, I share the rent with Allegra—though she is seldom present to enjoy the trappin's of such a fine residence. As you may have discovered, she lives everywhere but here in the States."

"I see. Well, good-bye, Sonata. You'll hear from me." She reached for me impulsively and hugged me, pressing those marvelous breasts of hers hard against my shirt. Then she was gone. Hmmm...I'd say she left a good impression on me! Now that's a lover girl!

## Surprises Come on Wednesdays

Wednesday is the garbage pick-up day. I heard the truck in the alley and the men emptying the trash cans. I had a little time to kill and before I forgot it, I thought I'd best see about Sonata McCambridge and her little dilemma. Maybe I could help. The address was in Beverly Hills, on Carmelita right off North Canon Drive. It just so happened the landlord lived several houses down from the very nice home Sonata supposedly shared with her sister. The landlord's name was James Rick. He was tall and slim with that stern bookkeeper look. He was cordial, but I knew he was being paid a special "move-in" price by the new renters and Sonata and Allegra were dispensable. "Miss McCambridge hired me to tell you she's rather put out by her sudden expulsion. Ya know what I think? I think someone bought their way into that nice house you own down the street. Miss McCambridge was feeling pretty displaced, Mr. Rick. May I inquire who is that rich and important to be taking possession that you should dispossess another tenant?"

"You may think what you like, sir. You may inquire, Mr. Denning, but I cannot divulge the names of the new residents. Now, if you don't mind, I'm a very busy man." Just then the phone rang and he excused himself to answer it. I glanced down at his desk and was very surprised to see the names of some very interesting people in Rick's schedule book: *Mr. and Mrs. Sydney B. Factor!* The date of October 1st was notated as when they would take possession. *Now* I knew where Marla Felix, real name Evelyn Gossman, lived...or will live! What a small world we this is, I thought.

I got back to the office and called Theodore Gossman. He was elated that I found out where his estranged, bigamist wife would be living soon. He said he was going to present me with a bonus for my efforts. I felt pretty good about that. He told me our business association was now at an end and he would appreciate it if I no longer contacted him, unless he got a hold of me first. I agreed. I also called Sonata McCambridge and told her no soap, the landlord would not budge and she'd have to move pronto. She was disappointed but thanked me.

That night I went back out to watch the dazzling Scarlett O'Hara sing at the old *Bella Notte.* She was singing *Look To the Rainbow* from a recent Broadway show called *Finian's Rainbow.* I liked the way she sang it. The club was half-full and Scarlett seemed oblivious to the audience this night. Her eyes were far away in some unreachable clime known only to her—or maybe not even to her. She was wearing a very thin shimmering red dress that clung to her like a second skin. I didn't know what was so fascinating about this doll, because some of her was absent, I thought...but she sure held the audience. When she finished that song, she went into a danceable version of *Maybe You'll Be There.* I thought then that someone had broken her heart a while back and she was carrying that inside somewhere. But I couldn't be sure. Who could? I also suspected she was still searching for something or someone who wasn't either in the crowd that night—or in her life.

About 1:30 a.m. I got back into my office. It felt lonely. I picked up the phone and wanted to dial Ida. Then I wanted to call Maggie. I ended up phoning no one and sat back in the dark, watching the neon sign across the street blink its colors onto my office floor as I smoked and fell into a drunken stupor.

# Chapter 5

## GOD TALK

It was Thursday, October the 2nd. I'd given Ida four days off to go visit her mother and father near Thousand Palms. Two things of significance happened that day. One, I found out that Evelyn Gossman had moved into her newly rented home the day before and second, I got a large package sent special delivery from some address in San Francisco, that *wasn't* Theodore Gossman's address at 2222 Broadway. That was odd, I thought.

Just then the door opened and in walked Tommy Knockers, my newspaper boy. "Here's a free one, Mr. Denning—they counted too many papers."

He handed me the paper. "Are you sure?"

"Yep. It happens a lot—I was supposed to get fifty papers. I got fifty-one instead.

I took a buck out of my pocket and handed it to the young lad with the sad face. "Here—buy yourself something...I mean something you'd really like to have," I said.

His face lit up. "Gees—that's great! Do you think that's enough to run away on?"

I chuckled. "Still thinking about that, eh? Being out there in the world ain't all it's cracked up to be, Tommy. It can get mighty lonely at times."

"I don't care!" he said rather decidedly. "I don't wanna be at my house any more—and besides, I already thought about what I wanted to do when I run away."

"Yeah? What?"

"I wanna travel the seven seas—I wanna be a Merkant Marine."

"Oh? I think you mean *merchant* marine. I think that's a good idea—but I don't think they'd take you—not just yet..."

"Why not?"

"You're just a little wet behind the ears, kid—too young to be striking off into the world alone."

"They took Jim Hawkins—I'd say he's my age-- and he had to fight off pirates and things."

I smiled. "Ah, *Treasure Island*—to be sure, Jim was about your age—but it's a *fiction story*, Tommy, and adult men he knew took him with them. A very different story than striking out on your own..."

"Maybe you could come with me, Mr. Denning. I sure bet you could show me a lotta things I'd like."

I thought about smoking, drinking, woman-chasing. "I don't think so, Tommy...you see, I'm not the best example you could expect—besides, I think you oughta wait a year or so before you fly the co-op."

"Well, I gotta get back to my corner. See ya, Mr. Denning..." His voice perked back up as if we hadn't discussed this serious subject. But hell, after all he was just a kid. He disappeared through the doorway.

Late that afternoon, I drove over to Carmelita Drive off Canon in Beverly Hills. There was no activity. I sat low in my car and had a smoke. Soon I saw her. That lovely blonde woman with the Lana Turner look and smile, sleek, intelligent. I wondered what *she* wondered about life. Who was she, really? What did she feel when she changed identities so often? Marla Felix? Did she fashion herself after the likes of Maria Felix, the Mexican movie star? What did she feel when she slinked into bed at night with a new husband she didn't love? Or maybe nobody has to love anybody to have sex. She walked up to her new address and put the key into the lock. She was wearing a tight beige skirt and her bottom moved back and forth nicely as she entered. Quite a babe, I thought. Why did Eddie Grant leave her? I wondered. Had they a master plan together? She gets rich and he joins her later? And why does he maintain Evelyn didn't kill anyone? Maybe *he* was the killer!

Why should I care? I did my job and got paid for it. I had no further obligation to Gossman or his beautiful deceitful wife. Hell, I had other fish to fry, and some life to live. Maybe I'd give Maggie a call later!

## The Holographic Phonograph

Thursday evenings were close enough to the end of the week for me to start drinking a bit more. So I plopped down on my comfy chair behind the desk and lit up, poured a tall one and sat, looking at that big package sitting on the floor across from me. I had no idea what Gossman would've sent me. Also strange, it had no post office markings on it. That meant someone had simply delivered it in person and left. As darkness fell and the phone hadn't rung, I felt that empty loneliness again in my gut. But I was too drunk to put myself together and go out night-clubbing. So I cleared some of the crap off my desk, got up and put the package on top of it. I carefully unwrapped the damn thing. One never knew if someone who didn't like me had planted a bomb and all I had to do was pull the wrong string and bang! you're dead. I was somewhat surprised to see what Gossman had sent me. He knew I liked it a lot, but to send it to me—that was a bit much, I thought. Naw, there had to be another angle to it. There sitting in front of me was Gossman's *magic phonograph*! The thing was about two-feet by eighteen inches and maybe it stood about a foot above my desk surface. The turntable was pitch black. I'd recalled that Gossman had an L-shaped gizmo of some kind and maybe a 10" disc on the turntable. The phonograph had a little side pocket. I reach in and found the tubular substitute for a tone arm and indeed, a thick disc was also in the pocket. The record somehow reminded me of the early Thomas Edison cylinders in the late 19th century. Then discs competed with the *Columbia* and *Victor Talking Machine Company*. But the Edison discs came late, played longer and were more expensive and many folks preferred the simple 78-rpm records that only played about 3-minutes per side, tops. I recalled an irate father of one of my early Italian buddies across the river. He was pissed because he'd bought Enrico Caruso's version of *Cielo e Mar*, some operatic aria for his *Victro-*

*la*. But because of time restrictions, a whole verse was left out of the recording and Mario's Dad was really pissed! I was about 12 when my neighbor played an Edison disc for me—maybe around 1913 or so.

But Gossman's phonograph was another animal altogether. I had seen the images escape from that disc into three-dimensional displays before my very eyes. So I put the gold tube into place and set the disc on the platter. What I heard and saw made me believe I'd finally become a delirious alcoholic and at last the delusions had come to haunt me. Voices moaned and cried out in the night, my lights went out in the office and I stood there in the darkness with dazzling colors emitting from the air around me. Now I saw letters, and there was something spelled out in symbols right above my head! Some letters fell below that—**L-a-z-z-e-r-i-a** appeared below the symbols...**Lazzeria.** Maybe that was the brand name or something. What in the hell did it mean?! The voices pulled me toward a rising column of light and swirling colors, sort of like a whirlpool. It gained momentum and I found myself becoming weightless as I was sucked up into the quickening vortex of sound, light and color! The moaning voices calmed into those of lovely angelic voices. I'd heard the music of the spheres years ago and maybe this was it again, pulling the plug on me and I was gonna die. But then again, maybe not—and suddenly I was less drunk.

One thing I knew for sure. I wasn't in my office any more. I stood at the shore of a roiling ocean. The beaches were sandy and as far as the eye could see in either direction, nothing stirred, not a soul, a seagull, a crab, a sand flea. There was no wind to stir the breakers, either, which seemed strange to me. Above me in the distance loomed a huge mountain, high and craggy with clouds swirling at its top. But what was even stranger was at the base of the tide-line stood a rope ladder ascending from the seashore straight up to that giant peak! Out of nowhere a gentle, masculine voice spoke: "Will you walk to me?"

I looked around. I saw no one. "Walk to you?" I questioned. "Who are you and why should I?—besides, I don't swim that much and I'm afraid of heights. So, thanks all the same, but I don't think so." I looked at my body. I was naked. But the temperature was perfect. "Uh…again, who *are* you and whatta ya want?"

He didn't answer me directly. Instead he urged me toward the longest, highest rope-bridge I'd ever seen. "Now…when the waves recede, grab the side ropes with both hands and climb aboard. Do so quickly. You will then ascend until you are safe from the billowing waters below you."

"Why should I? I'm really not anxious to drown today. And by the way, where am I?"

Again he didn't give me a direct answer. "If you wish to grow, walk to the ladder and ascend. I will be with you." From some deep instinct within me I felt the urge to listen to the voice. So I waited until the cycle of the waves had diminished and then I dashed for the rope ladder. Just in time, too, for as I scrambled up the first few feet a huge surge of sea came at me, wetting my behind. I scurried on up the ropes until I had cleared the cliffs that divided land from beach. The damn thing ascended at about a 20% pitch and I found myself huffing and puffing as I got higher. Then I looked down and stopped. I was a good one-hundred feet above the land now! Good grief! What in the hell was I doing? Where was I? Who belonged to the strange voice? And what happened to the magic phonograph and my office?

The height made me dizzy. "Ya know, mister, I can't go on—I have *acrophobia* and I'm getting pretty dizzy."

"But the tide grows higher and soon will consume you. If you do not climb to me without fear, you will never reach what you came for."

"What did I come for?" I asked. "I'm in the dark here, buddy!"

"You came for the completion of your earth life and the preparation for your leaving your gross molecular body behind. Climb to me and you will accomplish that."

I thought for a minute, suspended as I was on that damned rope bridge looking up to the mountain looming above me. "Is that what this is all about—am I dying—dead—or what?"

"No, you are still an earthling, such as you are. But you are yet precious. So trust and walk forward, do not look behind you, for even now a wall of water rises up out of the sea and will inundate you unless you come forth briskly and do not turn to look back. Trust."

Hesitatingly, I did so. I felt nausea as I ascended. I fought for air as I approached the mountain. Finally I reached the base of it, but the sea didn't sound any more distant than it had before. That was weird, I thought. But I kept climbing, as out of breath as I was. "I don't think I can go on much longer—you know, all the booze, smoking—"

"—and sexual indulgence, mustn't forget that," the voice spoke. "You have senselessly dissipated much of your inner reserves. Thus I give to you *The Ten Tenants of Joy.*"

"This is hardly the time, buddy—now it's cold and I'm shivering here!"

He ignored me and began to spiel out these directives: "*One, BE OPEN, Two, BE STILL, then LISTEN TO YOUR INNER RESERVES, PREPARE FOR ANYTHING, RID THE SELF OF ALL SOURCES OF POLLUTION, INWARDLY, OUTWARDLY, TAKE STEPS TO PREPARE THE ENVIRONMENT AND TEACHING, BE AMBIENT, BE PART OF GOD: TAKE REASON AS ITS OWN ANSWER, and finally, BE PRECIOUS TO YOUR OWN CONDUCT.*" Then the voice fell silent. I was struck dumb.

"What am I, a priest or something? Hell, if I did all of those things, I'd—I'd—well, I'd be a saint or some guru!"

"Well...? So...? We are always teachers, we are always students."

I was feeling a bit weak, but there I stood at the foot of the great mountain. "Okay, okay—so what's next?"

"Keep climbing. One foot in front of the other...I am here with you."

"Yeah? Well, how come I can't see the way?"

"Because I *am* the way." I didn't try and figure out that one. So I, again, continued to climb. In what seemed but a few minutes I was at the three-quarter point up the peak. But I was exhausted. I told the voice I didn't wanna go on, but he remanded me and told me not to look back, that a giant wave would break over me and I would perish if I stopped. And therefore, he told me, I must press on, and no matter what, don't look behind.

"I—I don't think I can go on, buddy," I said, out of breath.

"Then I will place my love into your chest and we shall climb together," he said in a kindly way. I felt a warmth enter into me and I could breathe deeper than I ever had before.

"What the hell did ya do? I can gulp in this fresh air like a new-born baby!"

"I simply loved you as I would myself," he replied. "Love is always the answer, no matter what form it comes in.

"You're not some religionist, are you? I hate religionists! You divide everyone by having a new ball of wax to spin onto the stupid idiots who'd listen to you! Bah! Just the thought of it gives me a bad taste in my mouth."

I guess he thought the comment wasn't worth responding to. But whatever he injected into my chest gave me the strength to complete the climb and before I knew it, I stood at the end of the rope ladder. But my worst fears confronted me: the damn thing was suspended in mid-air and there was a huge thousand-foot drop as if the mountain had shrunk and I was now above it! "Now...walk...walk out onto the air. It will support you."

"Are you kiddin', mister? I may have fallen for your 'love-in-the-chest' thing, but I know for certain I'd fall to my death if I did what you suggest." Just then I made the mistake of looking behind me for a way out and a gigantic wave loomed over me about to break and drown everything in sight. I had no choice. I jumped off the precipice, thinking this was the last of Cable Denning and that would be that! But I was wrong. Instead, the wave receded and I floated like a feather ever downward until I settled into the most beautiful place I had ever seen.

"Well, you did it hesitantly, but you did it, and in doing so, halted the water from inundating you," the voice reminded me.

I looked around. "So...where's this and how come I'm not dead?"

"This...is inside *you*...everything you see...your true self...and you already know on some level that you cannot perish—not really."

I felt pretty good. "Okay, buddy, so even though I don't believe in a one God thing, are you some kind of god? Did you create Creation?"

"No one can create creation. I simply fashioned your species," he answered matter-of-factly. "Not a very good job, was it?"

"No, as a matter of fact—the frickin' human race stinks! Are you male or female?" I inquired.

"We are all both." He changed his voice into that of a female's. "Or would you prefer that I speak like this? You particularly respond to the feminine quality in your earth-life journey, do you not?"

"I suppose so. But I think I liked your other voice better."

"Humans are so primitive—but some are precious as well—to be looked after now and then…"

"Oh, yeah? Then why did you create us and then write us off your list of things to improve—and abandon us without a roadmap?"

"I didn't. Humans wrote themselves off, as you suggest the phrase. A man and wife are riding together in a motorcar. The wife says, 'When we first dated, we sat so close together. Now we're on opposite sides of the car' The husband smiled to himself. 'But I'm the driver, and so I've been anchored to this steering wheel since that first date. It's *you* who have moved away from me'. Perhaps unknowingly, my creations have forgotten…and moved away from me."

"Why didn't you interfere?"

"Because free will allows *when* they shall question their true origins, not that they *shall*. When they ask, I shall answer."

"But it's such a beautiful planet—why destroy everything else if humans keep killing each other and messing up nature?"

"The planet will outlive humans, by many eons…nature is constantly adjusting towards balance. Your present Western civilization is material-driven, so to speak, and caused the initial downfall of humans. The other seven deadly sins did the remainder. Western culture is based upon warfare, political and financial controls, secretive scientific subversion of private rights and health—and lack of true education for subsequent generations of vipers."

"Vipers?"

"The reptilians' science invaded my creations long ago on earth. They mixed up a soup of genes. I did not intend that. Now the human is generally less than nothing, in a way. The species is without direction. Tribe and class-consciousness rule while they are dominated and controlled by the invisible ones who plot and plan behind closed doors. Only a few remain pure."

"But haven't all nations and cultures had invisible, ruling classes that control their populations as long as there have been humans stupid enough to be ruled over?"

"*In your history*, yes. But what is meant by '*Heaven*' is that state of being where larceny cannot exist within the souls of my creations and everything is in perpetual equilibrium. That's how I originally designed them. In giving them free will and choice, I subtracted that natural filial love they might have for me and converted it into a desire only to be expressed by a *voluntary* heart, with a wish to know me."

"You mean you commanded them to love you originally?"

"No...you do not understand. *They were consciously created with my love within them.* But I wished that they *earn* my love and their eternal estate. So...I gave them free will to seek me out and hold me in reverence and love. But that has gotten lost, and my creations shall not seek me deeply enough to find their complete love for me within them."

"Certainly not in this earth existence. Besides, there are too many of us. We are quickly overpopulating the planet and quality of life will diminish."

"Yes, you are right...there must be a purging...but there have been many such rises and falls before. There are *controls* in the cosmos you know nothing about."

"Why did you create humans in the first place?"

"Children...children are so innocent, unsuspecting and willing to learn and grow. We were lonely for those who would love us as family, embrace and honor what we had done for them—and since I was the chief designer—we—I—thought it a pretty good idea. But as you see, even the best ideas are not foolproof."

"So why am I here?"

"I told you...to prepare for a higher life. Other than that, I don't know...why *are* you here?

"All I know is I was a bit drunk, I started playing the magic phonograph and all of a sudden I was on the beach walking toward the rope ladder."

"I see. Then we must have called you."

"*We?* Who's we?" I asked, still unable to see anyone. "What do you look like, by the way?"

"Look like? Oh, you mean as perceived by your three-dimensional eyes. Hmmm...let me see..." Then this figure of a kindly-faced old man with a long white beard and hair stood before me. "How's that? More like what you had in mind?"

"Yeah...thanks, at least I can talk to someone I can see. What do you really look like?"

He pointed up into the gloriously colored sky. "That...this...you...everything you can see or hope to see—we are those things."

"You mean you don't have specific form—like a body?"

"No, not really. We are *consciousness*. You too are consciousness in your highest state of being. You must learn to be conscious of consciousness. That is *awareness without form*. You have the power and will to transmute. You can be anything you wish within your frequency field."

"What does that mean?"

"You are a *vibration*, tuned within specific perimeters—you cannot be a snail or swordfish or mountain lion. Your vibration is frequency-restricted within certain transmutation boundaries. That maintains order. Order is important for an infinite cosmos. But I do not know everything there is to know, either. No one does. I created your form from the ape in order to expand my own knowing. We are that way, you know, curious about things. But in the end, it is only love that counts. That is the highest vibration. It is no colors and all colors at one time."

"I don't understand that. Anyway, do I have to leave here with a lesson or something?"

"Not necessarily. Not if you don't wish a lesson. The experience is sufficient to prepare you—for all is done silently in the higher worlds. You probably came here through that device that plays holograms and it increased in frequency until it tripped you here! Was it fun?"

"Not particularly. Especially the wave and height thing."

"We are always attracted to the things we fear most, so that we have opportunity to overcome them by facing them. You are not known to have fear, as I see into you. Why did you fear this? You did that today. Perhaps that is your lesson. Walk through your fear."

Suddenly next to the figure in the white robe stood a lovely young angelic looking female. Her diaphanous gown was pretty see-through and her figure was exemplary. She whispered into the ear of the old one.

"Ah, your last appointment on earth shall be September 13, 1955, Templa reminds me. Prepare for that day."

"C'mon, now—how can you know those things?! For all you know, I could get shot to hell in a dark alley chasin' a hoodlum, mister whoever-you-are."

"True, but you won't be," the male's voice answered. "Templa keeps accountings of all such things—quite accurately, I might say."

"Now can I go back home?" I asked, a little annoyed.

"Are you willing to go back the same way you arrived?"

"No…"

"I thought not. Well, then, take Templa's hand and she shall take you upon a different route."

"You haven't explained why you called me."

"Oh, I didn't?" Again, the young angel whispered into the old one's ear. "Oh, yes—of course—it was simply to remind you of *love*. You earthlings are so devoid of true love…the love you are born with that became buried in you so deeply. Now you cannot find it. But sooner or later you will. When they stop fear. Then you will let go. Then you will know love and joy, even with someone who can love you equally, deeply." The young angel came forth and took my hand. She did not speak but the second her fingers intertwined with mine, I felt a wondrous warmth in my gut. The elder waved good-bye and Templa walked away with me into a golden pyramid that had no walls! We stood in the middle of it. A rain of energy poured over me and I breathed like a brand new baby once more. Next thing —I was on the floor in front of my desk, just waking up!

## Death On the Golden Gate

Eventually I made my way to my comfy chair and sat. I lit up a Lucky Strike. The phonograph was still now. I glanced at my watch. It was about 8:35 p.m. It seemed I had been gone for many hours. But actually, in less than an hour or so I had experienced what the magic phonograph had granted me—a peak into yet another dimension of being.

Just then I saw a shadow in the hallway. It approached my door. There was a knock. "Yeah, come in, the door's open…"

In walked Lester Keith. "Denning? I need to talk to you. You didn't answer your goddamned phone—how in the hell do you expect to do business when you never answer your phone?" he admonished me.

"Easy…if I ignore calls from people like you, Lester…then I can drink and smoke all day without a smidgeon of guilt."

"Well, I wouldn't be too pompous if I were you, big shot. You never know if I've come to arrest you and put you behind bars where you belong." He glanced at the magic phonograph. "What's that—your confession machine—Dictaphone?"

"No, it's a *teleporter* to other planes of existence, dimensions you couldn't even fantasize about, Lester," I answered pretty smart-mouthed. "You know why? Because you have no imagination."

"Don't be a smart ass, Denning. Your number's gonna come up one of these days." He took his hat off and sat opposite me. "So…now to business. Just what do you know about this Gossman fellow you mentioned about a few weeks ago?"

"Yeah, Theodore Gossman, San Francisco, California. Music teacher, a few mysteries—married a trophy wife. What about him?"

"He's dead. The San Francisco police think he jumped off the Golden Gate Bridge. Pending the autopsy, you would've had enough time to get to Frisco, snuff Gossman out, take some of his counterfeit dough and nobody would know the difference.

171

Plus your name was on his appointment book." I saw that Lester knew about the counterfeit money downstairs at 2222 Broadway. "Minting dough on church property—tch! tch!—he oughtta be ashamed of himself!"

I mulled this new development over in my head. "I would've had to push if I did do it—the man was a cripple, confined to a wheelchair. Besides, what motive would I have to kill Gossman? I could've stolen from him at least on two occasions."

"You knew about the phony dough?"

"Yeah, he paid me with it, I'm sure."

"How much?"

"A lot. Maggie and I found it the second time I was in that building."

"Maggie? Who's that?"

"Oh, a librarian who's a part-time sleuth."

"Would she have knocked over Gossman? I think the FBI might wanna meet her. They already know about you, so they tell me."

"Nope, she hardly knew him—she'd met him through me. Leave Maggie outta this. And leave me out. I'd check out the broad who looks like Lana Turner and acts like a snake. Remember? The one who most likely did her four husbands in and is working on number five now?"

"Yeah, but you didn't know where she lived."

I decided to keep that a secret for the moment. "And still don't."

"Don't hold out on me, Denning—or you'll get the shit kicked outta you one way or another. I'd be first in line."

"When I know, you'll know," I lied.

He got up. "So, depending on what the Frisco coroner says, you're a free man—for now. But you do know, private detective bullshitter, how much I wanna pin something on you that'll stick. And ya really wanna know something else? In truth I hate guys of your ilk."

I smiled. "That's too bad, Lester—look in the mirror sometime—there's a criminal behind every face—the next thug's mug you see might be your own!"

"Shaddup, you—I'm tired of your fast mouth and big talk. I don't want you to sleep at night, Denning, cause sooner or later the Devil's gonna come and take you off to Hell and Damnation where you belong!"

"I don't think he's interested. Don't sweat it, Lieutenant—we all get there sooner or later. Good night and—uh, oh, I'll sleep just fine tonight, thank you."

"You look like shit. You been drinkin' and cavorting with women again?" he snarled.

"No more than usual. What about you? I'd drink if I was in your business, Inspector Keith."

"Up your ass, Denning!"

"Sorry, Lester, it's just your high and mighty authoritative crap that gets to me now and then. Most of the rest of you I can stomach on a good day."

He ignored what I said. "Oh, Gossman left a note with your name on it. That happens to be one of the reasons you're under suspicion."

"Oh? What did the note say, Lieutenant—was it a love letter?"

"None of your goddamn business."

"Maybe if you tell me I can help."

He took a folded piece of paper out of his breast pocket. "Okay, wise guy, see what you can make of this." He tossed the note and it landed right on the magic phonograph. I opened it. "*Dear Dinsie: I have to keep it out of the wrong hands, so I'm sending the Lazzeria to someone I've employed to 'find you' who also resides in Los Angeles. Someday, dove, I'll return to my svelt youth and women will have me—TG.'* I read out loud. It began to sound like Gossman had set me up to find his wife. But why? Why would he pay me to find someone whose whereabouts he knew already?

"So, who in the hell is this 'Dinsie' and what's the 'Lazzeria'" the curious inspector demanded in a gruff voice.

"Well, I can answer one of those. *This* is the so-called *Lazzeria*, a holographic imaging machine of some sort. Anyway, that's what I think." I didn't wanna tell Keith anymore. He wouldn't get it anyway. "And Dinsie? I think that's a nickname for his errant wife, Evelyn Gossman."

"Ya don't say? They're in collusion? Why hire you, then? It smells, Denning." He scratched his head. "So, what you're sayin', track down this bimbo wife of his and you'll solve the case, eh?"

"Well, that was the original intent, but not exactly. My job's through, Lester. Gossman hired me to find his ex and I think I did. I earned my dough. Over and out..."

Lester fumed. I realized I'd made a slip. "I thought you told me you didn't know where she was—I'll tell ya, Denning—"

"—look, Lieutenant, Los Angeles, okay? Fucking *Los Angeles*! I told you I *think* I did. You never know nowadays."

"Yeah? If you're lying and you're implicated in Gossman's murder, I'll string you up myself! Friendship goes so far, Denning, up to the point of murder!"

"So be it, Lt. Keith...good night. Flatfeet like you go around with your attitude up your ass, mister, you hold your hands over the sides of your eyes like blinders, you're myopic and don't bend the law because you don't wanna lose your job—or your retirement...to hell with justice! You know who you should be stringing up, Lester?—all those goddamned politicians downtown who are on the take, judges included, or the cops on the vice-squad who take money from the Mafia and the like and allow 14-year old girls to be sold on the street or deported to some foreign port of call! Don't tell me about murder, Mr. Policeman, we've both seen enough for a hundred lifetimes—so let it rest, Lester...I'll tell you what I think you need to know when the time comes. Now, go home and do your work. You are a public servant, ya know—and I'm the public..."

He said no more, but put on his hat and stomped out of my office.

# Chapter 6

## ZOMBIES IN THE PANTRY

### The Case of the Missing Movie

It was Halloween Eve, October 31, 1947. Days had whisked by and my business was so-so. The times were changing along with the laws. Lawyers started to make inroads in hiring their own on-staff investigators to trace some dirty mud on the defendant to stick on the case so it'd swing toward benefitting the plaintiff. That left guys in my profession scrambling to make up for the lost work. Soon, I suspected, I'd have to find a new angle in my business because people like me were left outta the loop. I'd seen Maggie a couple of times. I knew she was becoming more attached each time we made love, but what's a guy to do? Even after ya tell the truth, people believe what they wanna believe.

I decided to hang out in a seedy bar until after the kids got off the street and Halloween was officially over. That meant well after midnight. The bar was *Halloran's* on Sunset Boulevard near Ivar. It was a dump that ya walked down into and it smelled like beer and piss as you descended. Inside, cigarette smoke masked some of the smell, and scurrilous people having a ribald drunken time filled your senses with a thousand memories I'd lived throughout the years. Instead of a babe singing up there with a little combo, there was a guy with a nice croon to his voice. I thought I'd seen him somewhere in the movies, but maybe not. He looked a little like Vaughn Monroe, but I knew it wasn't him. I found out his name was Denny Rivers and he hailed from the east coast. He *was* singing a Vaughn Monroe song from 1945, however. *There I've Said It Again* came from a time I was chasing down Einstein and nearly missed getting blown up in the Nevada desert. It was a tense time, to say the least, when I almost bought the candy store by the A-Bomb test when Oppenheimer's military men tied me and a couple of babes to the top of the tower to explode us. Well, that didn't happen. Someone unexpectedly saved our asses. But that's another story.

I walked up to the bar, sat on a stool and ordered. Then I pivoted around to watch the singer and the band. To my left sat a middle-aged woman with a black hat and small veil. She looked like she was down on her luck, not because she wasn't dressed well, but her face seemed somber and she sat still and looked toward the mirror behind the bar. When the male singer took a break, I went up to him and tossed a couple of bucks in his jar. "You remind me a little of someone else who sings, but I still think you have a personable style all your own," I complimented him.

"You don't say! Well, that's the best compliment I've had all night from the customers in this dump. Most of 'em say, 'what time do you get off, pal?' But thanks, buddy."

"Think I've seen you in a couple of movies—or are you just a look-alike?" I inquired.

"Ha! Look alike? Nope, I'm a B-actor's B-actor—been in a few movies lately—bit parts, ya know. I'm really a singer. I played a tough guy in John Garfield's *Body and Soul*—you know, small parts."

"Oh, I think I saw you in that—I'm a big fight fan, ya know."

"Yeah, a lotta guys are. What—what do you do?"

"Oh, I'm just a lowly private dick—I take Kodak photos of men and women in compromising positions...or men and men, or women with women—" I chuckled. He laughed lightly.

"—figure me this one, then, Mr.—Mr.—"

"—Denning—Cable Denning..."

"Mr. Denning... You see, recently I went to work for Bob Lippert—a really cheap B-movie maker—but despite that, we made a hell of a good film—*'Aliens On Mars'* it was called. Now the damn thing's disappeared...just three months to a release date, too!" He took out a cigarette and I lit it for him. "Lippert's beside himself—but who would steal a science fiction movie about earth people ending up on Mars? And—"

"—depends who's on the *inside*, Mr. Rivers—and if the movie revealed a little too much—more than the public ought to know—well, then you can count on your movie vanishing into thin air. Sometimes scripts and movies get made that are too touchy or revealing to the powers that be. And that's a no-no."

"Just call me Denny. Maybe I can call you Cable? What a strange name for a person—how'd you get that name?"

"Ask my mother..."

"Maybe I will."

"Ya can't."

"No? Why not?"

"She's dead."

"Oh. Well, anyway, you sound like a conspiracy is going on or something. You really don't believe in that horseshit, do you?"

"Some of it I do, I'm afraid. I've seen too damn much to sweep things like this under the rug. We're being watched all the time. Remember such things are more common than you might think—*and* sometimes right under your nose."

"Well, now that you mention it, an agent for a Brit author named George Orwell inquired of Mr. Lippert whether he'd be interested in making a futuristic movie of some kind. *1984*, I think it was called. But he hasn't finished the book yet. Small chance of that being a Lippert film. Hell, the other movie companies wouldn't touch it, I hear."

"Oh? And why not?"

"I don't know. Think back a couple of years, Orwell's *Animal Farm* and the controversy that caused. Too intellectual, maybe—you know, not enough blood and guts—too controversial—maybe people hate to think...who knows?" He walked over to an empty table, put out his cigarette in an ashtray and returned to face me. "Well, back to the salt mines for me." He extended his hand. "Good to meet you, Cable. And thanks again for the compliment. Makes a guy know he's getting through to someone amongst all these drunks in here." Then he walked away and I went back to my barstool next to the attractive lady.

As Denny Rivers began his version of *1944's Besame Mucho,* the lady looked up from her drink and turned to me. "He knows how to tear out your heart, eh?" she said in a slightly slurred voice. I could tell she'd been drinking.

"Maybe for some, lady. It doesn't have to be the end—it could mean the beginning of a torrid love affair, couldn't it?"

"I've already had that...wha—what I *don't want* is any more entangle—hic!—entanglements! Had enough...what do you do, mister?"

"I'm a winding down private dick, lady...that's all..."

"You mean a private detective? The kind that snoops into everyone else's business?"

"Yep, that's me. What do you do?"

"I'm—I'm a film editor—just finished a nice cut, too. But something went wrong."

"Something went wrong?"

"Yeah, the damn film got stolen..."

Then I made the connection. "Ah, you and Denny Rivers worked on the same movie?"

"Yeah, for all the good it did me. I've had a big crush on that bloke ever since he came on the set. Kurt Neumann hired him. I think he's a handsome hunk, don't—don't you?"

"Well, that wouldn't be my reaction, lady, but I see what you mean—he's quite a good-looking bloke with a fine set of pipes."

"Yeah, I'd like to know the rest of his plumbing," she intoned. She sipped from her drink. "You—you have a steady girlfriend, Mr.—Mr.—?"

"—Denning, Cable Denning." I handed her a card of mine. "I'm over on Franklin near Cahuenga. I can't afford to have a steady girlfriend—it's too hazardous to the health."

"Oh?" She glanced at my card. "What if I hired you to find my lost movie?"

"I don't know. I get $25 a day plus expenses...you know, gas, phone calls from phone booths, getting shot at, dispositions, shoe leather—"

"—shoe leather?!" she laughed. "That's kinda nervy, wouldn't you say, Mr. Denning?"

I chuckled. "That's in a manner of speaking, Miss—Miss—"

"—*Mrs.* Thelma Rhodes. Believe it or not, I have a husband roaming around out there somewhere dressed in his ego. He hasn't wanted me for years—but he sure in hell screws all the young starlets that'll say 'yes' to him."

"I see. Yeah, sometimes that happens...I'm sorry. You seem like a straight shooter."

"They—they—hic!—they don't come any straighter, mister."

"So...do you have any clues who'd possibly wanna steal the movie? By the way, what's the name of the company?"

"Robert I. Lippert—a theatrical con man of sorts, I guess you'd say—goes under the current name of *Action Pictures.*"

"Okay...so...do you have any clues as to where the movie might have disappeared to? What's the motive? And why would someone steal an unreleased motion picture?"

"You got me. I edited the damn thing. It was a science fiction film, you...you—hic!—know...about five crew members going to the moon—but their orbit gets deflected and—and they end up on Mars and find a bunch of zombies!"

I flinched inside. "*Zombies*? What in the hell would zombies be doing in a modern science fiction movie?"

"Hell if I know—ask Mr. Lippert—he bought the story."

"So I need to know who paid for the film's production, what's Lippert's interest, who objected to the movie being made—if anyone—and would there be anything in the content that might offend someone?"

"Are you kidding? Someone's *always* offended. That's the movie business. Ya try and make films that—hic!—that are benign—yet appealing—but really, they're just pap for the masses."

"Maybe I oughtta talk to Mr. Lippert. He's the guy who bought the story from someone, eh?"

"Yep, he did. *Ardel Wray*...she's a screenwriter and the author. She's the one that wrote *Isle of the Dead* with Boris Karloff in mind. Val Lewton made it at RKO for under $250 grand about two years ago. That's about all I know, Mr.—Mr. Denning."

"Don't you think Lippert oughta be footing the bill?"

"He's cheap. He makes movies to sell to the smaller venues that have a large turnover. Everybody goes to the movies...you know that."

"If you want me to handle the case, then, phone me—the number's on the card I gave you. Just maybe we'll find your lost movie."

She extended her hand and we shook. "You got it, handsome!" she said and I dodged out listening to Denny Rivers singing *Life is Just a Bowl of Cherries.* Oh, yeah, sure it was!

## The Picture in the Compact

The next day was Saturday, November 1st. The phone rang about 10:30 as I was stumbling outta bed, so I answered it. "Yeah, Cable Denning here…"

"Cable, it's me, Maggie. What are you doing?"

"What am I doing? I'm trying to wake up, Maggie. Long night last evening. What's up?"

"I wish *you* were, handsome. Can you come over—I'm feeling a lot of…of desire for you just now. It's been a couple of weeks, you know…"

Maybe sweet, innocent Maggie was what I needed today. "Yeah, I think we can arrange that. It might be a couple of hours. We can grab some breakfast."

"Breakfast in the afternoon?" she queried me. "Why don't you have *me* for breakfast, and then we can go for lunch?" she said naughtily.

"Yeah, why not?" We agreed and I hung up. Then the phone rang again. "Yeah, Cable Denning here…"

"Mr. Denning, this is Thelma Rhodes, the drunken film editor you met last night."

"Oh, yeah, Mrs. Rhodes, how are you today?"

"I didn't score with Denny, if that's what you mean. Like my husband, I guess I'm too old for him.

Anyway, I'll send you a check if you'll take the case. Here's the starting information you'll need." I got a pencil and pad and told her to shoot. "Ardel Wray wrote the story and script. She lives at the Beverly Carlton Residential Hotel on Olympic. Val Lewton uses her to script write a lot. Ardel may be a bit touchy, so be on your toes. But there's another person she hangs out with who's *really* scary. His name is Ryke Simpkins—you'll find him at the *Orange Cockatiel* on Wilshire, a dive where a lot of weird people hang out. I don't think Lewton or Lippert know anything. I just have this gut feeling Ardel's friends might know something about the missing movie. Okay?"

"Yeah, swell, Mrs. Rhodes, at least it's a place to start. I'll get right on it. Twenty-five bucks a day plus expenses. Thanks..." I hung up.

I knocked on Maggie's door. She was wrapped in a towel. She sure had changed from a bashful librarian to a more or less aggressive femme fatale—at least in our private moments. "Hello, Cable," she purred as she pulled me in. She reached for my body and drew it close to hers, dropping her towel in the process. I didn't say a word because I knew exactly what Maggie Loggins had in mind. We went over to her mussed up double bed and she began to undress me. It wasn't long before she had drawn me between the sheets with her and we were kissing and touching each other everywhere. "I've been thinking about you since the last time you left, mister," she sighed. She spread her legs and wrapped them

184

around me, drawing my body between them. She let out a whimper as I entered her. And all the rest? I felt amorous and guilty at the same time. What a hell of a way to exist, I thought. But what's a guy to do?

Later that afternoon we went for a late lunch. I had bacon and eggs with toast and coffee, while Maggie had an olive sandwich. "I've been thinking, Cable. If Gossman is dead—and I don't think he killed Evelyn's husbands—then I thought Eddie Grant is in collusion with Evelyn and they plan on being together and splitting the money. But I did some checking. Eddie Grant is actually a wealthy man. His Dad was a big banker or someone in the financial world—lots of money on both sides of the family. Eddie doesn't need the money. I don't think he needs Evelyn, either. You know what I think?"

"No, what do you think?"

"I think it's Evelyn who's holding on to Eddie. No, I believe there's someone else bumping off Evelyn's husbands."

"Why couldn't it be Evelyn? She sure has motivation."

"It's too obvious. Here's what I think. I think Gossman was blackmailing Evelyn to get back at her. I think he knew something. But his killer knew he knew it. So he killed him. Besides, Eddie's been dating someone else who's much younger and very pretty. She's also a singer, so they probably have a lot in common."

"Yeah? Who's that?" I answered, sitting back and lighting up.

"Her name is *Scarlett O'Hara*—she's a headliner at *Roscoe's Hideaway.*" I almost swallowed my cigarette!

"Yeah, I've heard her—and she's a dish alright," I covered.

"You probably drooled over her, if I know you," she kidded me.

A strange chill ran through me. Eddie and Scarlett? What an odd combination. But as Maggie said, they were both singers and maybe shared more things together than most people. "Not drooled, just admired, Maggie. Well, at least Eddie's enjoying life with someone who's got a lot in common with him, eh?"

"Yes...it's funny what attracts people, isn't it?"

"Yep. So any other bright ideas as to who killed Evelyn's husbands? And why should I care? I did my job, Gossman's dead and I've a new case to pursue."

"Oh? What case is that?"

"I guess you could call it, *The Case of the Missing Movie.* Some science fiction film just got edited and subsequently was stolen. A guy named Robert I. Lippert has this B-movie company, I guess. I met the editor last night. She had the hots for a singer named Denny Rivers. She's paying me to find the movie. If we find it, maybe she'll get some brownie points and a promotion."

She giggled. "And maybe Denny Rivers, eh? Doesn't the owner of the film care?"

"I don't know. Maybe he's got a lotta irons in the fire."

"Talking about fire, I'm still on fire for you, mister. What are the chances we might go back to my apartment for—"

"—sorry, Maggie, got a busy day...or what's left of it. I just got hired to go find that missing movie."

"Can I go?""

"Not where I'm going, kid. I hear it's pretty sleazy, starting from the ooze up."

"What do you mean?"

"I gotta start in some pretty rough neighborhoods. It ain't safe for a Puritan librarian who belongs with a lot younger man."

She pouted. "There aren't any younger men out there who are better then you are, Cable. I mean that." She looked at me and took my hand. "Honest...believe me? I don't ever want you to stop loving me."

"Whoever said I loved you? We have sex two or three times a month, that's it. Why do dames assume things so fast? Did you ever hear me say I love you?"

She took her hand away and looked down at her lap. "No, you never have, Cable. I'm a girl—and girls assume things sometimes, I guess. Or maybe it's wishful thinking. I'm sorry...I keep building castles in the air, don't I?"

"Yeah, I'm sorry, but I think you do, Maggie. But if there's a prince inside one of those castles, it ain't me. I know that sounds hard. You know my life and the way I exist on this planet—I'm still considered dangerous territory, babe—even to myself. Please keep that in mind next time you go day dreamin' about our relationship. I shouldn't even be with you right now."

She lifted her eyes. "But you are, aren't you?"

"Yeah, I guess I am. Look, kid, it isn't that I don't desire you—"

"—there you go again—I'm not a kid. I'm a grown woman who happens to sleep with you now and again, okay? Maybe you forgot, but on the first day we met you asked, where can *two people in love* go to get something to eat? So we went somewhere. But only one of us fell in love eventually, and it wasn't you. How can you throw words around so loosely? Don't they mean something to you?"

"I think you knew what I meant, Maggie. Sometimes people say things. Especially big loud mouths like me. Maybe I felt frisky that day." I lit up a Lucky Strike. "I'll tell ya what, before I go sleazing it later—how would you like to go see and hear a fine young singer?"

Her face flushed and she began to glow. "I'd love it! You mean tonight?"

"Yep."

She glanced at a clock on the wall. "It's Saturday *afternoon*, Cable. I've—I've got to get home and change into—into, well, something more appropriate—you know something more presentable. What will we do in the meantime?"

I gave her a naughty smile. "Oh, I don't know. I suppose we could go back to your place and take a nap..."

She grabbed my leg—pretty far up. "Oh, Cable, I can't believe it—you'd actually be with me for like a whole day and night?"

"I didn't say anything about all night. Just part of it, okay?"

"Yes, sure! That's swell, Cable!"

We got back to Maggie's apartment and I undressed and crept between the sheets while my young librarian friend went to take a shower. Soon she came out and watched me for a minute or two. Then I felt a finger by my nose. I started. "Yes?" I said, smiling at her.

"That's us, Cable. I was going to take a shower, but I was, uh, leaking a little and I felt myself and this is what it smelled like. It's divine, Cable, I mean, really divine—just to think our combined juices intermingled and—and—"

"—yes? and what?" I whispered to her.

"And I just wondered if there was any more where that came from. We've never made love when I was still wet with us." I pulled her toward me and kissed this sweet young woman of the universe. As a matter of fact, I was still hankering for the little lady from earlier in the day. I felt between her legs. She was wet and swollen. It wasn't long before we were inter-twined in one another and I was jamming the love of Eros into Maggie Loggins!

Women can and do surprise sometimes. Maggie was dressed in a tan tight skirt with a light peach blouse, nylons and heels. Her hair was pulled back and to the side and she could've been anyone's model—except she still looked like a librarian. Maybe that's a stigma people have a hard time getting rid of.

*Roscoe's* was pretty crowded, but we managed to get a small table near the back of the old *Bella Notte.* Suddenly I had a flashback. Ol' Jedadiah Penn was calling to me from a table. Honey Combes was up on the stage singing her little heart out and I was happy. That was 1928. Now the crowds were younger and different. The vibration was changing. Scarlett O'Hara was singing a 1941 Glenn Miller hit song entitled *I Know Why* and for a minute it sounded very much like Evelyn Gossman's voice was coming out of her mouth. Naw, must be my imagination. Her rendition was a bit more separated and faster than the lady who now goes under the name of Marla Felix. But there was an amazing similarity in their voices. Or maybe I'd heard too many female singers through the years and they were all starting to jumble together.

About 10:30 p.m. who should walk in but Eddie Grant. "Wanna dance?" I asked Maggie.

"Dance? I'm—I'm not sure I know how, Cable," she confessed.

"Yeah? Well, just grab me in the dark and circle around."

"It's that easy? Well, I guess I could try. But don't laugh."

"Wouldn't think of it," I smiled at her. Maggie fit just swell into my arms and we slowly whirled around the crowded dance floor. I kept my eye on

Eddie Grant. As soon as Scarlett had finished her number, we clapped while Eddie bee-lined it for the stage. He followed her to the back, into Honey's old dressing room, I'd bet. I congratulated Maggie for dancing so well, returned her to our table and excused myself, telling her I'd be right back. I rounded the corner in time to hear Scarlett and Eddie arguing wildly. I hid behind a curtain as Eddie came stomping out. I waited. A few minutes later Scarlett came out pampering her hair a little. As soon as she'd passed me, I went for the dressing room. It was open. I nosed around on her vanity dresser. Combs, brushes, lipstick, eyeliner, eyebrow pencil, shadow and a circular brass compact. For the hell of it I opened the compact and where there should have been a mirror there was a small photo. Only it wasn't an ordinary photo. Nope, it was a photo of *Evelyn Gossman!* Just then I heard a key turn in the lock from outside. Now I was locked in! Shit! Scarlett must've forgotten to lock it, being so upset with Eddie and all. I searched around the room. Finally I found a strong metal fingernail file and sandwiched it between the door jam and managed to push the latch back far enough to open the damn thing. I then joined Maggie. "

"I thought you'd fallen in," she kidded me.

"No...I—I was doing some work, Maggie."

"Oh...you mean snooping kind of work?"

"Yep. I found something out, too. But I ain't gonna tell you—just yet."

"Darn it, Cable! That's not fair! I'll bet you found a crucial bit of evidence. But where?"

"In the singer's dressing room."

"Shame on you—legally, that's breaking and entering." She leaned toward me and looked at me with those intense light-blue eyes. "So...? What did you find?"

"I was tempted to grab it and use it as evidence. But I thought I'd let it play out a bit first."

"Cable..." she whispered intensely in my ear. "*What?!*"

"Okay, let's go. I'll tell you on the way to your apartment."

We left without Eddie Grant seeing us and soon we were cruising along toward Maggie's apartment complex. "I'm waiting..." she said impatiently.

"Okay...okay...let's just say I found a very odd and possibly incriminating bit of evidence."

"Yeah, yeah, yeah...but what?"

"A woman's compact—you know for face powder or the like."

"A compact? How could that be incriminating?"

"It could be—*if it contained Evelyn Gossman's photograph!*"

Maggie's face lit up like a Christmas tree. "You mean...you found a picture of Evelyn Gossman in Scarlett O'Hara's compact—like hidden?"

"Well, I don't know if that was the intention. Maybe she admired Evelyn at one time in one of her other incarnations. And maybe she stuck it in her compact in place of the mirror that's probably under it."

"What did you say?"

"That maybe Scarlett O'Hara admired Evelyn Gossman at one time in one of Evelyn's other incarnations—"

"—no! That's not what I heard. I heard that maybe *Scarlett* had had another incarnation. What's her real name? Where was she born? Where has she lived and all the rest."

I dropped my enthusiasm. "Oh...Well, maybe that too..."

"Oh, Cable, you should have removed the picture and looked on the back—you know, for dates, comments, names?"

"Well, I felt time was running out and indeed, Scarlett returned before I finished all of my snooping and locked the door—from the outside. So there I was, locked in her dressing room."

"No wonder you took so long to get back. So, how'd you get out?"

"Oh, the old fingernail file trick. It worked, and here I am."

She cuddled up to my shoulder. "Oh, Cable, I'm so proud of you. But you know what?"

"What?"

"We've gotta get back into that dressing room and find out what's on the other side of that photo."

"Not tonight, honey. It's been a long day and I've got other fish to fry in the less savory parts of town."

# Vorvolaka

As soon as I dropped Maggie off, I headed for Part II of my evening's adventures—the one I was getting paid for. So I drove to *The Orange Cockatiel*. It really *was* a dump, as Thelma Rhodes had explained. One entered at street level alright, but the guys hanging around outside made ya think about changin' your mind. Inside it was dark and noisy with men's voices, mostly. There was an old Seeburg jukebox in the corner spitting out popular tunes and some strung out babe and a guy in a T-shirt dancing with her by the jukebox. Many a probing eye was watching me. I knew I was outta place with my fedora, trench coat and my trusty .38 buried underneath the coat.

I approached the burly bartender. "I'm—I'm looking for a man by the name of Ryke Simpkins," I said.

He had a toothpick in his mouth and shifted it to the other side of his lip. He didn't say a word, but his eyes looked straight down. I didn't know if that meant dead or downstairs. I assumed it meant there was a lower floor. "Ya gotta buy a drink first, buddy. That's the rule—no drink, no go."

"Whatta ya got?" I asked.

"Whatta ya want?"

"Gin, straight."

I ordered a cheap American gin that tasted like rubbing alcohol. The bartender took the longest time to get me that drink. I paid the man and gulped it down, but it tasted bitterer than any Juniper plant derivative I'd ever tasted. Then I headed toward the rear of the dive. The jukebox was blaring and the bass hurt my ears as I descended the wide wooden stairs. It brought me back to the war years as Duke Ellington's band ploughed its way through *Take The A Train*. As I descended the stairs, the music faded into the back of my mind and I smelled something odd—and ominous. Just as I reached the bottom I heard a creaking noise and huge black iron doors slammed shut behind me. Now it was pitch dark and I could hear sneering and giggling down the hall. I lit a match and followed the sounds. I felt a little woozy and staggered up against the wall. But I kept moving. Soon I saw a folding door to my right and entered. The whole far wall glowed a sickly, pale green. It was a row of monstrous cupboards, maybe some kind of pantry, I figured. "Ouch!" I complained as the match burned down to my fingers. I quickly lit another.

My mouth went agape when a cupboard door opened and out walked a huge greenish humanoid creature of some kind. He walked like the living dead, slowly, surely toward me. "Put a coin in its mouth!" a female voice with a thick European accent spoke behind me.

"A coin? For what? Look lady, I don't think a coin is gonna stop this thing from comin' at me!" I said loudly.

"It will, he is a *vorvolaka*, one of the living dead—you would say perhaps 'zombie' in your language. A coin placed in his mouth will prevent him from crossing over the Black River forever."

"Look, I don't even know who you are, let alone that thing coming for me—but how do you suppose I get the damned thing in his mouth without getting strangled by those huge hands?!"

"What are you doing here?" she asked.

"Looking for a guy named Ryke Simpkins, and trying to find a lost movie. I'm a private detective—hired by someone to find it. I was led here, somehow. It's nuts, now ain't it?"

She was a bit nervous but held steady. "He's not here." Then she approached me closer. "The coin, sir, place the coin in the mouth while you speak *'nyugodjék bekében'*."

"Beg pardon?" I exclaimed. The barely animate dead-looking thing that approached me was silent but almost upon me. But it moved laboriously, so I grabbed a nickel out of my pocket, jumped up to toss it into the dark hole that was his mouth and yelled clumsily, *'nyugodjék bekében!'* Instantly the hairy creature that stood about 7 feet tall stopped. "What the hell did that mean?"

"It's Hungarian ... 'rest in peace'—and now he shall!"

"Why in the hell didn't *you* do it?" I asked the lady as the creature undulated back and forth in front of me, trying to keep its balance.

"I was not tall enough. Besides, *Ryke Simpkins* would kill me if he knew!" The thing collapsed onto the floor. I detected no sounds. "I am Borlanka Schrievnck." I couldn't get much of a look at her, but she seemed to be in her middle forties, a little stout with short hair and piercing blue eyes.

196

Then my match went out and we were in the dark except for the fuzzy green glow coming from the pantries. Suddenly her hand grabbed mine and she led me out of the room down the hall, away from where I had entered. Soon there was a dim light as we turned left and I could hear the gurgle of water. "Where are we going, lady?"

"To have you meet someone I'd rather not have you meet," she answered, still pulling me along down the dimly lit hallway.

"Oh?"

"Did you say you're looking for a lost movie?"

"Yeah, something like that. My client put a lotta work into it. I'd like to get it back for her."

We walked into the room which was semi-lighted by a pinkish-red light bulb mounted on a professional reflector, the kind they use in movies to focus the light. A small man with no chin greeted us. His face was unshaven, his eyes a dirty black and squinty, his manner brusque. "I wanted to be a movie director...but a life of iniquities was more fun!" Then I glanced at a corner and in the dusky pink light there stood what appeared to be a very young Asian girl shackled to the walls! He saw me raise my eyebrows. "Oh, her...a little Japanese tidbit—you remember the Japs, don't you? Only two years ago when we 'ceased hostilities'—but I'm still at it, I guess, huh?" he laughed. "You weren't there to see it, but those bastards had 16 miles of tunnels—hell, they were Lords of Darkness, little fucking Princes of War and murder. Yeah, I was there. We landed on Iwo Jima on February 19, 1945. It took us more than a month to blow those bastards to hell and sear their fucking little asses with the *Dragon's Fire*—that was our affectionate term for the flamethrower. Without them, we'd never have flushed those little slant-eyed bastards out of those damn hills. Eight thousand men were lost—*our* men—twenty six thousand were injured. So...you see, I'm not all that fond of those merciless little shits." He glanced at the woman who had led me there. She had been standing in the background. "I see you already met Borlanka—she is an Hungarian, born and bred you might say, to look after those creeps in the other room down the hall."

"You'll have to excuse me, Mr.—Mr.—"

"—Ryke Simpkins is the name. And yours?"

"Denning, Cable Denning. I'm a private—"

"—I know what you are, Mr. Denning. I just didn't know who."

"Anyway, I'm a bit confused here. First of all a lady editor tells me a movie script writer knows about you, or at least about the disappearance of a certain Action Picture movie, written by Ardel Wray—and thought you might know about it. So I make it into the bar upstairs, the bartender looks down when I mentioned your name—then he proceeds to dope me up with a shot of gin. Next, I run into zombies, a weird Hungarian caretaker, a young Japanese hostage or sex slave or whatever she is—and you. Care to explain?"

"I never explain the past. Just the present." He looked at my face in the dim light. "How much do you want that missing motion picture, Mr. Denning?"

"Not enough to go through this shit, I'll tell you."

"How much do you value your life?"

"Not very much...why do you ask?"

He walked a few paces, then turned to look at me. "I was going to propose something...something *fun*—like you get your missing movie and your life—*if* I can watch you seduce my little captured Nip over there. And oh, there are a few feet missing from the film. Certain...uh...powers that be...took objection to the 'unedited version', so it seems. So now it's properly edited. I am its 'caretaker' until the right offer came along—which could be you on behalf of your client, Denning..."

I was beginning to connect the pieces: Simpkins worked for the really bad guys and was up to as much no good as he could get himself into. The zombie, the caretaking broad, the little Japanese sex-slave were all a confusing mess, a result of people grabbing for straws and stirring the mix. I thought it over for a minute. "I'll tell you what, Simpkins, you take your movie, your little Japanese sex-slave, your zombies and your nice little secretary-caretaker—and shove it!" I started for the door, but Simpkins drew a gun and before I knew it he shot me in the arm. It hurt like hell. "You son-of-a-bitch!"

"I want you to rape her, taunt her, take her, big tall and handsome. And I will watch, I wanna see those nip females get theirs right up their tight little twats! After all, they are the ones responsible for breeding those goddamned Nips."

I glanced at my arm. It was bleeding. "Okay, okay...get your lady to fix me up so I don't bleed to death all over the nip."

He looked delighted, as sick as he was. I think the war had damaged his brain. Or maybe he was that way before. "Oh, no, we won't do it that way...we will have Miss Toyami lick your blood clean. But first you must be naked in my pink-orange mood light—and Borlanka will dress Miss Toyami in a revealing silken red nighty—and you, Mr. Denning, must aggress upon her, take her, force yourself on her skinny little thighs and plump but firm small breasts—and penetrate her, releasing your spermatozoa into her crotch so we will breed out their pure race and evil misdeeds against humanity. You will kiss the blood off her lips as well. If...I say, *if* I am satisfied with your performance, I just might release you with all nine reels of the movie. But you'll need help carrying it in those clumsy metal cans."

"Don't bullshit me, Simpkins—I don't think you wanna be discovered and real life ain't radio. I don't expect Mr. Keen, Tracer of Lost Persons to come to my rescue."

"Very well, then have it your way."

I took a deep breath and glanced over at the nervous Borlanka Schrievnck. Miss Toyami whimpered as the older woman left and returned with a glistening red silk nighty. Her eyes began to tear as Borlanka stripped her of a few rags she was wearing and slipped the negligee over her head. "You guys disappear and be happy little voyeurs through a peephole somewhere, okay?" I said. Surprisingly they both left without another word. I took off my clothes and approached the young lady. I bent down and looked into her face. "I'm sorry you've had to endure this. Don't worry, I won't do anything to you—we'll figure a way out of this together, okay?"

She touched my shoulder near the bullet wound. "I am a Japanese American," she muttered in clear English. "That monster kidnapped me from my family." She was shaking.

"I'm sorry, kid. I don't know exactly how we're gonna get outta here, but I'm going to have to pretend to accost you..."

"What's that mean?" she asked in earnest.

"Attack you, do what that bastard Simpkins wanted me to do. Has he hurt you?"

"No, not really. He's incapable of having sex, I think. But he uses all kinds of instruments on me, some rubber, some other terrible things, like clothespins on my nipples. Oooo! Terrible!"

"Yeah, I know how those perverts can be. So, now I'm gonna take you in my arms gently and pretend I'm making love to you, okay?"

She looked up into my face with her intense black eyes. "You are bleeding still. What shall I do?"

"Nothing...let's just get on with the play acting..."

"Promise...promise you will not hurt me—if you—if you have to—do it."

Just then I remembered my clothes lay on the floor in a pile a few feet away—with my .38 buried under my trench coat. Why hadn't Simpkins noticed and confiscated it? That made me wonder until I glanced at the entrance to our little prison room.

There at the threshold stood yet another horrible vorvolaka! Simpkins' voice pierced the silence. "I wouldn't hesitate if were you, Denning! That particular kind of zombie is brain-washed to kill anything in his way, but he will hesitate until I press the right button, if you know what I mean..."

I turned to Miss Toyami. She was trembling at the sight of the huge beast in the doorway. "Okay, here goes...listen carefully...I'm going to touch you now, please don't be too squeamish. I have a gun hidden over there under my coat—and I'll go for it at what will hopefully be the right moment. In the meantime, you can resist me and squeal a little. I think that's what he wants. I think he hates females and wants to see you vulnerable, helpless as you suffer at my hands. Is that clear?"

"Yes...!" she whispered. I drew her very small naked body to me. My penis fit between her breasts and her head barely above my belly button. I began to stroke her and put my arms onto her butt. She whimpered a little but I persisted.

"It's not very convincing, Denning—it sounds like you have a secret pack not to hurt her—well, let me assure you—you *will* hurt her! Or if you refuse, the vorvolaka can do it, feeling nothing, enjoying nothing, mindlessly ripping her apart while you stand by helplessly. Take her and have a chance for life, detective!"

Just as he finished speaking I raced the few feet to my overcoat, pulled out my gun and fired upon the zombie. Then it occurred to me he was already dead! "Okay, Simpkins—where are you?"

202

"Ha! That's why I didn't take your gun, stupid man! No, Denning, get over to Miss Toyami and finish the job. I'll give you five minutes to properly seduce her. After that...guess what? Time's up! Everybody dies!"

Dismayed, I walked back toward Miss Toyami. "I am a Buddhist," she informed me under her breath. "We must become *shunyata*—a zero, a nothing. Then we must close our eyes and think of the ultimate, above all things—*nirvana*—release our candle and let it blow out!"

I didn't understand. "What do you mean?"

"We must *become* the experience, not experience it! There is no time now. Take my hand," she whispered. I did so. Instinctively I reached into my pocket for my pocketknife and opened it.

"Good—good! Now fuck her and kill her!" the madman shouted from behind a wall at us.

But there are more dimensions than three, and I knew somehow Miss Toyami knew this. "Cut my bonds!" she declared softly.

As soon as her hands and feet were free, she took my hand and began walking briskly toward the damn zombie. I had faith in this little slip of a thing from an alien culture. But she didn't stop and walked right into the zombie as Simpkins shouted to stop. But she didn't stop, and the monster in front of us gave us no resistance, as if we were not there at all. We comfortably slipped between its huge, widespread legs. As soon as we were out into the hallway we ran as fast as we could toward the sound of that gurgling water I'd heard earlier. We came to a cement precipice and twenty feet below us a cauldron of churning, flowing water wended its way toward a huge gaping round hole. We didn't have time to think, as Ryke Simpkins and Borlanka Schrievnck were right behind us. We grabbed hands and plunged into the roiling waters below. Little did I know at the time that it was the main sewer outlet for this part of the city! We were swirled around until we fell together into the glory hole of eternal forgetfulness—a giant concrete hole that fell another thirty feet straight down into deep sewage waters. Somehow we survived it and swam downstream until what seemed like stinking, smelling, rotten hours later we got dumped by the large non-operational Hyperion outfall pipe into the Playa del Ray's oceanfront. But we were alive, naked and breathing. We made our way along the beachfront to a gas station. Immediately I grabbed a water hose used to fill up radiators and started washing down Miss Toyami. She did the same for me until a police car came by and arrested us. They gave us some ill-fitting clothes and some patchwork medical care on my superficial gunshot wound. Once downtown I requested Lt. Lester Keith and he straightened things out, more or less. "Jesus Christ, Denning—naked, early in the morning, on the beach coming out of a sewer pipe with an under-aged Japanese girl--and claiming to be the victim of some madman below a bar named *The Orange Cockatiel*? C'mon, you can do better than that!"

"Check it out yourself, Lester. Look, we may be contaminated here—will you have us checked out and please take Miss Toyami home?"

"You bet I'm gonna check it out! Downstairs zombies, a nutcase from an insane asylum, some Hungarian female assistant—how do you come up with all that crap? All I can verify is that there is a Miss Toyami who accompanied you here somewhat willingly, there's a main sewer system drain that empties into the sea from the point you described under the cocktail lounge. How you got there I don't know, but you can bet I'll find out."

"Yeah, you do that, Lieutenant. And don't forget to question Miss Toyami—she experienced a hell of a lot worse than I did."

"Oh, by the way, there are eight or nine cans of film in properties left for you. One Miss Schrievport brought them in. She said they'd been stolen. Who do they belong to? Is that your Hungarian?"

"Her name is Shrievnck. Shit, Lester, that's the lady you should have arrested! She was Simpkins' accomplice."

"Then why did she drop 'em off for you? You were looking for them, weren't you?"

"I don't know why she left 'em off. Yeah I was looking for the damn thing, my client paid me to find the stolen movie—*Mission To Mars* or some such title. It belongs to Lippert's *Action Pictures*, strictly a B-movie operation. But someone considered this particular talking picture too 'talky', I guess, and stole it, edited it and now it's acceptable, I guess."

"You expect me to believe that? I don't know about you, Denning. How you get yourself into these hair-brain investigations, I'll never know. Now get outta here. I'll question both you and the Japanese girl later."

A cop car took Miss Toyami and me to upper Alameda Street, to a little white house set back from the road. I thanked the cops and we went to the front door. As soon as her family saw Suzuki Toyami they wept happy tears and embraced me for bringing her home. I was questioned a little, but I left Miss Toyami in the arms of her adoring father with her mother and little brother embracing them. I left the house, but the father followed me to the street. "Where will you go now, Mr. Denning?" he asked me.

"Oh, home to my office in Hollywood."

"Oh, Hollywood...are you movie star? Hai?"

"Not hardly, Mr. Toyami...just a poor private dick."

"Oh, Charlie Chan private detective—but he not Japanese."

"No."

"I wish you well, and thank you from bottom of heart. Buddha says, so that you may not misunderstand my gladness: *'I can understand your compassion, and I would like to speak. For seven days I have been wavering between the two, whether to speak or not to speak, and every argument goes for not speaking. I have not been able to find a single argument in favor of speaking. I am going to be misunderstood—which is absolutely certain. I am going to be condemned, nobody is going to listen to me in the way that the words of an enlightened man have to be listened to. Listening needs a certain training, a discipline, it is not just hearing…'* He hesitated and looked into my eyes.

"And so, what's that got to do with me, Mr. Toyami?"

"Everything…let me finish, please. *'For even if somebody understands me, he is not going to take a single step, because every step is dangerous, it is walking on a razor's edge.'* You took action, Mr. Denning, you stepped onto the dangerous edge because you cared. You could have left my beautiful Suzuki in the hands of her kidnapper. But you took her with you. I salute you, if I may."

"But the truth is, Mr. Toyami, it was your daughter who saved us both—that Buddha stuff you were talking about—she quoted something about *shunyata* and *nirvana* and that damned zombie didn't even know if we were there anymore after we escaped. So, you see, I owe our being saved to Suzuki."

He bowed before me. "So be it, Mr. Denning. Yet somehow your bravery brought our daughter back to us. I bow to you." He did so and I left.

# Chapter 7

## WHAT HAUNTS OUR DREAMS

It was Thursday, November 13, 1947. They say 'All's well that ends well', but I'm not so sure. My client got her movie back, minus 22 minutes of something I will never know. My last experience set me back for a new trench coat, fedora, shorts, tee shirt, slacks, shoes and gun holster—not to mention my billfold with twenty-five bucks in cash, my driver's license and private detective I.D.

Living is as if in a fishbowl these days. Increasingly, everybody knows your business down to what kind of underwear you buy and it seems they can peak in at any time. Everyone from Uncle Sam to the Internal Revenue Service to radio pollsters checking into what you eat, what you sleep in, what car you drive and how much you pay for rent—they all wanna know about your habits. Ha! I got 'em fooled! Not every bloke they investigate lives outta the back room of his business like me. And even though my life was like an eternal turnstile, I kinda liked it that way. I had to admit I liked meeting new and interesting people. But part of me was getting tired of it. The variation got less varied and people tended to fall into certain categories I could pinpoint. So maybe things weren't that exciting after all anymore. Women were getting very independent, aggressive, almost masculine sometimes—and that certain air of surrender to a real man meant that real women were getting harder to find. Ida was a real woman. I had to stay away from her, though. I just couldn't see myself husband and Dad about this time in my life. My past had proved disastrous in that department. I already had a son who I don't think likes me much. Now *Maggie* has proven to be quite the young woman. Maybe she'd be more fun to hang out with. I knew that Ida pined for me, wanted to be with me, probably wanted to be married to me. But she was my Girl Friday and just now I couldn't risk losing her to home, hearth and apple pie—let alone motherhood!

The phone rang. "Yeah, Cable Denning here..."

"Hey, Cable, this is Eddie Grant. Found out anything about where Evelyn lives yet?" he queried. That always bothered me when he asked that. It was like *he* knew but was checking to make sure that *I* didn't.

"Yeah, as a matter of fact, Eddie, I know exactly where she lives."

"Oh? Where?"

"You oughta know—you've *been* there. Does Carmelita and North Canon Drive ring a bell?"

"Oh? I have?"

"Stop the bullshit, buddy. You also know that Theodore Gossman is dead, don't you?"

There was a pause. "Gossman dead? Naw, how?"

"Oh, it seems someone pushed him off the Golden Gate Bridge, according to the San Francisco PD. Could've been your lady fair—or even you, Eddie Grant. They're doin' an autopsy now."

There was a pause at the other end. "Honest, Cable—okay, so I'm lyin' about seein' Evelyn—I wanted to see her before she got too cozy with her new husband—"

"—oh, of course, Eddie—I'm sure he was out when you visited."

"But I didn't know Gossman was dead. Am I a suspect?"

"I donno. Maybe. Evelyn sure is. If Lt. Keith snoops around your private lives, I'm sure he'll find the connection between you two. And maybe even go so far as to check out who you've been dating lately in the area of talented young singers at certain nightclubs."

"So what? A guy can date who he wants—I think Scarlett's a knockout—a little testy, but I think we're gonna be an item before long. Maybe we'll even sing together."

"I wouldn't count on it, Eddie."

"Why not, Cable?"

"Oh...I don't know...I think Scarlett O'Hara is more than just a bit 'testy', buddy boy." I didn't wanna tell Eddie about Evelyn's picture in Scarlett's compact.

"So what in the hell do you mean?"

"I'm—I'm not sure, Eddie. I'll tell you when I find out myself."

"Don't go snooping, Cable—at least not into my business."

"That's what I get paid to do—snoop. Take it easy, Mr. Grant—no one is horning in on your territory. It might all be just a coincidence—your meeting up with Scarlett O'Hara. Who does she remind you of, Eddie?"

"I don't know—should she remind me of someone?"

"I donno. Just keep your ears open and your eyes peeled, okay?"

"Yeah, sure...talk to you later, Cable. Though now, I think I'm sorry I called." He hung up.

## The Unkind Ties That Bind

About 2:00 p.m. I made my way over to Carmelita Drive and knocked on Evelyn Gossman's door. She answered the door wearing a light blue silken robe with not much else on under it. "Miss Felix—we've—we've, uh, met before. See? I'm a big boy—I found my way to your house."

"Unpleasantly, yes. *How* did you find me?"

"Oh, how soon we forget. I'm a private detective, Miss Felix, remember? Mind if I come in for a few minutes?" She opened the door and let me in. I looked around the plush, decorated room. "You know, I've actually wondered what you think about, Miss Felix—you know, life in general, old flames, dead husbands, current ones, lovers—"

"—that's enough, Mr.—Mr.—"

"—Denning...Cable Denning...I have a few questions I'd like to toss your way, if you don't mind—"

"—but I do mind, Mr. Denning—I'm not inclined to talk much to strangers—now, if you'll excuse me—"

"—well, believe me, Miss Felix, it may not seem like it, but I'm no stranger—I know a lot about you. Where shall I start? Young and beautiful Evelyn Nesbitt meets and gets seduced by one Theodore Gossman, a cripple in a wheelchair. But he's got dough. Evelyn marries Gossman, but all does not go so hot."

She lit up a cigarette and turned away from me, nervously puffing. "Go on," she said impatiently.

"So she leaves ol' Teddy boy for other climes. She meets up with a handsome bloke who sings named Eddie Grant. They become flaming lovers for a while. But then our heroine becomes bored and trades poor Eddie off for some Mexican millionaire. In the process of playing the game of incognito and killing off subsequent husbands, Evelyn Gossman becomes Anne Shirley, Lucie Mannette, Cathy Trask, Hester Prynne—and now as Marla Felix, she is married to one Mr. Sidney B. Factor. She seems quite nonplussed when her mates seem to kick the ol' bucket and nobody can prove that it might be murder!" I stopped and looked at the beautiful woman with the wonderful figure. She seemed unperturbed. She had her blonde hair up like Lana Turner and possessed those wonderful high cheekbones distinctive of beautiful women. "So now come the touchy parts, Miss Felix—Gossman knows his wife has this love affair with Eddie Grant in Mexico, yet he does nothing. He also happens to manufacture phony money in the basement of his so-called 'singing school' in San Francisco. He tolerates at least four husbands and claims he can't find you, so he hires me to find you—and then lo and behold—a cripple in a wheel chair is somehow wheeled out to the Golden Gate Bridge late one foggy night and tossed over the railing, wheelchair and all!" I lit up a Lucky Strike. "Was he conscious at the time? Nobody knows but the killer."

Suddenly she spun around. "I didn't do it! Someone else has been framing me—maybe even Theodore did it —I don't know, leave me alone!"

"Not yet, lady. I don't buy it—even if he killed himself, how'd he get himself and the wheelchair overboard into the far and cold briny below? I've still got a few unanswered riddles. The cops get a hold of a letter the dearly deceased wrote, addressing a certain 'Dinsie' and a minor player in this scenario, one Mr. Cable Denning, just happens to see your picture on the inset of a compact mirror of an up and coming pretty young singer named Scarlett O'Hara currently performing at a local nightclub. Add to that Gossman had a very peculiar phonograph that projected holograms. What else did it do beside turn that Italian guy Caruso into a singing god or take alcoholic gumshoes on spiritual journeys? It all smacked of unorthodox, a bit unusual and quite ahead of its time, wouldn't you say? Maybe a little science fiction tossed in?"

"I don't know. Theodore was a scientist, musician and yes, a counterfeiter. Believe me, that's all I know."

"Oh? Answer me *these* questions, kiddo and I'll go. One...are you affectionately known as *'Dinsie'*?

Did you launder Gossman's play money? And three, did you kill your husbands?"

She ran to a sofa and threw her face into her hands. "Yes, yes!" she wept. "Dinsie was a nickname of mine, I laundered his money and he paid me a little for doing so. Otherwise he'd blackmail me and tell the police I poisoned my husbands. *But I did not kill my husbands*—someone set it up to make me look suspect—and I know nothing about this Scarlett O'Hara and why she'd have my photo in her compact—maybe she's a fan! Now, would you leave me alone...please?!"

I took a deep breath. "You've got a handy little mailbox, but no physical address. Just P.O. Box 1715, Main Post Office, Los Angeles, California. Keeping where you live a secret, Miss Felix? What are you hiding? You're well to do, you just married a multimillionaire and watch the bouncing ball, lady, maybe his number will come up pronto—hubby number five?"

"Get out! Get out!" She came at me flailing. I put on my hat and exited as quick as I could. But for the first time, I had the feeling Evelyn Nesbitt Gossman did not kill her husbands. But if not, then...who did?

By the time I got back to the office, Ida had gone home. I knew she was dating someone and might even marry him. In a way I was jealous, I guess. I was like an old rooster, and wanted to keep all the hens in the chicken house for as long as I could. But in truth, I knew you couldn't keep people from fulfilling their lives and destinies. Hell, after all, I was still expecting the last of the Seven Fates—maybe more. I was never certain I'd experienced *Amorti*, the Goddess of Love—I've had so many kinds of love in my life. And consciousness? I'd even forgotten the last two names of the Fates whom I somehow had agreed to let guide me. But I know the Goddess of Death couldn't be very far behind.

I felt lonely so I called Maggie. She'd just gotten home and we decided to take a ride to the beach—in the dark. We went to a place called Paradise Cove, just south of Malibu. I parked and we walked out onto the small wharf that was deserted this time of night. "So you say you saw Evelyn Gossman this afternoon? Was she nervous?" Maggie asked me.

"Yeah, but as I said, I'm beginning to believe as you do—she didn't kill her husbands. There's a master marionette pulling the strings behind the scenes. Someone who wants to get back at her for something she did—or didn't do."

"Eddie Grant?"

"I don't think so."

"It can't be Gossman, he's dead."

"Right..."

"So who's the missing person? Did you make any sense out of finding Evelyn's photo in Scarlett O'Hara's compact? I've thought a lot about that. But why would a young singer possibly be implicated in the murder of several old men with money? Unless she wanted some of that money and was blackmailing—"

"—whoa, there, Nellie! I think you're heading way off base. When I mentioned it to Evelyn this afternoon, she confirmed that maybe Scarlett O'Hara was simply just a fan. After all, you have to admit, Evelyn is a knockout chick with class and talent. And so what if she was running money for her husband? That ain't murder."

"Maybe...there are still some missing pieces. You say Evelyn admitted she was somehow circulating Gossman's phony money?"

"Yep."

"Why would she do it? She didn't have to. She's rich." Maggie took my arm and we started back toward the shore. "Just for a minute—let's assume that Evelyn killed her husbands, okay? Now, no one has identified the chemicals used to kill them, right? And Theodore Gossman was a kind of weird scientist type, right? So...what if he provided Evelyn with an unidentifiable poison that killed her husbands and Gossman's price for it was that she filter his counterfeit money?"

"Laundering...that's what it's called. Yeah, could be...so that means complicity and collusion."

"Yes, and that would keep it all tidy for both of them. They may not have been good romantic partners, but really good partners in crime." She stopped. "But if that's true, then why kill Gossman—the goose who was laying all the golden eggs?"

"I don't know. As you said, Gossman and Miss Priss were not great partners in the bedroom—and what are the thousands of deliciously sinister fates waiting for lovers whose romance gets twisted out of shape along the way?"

Maggie bent up to kiss me. "Not like us...we're great romantic partners, don't you think? I never knew, Cable...being with you means so much to me. Can you come home with me?"

I kissed Maggie Loggins. "Oh, I don't know...I'm more expensive after midnight..."

She grabbed my neck and her lips clung tightly to mine. "That'll be just fine, mister—so am I."

## Don't Bug Me Baby!

I had a hunch. The following night I decided to travel over to the old Bella Notte where Scarlett O'Hara was singing. I sneaked in the back about 11:00 p.m. As I suspected, Eddie Grant was sitting at a table right beneath the stage and soon the two of them were in a boogie duet version of *House of Blue Lights*. As the house spotlight went blue, I looked around in the shadows and sure enough, sitting in the darkness by herself was the inimitable Marla Felix, her blonde hair done up in braids on the top of her head. She smoked a cigarette slowly, pensively, watching her ex-lover and Scarlett O'Hara make their own brand of love. Was she jealous? Did she need to find out what Eddie was up to—if not her? And did I pique her interest when I mentioned finding her photo tucked away in Scarlett's brass compact? That was all I needed to see, the fact that she was there and something had bothered her.

I left the club and crossed the street to my car. But before I could reach it, two punks came out from a storefront entry with their guns drawn. They said nothing but were on me like bees in a poppy field! I didn't have time to draw my .38 so they were upon me and slugging away with fists and gun butts until I went down. That's all I remember until I woke up in a nice penthouse with someone humming in a bathtub. It was a female voice. I felt my face, it was swollen and sore and my lips had bled onto the carpet below me. I felt a tooth was loose, third over on the upper left. My hat and gun were scattered about the spacious room. I crawled over to get my .38, but it was empty. Just then a lovely vision of a babe stood in the doorway to her bathroom, the backlighting revealing a fabulous figure through a thin yellow bathrobe.

"Oh, poopsy-woopsy—did those bad men beat you all up?" she simpered paraphrasing Betty Boop. "I knew if they were kind you would never come to see dear Mimsie-Pimsie here."

"Who—who are you—where the hell am I—and what am I doing here?" I flustered.

"Oh, he's upset at me!" She meandered over to a sofa and sat, her robe parting enough for me to get a good look at what was all the way up her legs. And from the floor it didn't look bad. "I, detective? I am *Mimi Marchand*...you are one Cable Denning—according to your driver's license—and...you have taken temporary residence in my apartments...but I cannot tell you why you are here—*yet.*" She spoke with a decided French accent that had a slightly Americanized coloring to it. My head began to spin, I felt nauseated and my body felt weak and helpless. "Oh...and about how you are feeling. I—I had you drugged a little bitty because I could not have a strange and perhaps aggressive male in my boudoir. I shall have you secured soon and then we can speak...freely."

Just then another good looking babe entered the room, her lithe body stopped in the middle of the floor and her curious face looked me over. She oozed sex appeal. "Yes? Is this the one, Mimi?" she asked my hostess.

"It is...so I am told. Rough around the edges—but who knows?" Then Mimi Marchand looked at me. "Oh, this is my sister, Mr. Denning, *Trisha Swinborne*. We are both single. I should say that immediately...so you will not get the wrong impression as to why I summoned you."

I looked at the reclining lady on the sofa. "So why *did* you summon me?" I asked, my head still not clear and my gut punching out a few bars of Yankee Doodle along with my heartbeat.

"You must rest first. Trish, would you scoot the chair over, please?"

The slightly younger Trisha Swinborne slid an armed chair in my direction. Then Mimi Marchand rose and the two of them helped me into the chair. One of them fetched a rope and soon I was tied up in the damn thing facing a wall with a large oval mirror on it. The older gal went into another room and emerged with a small snifter of something in her hand. "Now, drink this, if you will, please. We will not poison you. You are too valuable to us." She tipped the lip of the glass to my mouth and I sipped the sweet nectar-like green-yellow fluid down.

I must've slipped into a deep sleep because an hour or so later I awakened quite refreshed. The two women were fully dressed and stood by the oval mirror, looking me over. "So...what is it gonna be, ladies—truth or consequences—or do I get to go home and face some other horrible demons?"

They both snickered. "We are not demons," Mimi Marchand laughed. "We will not even keep you long. We simply need some...some information regarding who you think we are. And maybe a little teeny – weeny bit of something else."

I was puzzled. "Me—thinking who *you* are? Ha! Of course you're kidding! Besides being two females who happen to be sisters, both of you look as out of place as any two aliens can! Who do you think you're fooling? I'll bet I could scrape that nice skin right off your faces and see who *really* lives in there!"

They looked at each other, delighted. "Yes! That's what we were hoping for, Mr. Denning," Trisha Swinborne exclaimed. *"Who are we?!"*

"Ya know, it would be a lot more comfortable if I wasn't tied up in this chair. Obviously I'm no threat to you."

"While that may be true," Trisha Swinborne replied, "the security measures are for something other than keeping you from us."

"Oh?...dare I ask what?" I countered.

"You'll find out...soon..." Mimi Marchand answered.

"Let me ask this: who do *you* think you are?"

"Beetles! That's who we think we are!" Mimi Marchand flustered.

"Yes. Insects with—well, with intelligent brains." her sister added.

I turned my head from side to side because my neck hurt. "I'm not readin' ya here, girls. Beetles? What the hell are you talking about?"

Just then the lights flickered and I heard a fluttering metallic sound. "Those...those security measures I was talking about—it's father coming down the hallway!" Trisha Swinborne said anxiously.

I thought it sounded rather strange for a father of these two grown women to be with them—unless he was visiting, of course. But even if I was right, I was wrong—because what entered was not a human figure, but a huge six-legged luminescent creature about eight feet tall and maybe twelve feet long! It had a rather small head with big round eyes on either side, and humongous barbed feelers! It glowed shiny colors as the subdued light in the room hit the shell of the creature. Then the damned thing raised up a bit and colossal semi-transparent wings caused a wind that blew things about.

"Father!" both Mimi and Trisha shouted. The winged display stopped and the creature withdrew its wings. "Please! We want you to examine the human—not destroy him!" Mimi said in a distressed voice.

The monster insect tipped its head and then centered in on me. "So...let me see...," it remarked in a deep but somehow warming voice. "You are almost a human, but not quite." He took one of his long feelers and probed around my head gently. "Hmmm...a hybrid—I should have known..."

"Whoever you are, I am not comfortable and I'd wish you'd go blow and tell your so-called 'daughters' to let me go home!"

"You do not like my daughters? Why not? They are hybrids—just like you."

"Maybe, but not quite the same mix, Mr. Bugface! In case you haven't noticed, we're not the same shape!"

"Not me, stupid human man—*them!*" Then he swept his feelers slowly over the top of his body as if preening himself. "My daughters. They are the ones that must 'fit in' to your currently dominant species. So I had to make them look like your odd kind of creature. You are awfully vulnerable, you know, not to mention plain ugly. And that is why you must invent such destructive weapons to kill each other. In my species, when two males meet, it's simply a one-to-one battle with no weapons—until one of us is dead. Simple. What my daughters—wanted to know was...delicately put...would you breed with them—or would that repulse you?"

I looked at the comely young women. "Oh, no, I—I wouldn't say they would be objectionable at all—at first glance that is. But one never knows what's in the complete package—*inside.* Obviously you had to do a lot of work to shape-change and terra-form them to look like this. Just out of curiosity, what's 'mother' look like?"

"Ha!" the insect bandied. "A dish, a doll, a classic Madonna—a veritable Venus in the full-shell, if you know what I mean," he answered in a rather gay tone of voice.

222

"You mean you bred with a human female?" I asked, thinking of Joe Lorena, Honey Combes, Lily Norwood and all the Sens-Parafactors that had painfully made successes cross-breeding with humans.

"More or less," the parent insect answered. "One at a time my daughters are going to extract some semen from your erectile breeding gland. Their incubation receptors are at the side of their mouths. So they may have to *suck* somewhat to have you uh, 'give' some of your essential fluids to them. Let's hope it'll catch."

"Let—let me get this straight...you wanna have each daughter suck my male organ until they obtain enough sperm for them to conceive little human-insect babies? And, God forbid, if they are born into the world—what will they look like?"

"That's the wonderful thing—like you oddly, misshapen humans. Believe me, we are an improvement over this degraded species that now has dominion on your planet."

"And that's why you're tied in the chair!" Mimi Marchand spoke up. Her face was lighted and a big smile pulled across her face.

"Mimi will go first," Trisha Swinborne added. "I hope you'll have some left for me. Otherwise, I might have to suck a long time..."

At that moment I was wondering how Cable Denning could get himself in so many implausible messes! "You know, girls, I'm not a teenager anymore. Things take a little longer these days."

"So be it," the big bug said. "You need to *enjoy* it, guest! After all, it isn't every day you will have the opportunity to be a unique experiment in the evolution of the matrix lines of at least three different species!" Then the big bug turned and began to walk away. "Oh, by the way, my name is Oswald. And if this experiment is successful, you will be rewarded." Then he lumbered away.

The young women turned the lights down low, took off their clothes and had me stand up. They undid my belt and pulled my britches down along with my underwear. My schlonger was held at half-mast until the charming Miss Marchand gently took it into her mouth and began to stroke it in and out. She had some kind of very small "beads" or the like on her tongue and I don't mind telling you it felt very, very good! Within ten minutes I pumped enough sperm into her mouth to choke a horse! She didn't swallow it, though. Instead, she took that beaded tongue of hers and worked the spermatozoa into those side pockets in her cheeks. She actually thanked me and left.

That left me alone with the dark-haired and lovely Trisha Swinborne. "I hope my sister didn't take it all..."

"You already said that."

"Said what?"

"That you were afraid I wouldn't have any left."

"I said that?"

"Yes. Can you give me a half-hour break?"

She smiled at me, her lovely dark eyes sparkling in the subdued light. "As a matter of fact, what Mimi doesn't know won't hurt her." She went over to what looked like her purse on the table and took out two yellow pills. She fed them into my mouth. "Here. This is guaranteed to make your sperm production rise considerably—and fast. Perhaps you should lie down on the sofa over there. Can I trust you?"

"No...if I have a chance to run for it, sister, that's exactly what I'm gonna do." I felt a little woozy.

"I don't think so, Mr. Denning. You see, those tablets will make you weak in your brain but powerful in your genitals."

"Oh? That sounds just like most of the human race to me anyhow," I quipped. She helped me to the sofa and gave me a pillow. Soon I was reclining with my eyes closed. "So what's the life of a bug-woman like?"

"Not as exciting as you might think. Father hardly ever lets us visit mother. You see, she doesn't know she was used as a breeder. She works downtown at *Bullock's Department Store*. So when we visit, all we can say is hello and we're in the market for some hats or dresses. You see, she works in the women's apparel department."

"Yeah...okay, I get it. So what part of your life is exciting or fun?"

"Not much. We're kind of pioneers for our species. Father says we need to beat the reptilians at their own game. He says sooner or later the present humans will destroy themselves and we're more or less atomic radiation proof. So we can survive when most will die. I don't see what's so hot about hanging around when most people are dead. Think of the smell!"

"Yeah...I see what you mean..." I mumbled. Out of my control, my penis began to rise again after about twenty minutes. Trish noted it and began to manipulate my organ.

"Do you think I can suck it now?" she inquired innocently.

I was feeling no pain. "Oh, yeah...now would be great...you—you might want to lick it first...help stimulate it, you know."

"Oh...okay..." She began to lick and then soon she was sucking and soon after that I was exploding into her mouth with several teaspoons of jizz. She did the same as her sister and tucked it away in her two cheek-pockets. But when she stood up, I noticed a wetness running down her thighs. I asked her about it. She had no clue as to what that might be. I told her I thought it might be her human female organs responding to the sexual stimulus. She parted her outer lips and her vagina was very pink and swollen. "Oh! what do you think that is?"

"Stimulation, lady...you're also part human female. That's how *they* get inseminated."

"I see. But my Father told me I was sterile as a human female."

"That may very well be the case, Trisha Swinborne. But your female organs don't know that."

She looked at me sheepishly. "Oh...well, I guess our business is concluded, Mr. Denning." She untied my hands and foot halter. "May I show you how to get out?"

"Yeah, that'd be swell." She led me down a corridor into an elevator that descended and then into another elevator going up. Soon I was at street level.

She took my hand. "I don't know what being in love is all about, Mr. Denning. But if I ever did experience that—I'd like to experience it with you. You seem strong, gentle—and very virile. Daddy always said pick a real earth man—no mamby-pamby for me!"

"Look, lady, I'm crazy as a bed bug—uh...no offense! I'd be careful about who you mate with. By the way, how many young ones might you give birth to if things go right?"

"Oh, maybe about four or five thousand. The babies are very small when they are born."

"What do they look like?"

"Father—who else?"

"So, then, how do they get changed into human form?" I smiled as I asked.

"Oh, a process after about six or eight weeks, I think."

"Well, I'm off, young woman. Don't ever think it wasn't fun because it was—and despite the fact that you're half bug, I really had a class-A time!"

"Me, too, Cable Denning—goodbye now!" she lilted. We both walked away in opposite directions. Hell, on the street, who could tell if those babes were human or not?

On the way home I was thinking of the horrors lurking in the corners most people never see or experience. But a tide was rising out of a potboiler of a science fiction ocean, populated with creatures only dreamed about in the imaginations of great story-tellers. These are the things that haunt our dreams. Now I knew—some of them come true!

# Chapter 8

## MURDER'S A CHANCE

It was Tuesday, December 2, 1947. It was raining. I took Ida out for lunch that day. She seemed subdued. "Cat got your tongue or what?" I asked her.

"No, not exactly. It's—it's just that you haven't really seen me lately, Cable—or even talked to me except business stuff. I mean, you pay me on time and all but—"

"—you're gonna get married, Ida! What do you want me to say? I hope you found someone really good for you? Well, I do—and I wish you every happiness in the world."

Tears welled in her eyes. "Well, I'm not!"

"You're not what?"

"Getting married—I just couldn't—he's too young and immature. Besides, I'm three years older than he is. And he doesn't know how to please me in the—the more intimate ways—the way you did..."

I took a deep breath. It was like someone had come from behind me and knocked all the wind out of my sails. "Oh...I'm sorry..."

"Well, I'm not."

"You see, Ida—I thought this might happen. Did I spoil you for any other man? How many times have I told you—for six or seven years—go find yourself a young man—now, damn—you're no longer twenty and your child-bearing years are slipping away."

She lowered her eyes. "It wasn't just that. I didn't want him. And I wasn't in love with him." Then those periwinkle blues looked directly into my eyes. "I still want you, Cable. Is that so wrong? To desire someone who makes me feel like a real woman?"

"It is when it won't work in the long run, Ida. What'll happen when one of these days I'm dead and you're be out there in the world, lost, abandoned— oh, no, I don't want that responsibility pinned on me, babe."

Ida looked down at her empty plate. "I can't help it, Cable. But I can't force you. You either want me or you don't."

"Yeah, I guess that's about it, kid."

She looked at me directly. "Please don't call me kid. You know what a complete woman I can be— especially with you."

"Yes, that's true. You never heard me complain did you? But adult affection and sex is the tip of the iceberg, lady. There are a thousand other things to consider—my profession being one of them."

"I think part of that is a cop-out, Cable. It's a way for you to escape responsibility, something got stuck in you long ago and you're afraid. I don't know, maybe your love affairs, maybe women, maybe your mother—your father's wanderlust—who knows?"

"Maybe so, Ida, but it's too late to mend that fence. I am who I am and I'm almost fifteen years your senior. You still have time."

"Maybe, Cable, but will I still have your love?"

"Don't push the envelope, babe. Most of the time life comes in doses, not big gulps too hard to swallow. Let it rest, Ida..."

She didn't pursue the subject. We discussed some business items and then we walked back to the office.

## The Bones of Richard III

It was about 10:30 a.m. the next day, when the phone rang. "Yeah, Cable Denning here!" I said in my usual grumpy, morning voice.

"Oh, Mr. Denning, I'm happy to find you about! This is Sonata, Allegra's twin sister?"

"Oh, yeah, Sonata, how're ya doin'? By the way, I want to thank you for something."

There was a pause at the other end of the line. "Thank me? Whatever on earth for, sir?"

"Well, it so happens the rather presumptuous woman who took your residence over—you know, the one you got kicked out of?—it so happens she was a woman I was looking for—I mean professionally."

"I see—well, I'm happy you found your woman, Mr. Denning. If you really wanted to thank me for that inadvertent favor, I would not be opposed to your taking me to lunch—"

"—how about a nightclub for dinner and dancing?"

"Oh, sir, I would not impose on you for the world—I know you must be a busy man and I might blush bein' in your presence an' all—"

"—lunch it is then!" I flustered.

"But then again, on the other hand, Allegra informed me secretly how divinely you dance, Mr. Denning..."

"Oh? What else did she tell you?" I grinned.

"Well, now, some sisters do not have to express it verbally in order to decipher what one of the other sisters might have or might not have done. Let it suffice to say she enjoyed you very much, Mr. Denning."

"So what's it gonna be, Sonata?" I asked impatiently.

"I would be privileged to dance and dine with you, sir."

"Okay, that's swell. How about Friday night at *Roscoe's Hideaway*?"

"Oh, that would be delightful, Mr. Denning," she purred in that Southern accent of hers.

"Where do you live? I'll come pick you up about eight-thirty?"

"I do not see why that would not be appropriate, sir, thank you."

"Can we cut all the polite Southern crap, please? You call me Cable and I'll call you Sonata, okay?"

"Are you certain that is not too familiar? I was schooled in a prestigious Alabama girls' school, you know."

"No, I didn't know—but I'm uncomfortable with formality."

"I suppose I can break precedence in your company, Cable."

I liked the way she said my name. It was warm, sensuous.

"Okay, Sonata, thanks—where do I pick you up now?"

"Oh, mercy, I almost forgot! 513 North Rexford Drive, a little cottage with a wonderful rose trellis by the front window and interestingly, not far from Carmelita."

"Okay, Sonata, see you then."

"I am looking forward to bein' in the company of such a handsome and experienced gentleman, Cable, goodbye for now," she said and hung up.

It was obvious that Scarlett O'Hara was gaining notoriety as *Roscoe's Hideaway* was packed and the songstress up on that small stage held court with a peppy version of *It's Been a Long, Long Time,* written by the Tin Pan Alley writers Sammy Cahn and Jules Styne. I'd called for a table in the back of the room and I guess I hadn't noticed before, but Sonata looked like a million. Her hair and eyes shone in the candlelight as the waiter pushed her chair in and she faced me. She was wearing a purple, velvety dress, modestly cut. A lovely brooch in the form of a five-petal rose with white and a yellow core was pinned to the gown.

"You're a knockout tonight," I said, checking her out and smiling. "That's a very unusual brooch you're wearing."

"I am? Thank you, kind sir." She glanced at the brooch. "It's my family House's insignia. I'm a Tudor and all the women in my ancestry had to—well, had to look good for their men. I guess a rose was a feminine symbol—all Tudor girls were supposed to be feminine, you know..."

"Tudor?"

"Yes, our distant relative Henry Tudor married Elizabeth of York and began the family line. We're actually Welsh, you know."

"How long ago was that?"

"Oh, probably around the 1430's or so. Don't quote me—an historian I am not, Cable," she laughed. I liked her laugh.

"I—I never saw this charming side of you before, Sonata," I admitted. "Frankly, I thought you might be a bimbo of some sort—you know, a pretty skip-brained babe?"

"Skip-brained? Hardly, and actually I'm not even Southern." Suddenly her accent disappeared and she spoke in a slight British accent. "Would you like me better this way?" she asked.

"Ha! So that was a front?"

"Or a back," she teased. "I must tell you, Cable. Allegra has no twin. It's me, just made up different-ly—and my real name here in the states is Sonata." The wine was served and she toasted me. "Remember how we made love?"

I was astonished. "Uh...yeah...suppose you show me..."

She reached her finger across the table and asked me to touch it. I didn't dare in such a public joint! "This? Now do you believe me? I'm back for a job, Cable. Its code name is 'Richard's Bones'. Your government has a virulent spy in its midst. In 1946 your president signed a release form from military to civilian operation of the atomic energy commission. Seven men witnessed that signing by Harry Truman. One of them is a traitor to both America and England."

As an ex-cop I could see the pieces come together in this lovely woman's mind. She was about her business and I knew it. "Why '*Richard's Bones*'?"

"I imagine it's symbolic. In 1485 King Richard III was struck down in battle but the search for his bones continues to this day. But the tie-in is this: our spy had two young brothers killed because they knew too much about his presence in America. They were Brits and that reminded the internal forces here that Richard the Third possibly had two young men killed in the Tower of London because they might have threatened his ascendency to the throne. Hence the code name."

"I see." It was like walking through a dream of slow-motion firecrackers, as each went off I felt a blinding red flash, something warning me that I was too close to Death and could feel his breath down my collar. But Scarlett O'Hara continued singing and the audience continued drinking, smoking and carrying on as they'd always done. The singer was mesmerizing folks with her intimate portrayal of Duke Ellington's *Don't Explain.* It was romantic. Of that there was no doubt. I felt a toe touch my shoe under the table. I could also feel Sonata reaching for me because her own loneliness haunted her and she wanted to know there was a least one person in the world who maybe understood her a little, another bird of the same feather who'd say it's alright to continue to keep existing, alright to go on in this upside down parade of earth existence. And it was also okay to continue on in her world, the one that was labeled *'kill or be killed'* on the door. I was used to that. To meet someone else who dwelled in the dark corridors as I did was a treat. I chuckled. "Ha! Well, so much for this 'Southern belle' and her education in an Alabama school for girls. I've gotta say, Sonata, ya got a lot of nerve pullin' the wool over a compatriot's eyes!"

She smiled and I melted. "Compatriot? Hmmm. Well, I thought we might be more than that, Cable. I still tingle when I think of that night in Jirny. Didn't you say you wanted me to teach you more about making love the *Sens Parafactor's* way?"

"Yep, I did. You willing to teach me?"

"Are you willing to learn?"

"You bet." Just then I glanced over at the bar and saw Eddie Grant come in. He looked discouraged. But his eyes were glued to the stage and the exquisitely beautiful Scarlett O'Hara. I had this feeling Eddie had it bad for that elusive singer as she finished her song and bowed. Then she left the stage. Eddie followed her. I wondered how it would end up this time.

"Wanna dance?" I asked Sonata.

"With you? Anytime, Mr. Denning...please..."

I got up and took her hand. We went out onto the dance floor as the combo launched into a foxtrot version of 1947's *Beg Your Pardon*. I put my mouth next to her ear and sang to this lovely creature encompassed in my arms. *"If I lose my head, Beg Your*

*Pardon...for things that I've said, Beg Your Pardon, why should I worry the way that I do? When you're in no hurry to let me love you...I'll try for a kiss, in the garden, and if I should miss, Beg Your Pardon, but if some sunny day you'll let me have my way...then I won't have to say, Beg Your Pardon..."*

She clutched me tighter and reached her lips slowly up to mine. There in the semi-light of *Roscoe's* we kissed, warm, our mouths moving into each other's like they knew the way. "Will you stay with me tonight, Cable?" she whispered to me.

"What's in it for me?" I whispered back with a gentle bite to her cheek. "Plus I get more expensive after midnight."

She didn't answer but simply held me tighter and ground her hips into my front parts that gave me a rush. Oh, yeah, I'd go home with Sonata Blossom alright!

We ate and drank and danced. Scarlett O'Hara had gotten back up on the stage to sing 1939's *All or Nothing At All* with a sexy Latin beat in the background. I also saw Eddie Grant come storming out and make a beeline for the coatroom. He put on his hat and coat and left in a flurry. This was the second time I'd witnessed Eddie being rubbed the wrong way by Scarlett O'Hara. Maybe she just didn't dig him.

We arrived about 1:00 a.m. at 513 North Rexford Drive. It was a cool night and in Sonata's neighborhood, the world was quiet. She slipped the key into the front door. Then silently she turned to kiss me, as if to remind herself she had the right man by her side. She took my hand and led me directly to her bedroom. There she undid her pretty velvet dress, took off her shoes, turned her back to me so I'd undo her brassiere. Then she slipped her panties down and got into the bed. She lit a candle by the bedside and opened her arms to me. I took my trench coat and fedora off and sat down on the edge of the bed.

"What's the matter, Cable? Don't you want me?"

"Of course I do. I guess I just can't believe my good luck. Plus I've smoked and drunk too much tonight."

"You must stop destroying your body—until you finish what you agreed to do here on this plane of existence."

I glanced at her and combed my hair back with my hands. "I don't know, Sonata, seems like I've already lived a thousand lifetimes. Maybe I already did what I was supposed to do, now I'm coasting."

"Maybe...but I don't think so." She patted the bed. "Come...lay beside me before you go bonkers thinking about all the things you aren't or didn't do in this lifetime."

I unbuttoned my shirt and slid my trousers off. I took off my tee shirt and boxers and slid in next to her. She took her right hand and placed it on my forehead. It felt wonderful. Maybe she was a healer as well as a trained assassin. In that instant I went away with Sonata/Allegra Blossom—away to some dimension of tranquility and pink sunlight, crystal clear waters flowing down huge rocks from the mountains above. The grasses were green and blue, the sky orange and yellow, the horizon indigo and we stood before a large lake whose waters were changing between shimmering onyx and crystal blue sapphire. We were both spirits embracing within and without each other, frolicking like happy children in an endless landscape of beauty and peace. We saw no one else, but yet we knew we were surrounded by countless souls, light-hearted and smiling with us.

What must've been hours later, I awoke with a start. You know how it is about strange beds and waking up in an unfamiliar room. "Did you enjoy it?" Sonata asked me, her mouth smiling and her hair strewn across her face.

"Yeah...yeah...it was wonderful—where'd we go?"

"Inside, Cable, everywhere, nowhere, somewhere..."

"Oh...well, you don't have to tell me—I loved it. It was so familiar, even more familiar than this earth—except maybe for Bronson Park."

She snickered. "Ha! And now I suppose you want to make love?"

I reached out with my forefinger. Her own touched mine and off we were again as every fiber in my being began to take life and vibrate with desire and a marvelous buildup to an orgasm that I knew would blow the roof off the place! Sonata closed her eyes and I did so as well. We traveled through reds and greens and blues and oranges and maroons I'd never seen before. It's funny when something is so far above the conventional experience you aren't as aware of your physical organs as you are about the ecstatic joy you're feeling with the other person. Then it came, like a tidal wave of emotion and passion, all wrapped into the deepest humility and tenderness, a reverence for one another that finally burst into something more than an orgasm, more than an earthly five-senses experience. Maybe it was true universal love—that thing to which we are all connected, like it or not. But what's not to like? I loved it!

Once our cries and yells of orgasm settled down and we lay breathless side-by-side on Sonata's bed, I reached for her and she came crashing into my arms. "Oh, Cable!" That said it all. Just those two words. In them, I read she felt at one with me, at peace and happiness, but that perhaps we would never meet again in this life.

I left before dawn because I didn't want to see her beauty in the brash light of day. She escorted me to the door. "I suppose I could tell you...I don't know why you're going—I enjoy you so—but I understand. I've done the same for many years with men I didn't even love. But I do love *you*. You know we may never meet again...tomorrow I must go underground to smoke out the traitor in Truman's cabinet. It's dangerous because there's a lot of money hanging on AEC contracts."

"Yeah, I've known similar circumstances. Oppenheimer proved to be a rat along with Fermi and those guys who did the first atomic tests in the desert." I kissed her gently. "I guess I could say I love you too, kid, but frankly, I'm not even sure I know what love is anymore...if I ever did."

She kissed my nose. "Oh, yes you do—you've just lost your way, Cable. You'll get back on the beam one of these days. Good bye, my fellow traveler..." She quickly closed the door behind me. I didn't know if that meant she was crying or what. But that's the way it was for me. Years of good-byes in between hellos and nothingness. That feeling of Death lingering at the dinner table that night...I felt they'd kill her before she did her job. Then someone else would come in using a different method. That's how they did it.

In time maybe I would forget Sonata McCambridge. She'd get killed in some dark corner of the world on a case she probably didn't even like. But for me, she bloomed like a flower, and rose from the rich soil of her heart and spirit—then left silently and vanished from the face of the earth as having never been at all.

## Circumstantial Adhominem

It was late Saturday night, December 6th. I decided I needed to get to the bottom of this Evelyn Gossman case. Yeah, sure, I was already paid and the case was officially over. Or was it? As far as I was concerned, something was rotten in Denmark and the presumption that Evelyn's husbands were murdered and did not die of natural causes, still stuck in my craw. I had to find out one way or another.

I'd called Maggie before I left but she didn't answer. I thought she might be home later and I'd go visit her just before dawn. But no soap.

So I decided I'd start with a lead that was at least a possibility. I walked into *Roscoe's* that night and hid in the shadows. But Fate had a strange way of showing itself. Again, as the night before, Eddie Grant came in late and sat at the bar. I didn't think he'd seen me the night before with Sonata, so I decided to play my cards closer to the vest. I came out of hiding and approached the handsome singer.

"Hiya, Eddie. You still pursuing the same game?" I jested.

"Damn, Cable...*women*...how can ya figure 'em? Can I buy you a drink?" he asked.

"Yeah, sure, thanks...honeyed Canadian whiskey—hot water and a snifter."

"You like 'em sweet and fancy, eh?"

"Yeah...like my women. And speaking of women...should I assume we are still talking about the elusive Miss O'Hara up there on the stage?" The lady in question was singing a convertible version of *The Glory of Love* and the way she did it, the song was dripping with sex appeal.

"Yeah, I don't know *what* it is. I start smooching on her and ask her over to my place or let's go to hers—and she clams up. And that excites my Irish temper, so we argue. I end up here sulking. What would you do, Mr. Detective? You've had a lot of experience with the babes."

"I don't know. Some women are damaged and we don't know it up front. Others are just aloof. Should you persist? I'm not sure, some women aren't worth it, no matter how good looking or talented—maybe like Miss Priss up there on the stage."

"God, but I want her, Cable—I mean she drives me nuts just thinking of her! I've let my career slip a little trying to accommodate her. Everything seems like it's going just fine. But when I try to get any closer, she fluffs me off like I suddenly turn to poison or something."

"That's a red light in my book, Eddie. You let her get under your skin to that extent and it ain't gonna be healthy. Pull yourself together and find another fish in the sea. You do know the sea out there, is full of fish, don't you?"

"Yeah, but only one Scarlett O'Hara. I'll try once more tonight. I'm gonna corner her at the break in her dressing room. If she refuses me this time—shit, I'll—I'll just go my way with my tail between my legs."

"I think that's best—I get this feeling a lot of men have broken themselves over that babe singing up there. Why be one of them?"

When Scarlett O'Hara took her break, Eddie Grant joined her as she came down off the stage. I think he was cramping her style. Artists like her want to be alone after 45 minutes of singing. Eddie should have known that. He was a singer himself. And I was right. About ten minutes passed and out comes Eddie fuming. He went to the hatcheck, got his stuff and walked out.

I decided not to say anything but remained in the shadows because I had an idea I wanted to try. I was gonna find out where little Miss Scarlett went after hours. One night I'd followed her to a dump downtown near Temple that was supposed to be closed. But it wasn't. I found out it was called *'Nymphs'* and now was half boarded up. The entrance was down a few steps to a door that smelled of booze and urine, with trash strewn around. That's where I left her that night. Now I was gonna clear the mud stay with it.

I started toward the front door when a familiar voice called to me. "Oh, Mr. Denning. Good to see you," it said. It was Mrs. Thelma Rhodes, the film editor who had hired me to find a lost movie. The adventure ended up with me finding it okay, but I went through a villain, zombies and a fine young Japanese babe to get it.

"Oh, hello, Mrs. Rhodes."

"Will you join me for a drink? Someone at Mindy's told me you might be here watching that pretty little thing up there—singing on stage. You still are attracted, aren't you?"

"Not really. She's intriguing, Mrs. Rhodes—that's about all."

"Why so formal—you *could* call me Thelma, you know."

"I don't know...it might ruin my amateur standing," I kidded her. "After what I went through procuring that lost movie for you, I'm not sure I'd wanna do that gig again. Was it too edited to use as a full-length film? And as for Mr. Lippert?"

"No, it's being released just the way whoever edited it left it. They took the best parts away, you know. Mr. Lippert couldn't figure it. Who can? There are a lot of insane people out there."

"And just what was excised from the movie?"

"Oh, about thirty minutes---aliens hitch-hiking and coming to earth to intermingle with humans—the usual—looking like them but not really them?"

"Oh, yeah...I know that old worn out routine. But I'm glad all ended up okay. You'll have to excuse me, I'm on my way home—big day tomorrow," I lied.

"One question," Thelma Rhodes asked. "What *did* you have to go through to get it?"

"You don't wanna know, lady." I tipped my hat to her and left.

About 2:15 a.m. I was parked across the street from *Roscoe's*. Sure enough, the same little Dodge picked up Scarlett O'Hara and again I followed them to the place on North Grand near Temple. The joint once called *'Nymphs'* still looked closed down. But again, Scarlett O'Hara walked down to the piss-laden door and disappeared. I got out of my car and checked out the little alleyway that separated it from the adjacent building. All I could see were walls. What the hell was a gal like that doing in there, anyway? Who could she be seeing in such a lowly place far from the crowds of 1947 humanity? Discouraged, I went back into my coupe and lit up a cigarette. But luck was with me this night. Soon Scarlett stood out on the curb and got picked up again by the same car. Now I was getting somewhere. I followed the car along Grand until it turned left onto Alpine and right onto Bunker Hill. Scarlett got out just up from the corner. I parked and gave her a lead before I began to follow her. She went into a meat company's back door. She slammed the damn door shut and locked it. I looked for lights. Yep, soon up on the second story of the three-story building, a light went on. How in the hell was I gonna get up there? And even if I could, the risk of getting caught was too high.

Somewhere I must've slipped up because suddenly I felt a gun in my ribs. "Don't turn around and let me do the talking, buster," a stern female voice spoke. "Hands up. You don't ask questions—you just give answers, got it?"

I held my hands up high. "Yeah, got it..." I answered.

"What are you doing following my lady?"

"Your lady?" Then I got it. *Nymphs* was a secret hangout for faggot females. No wonder Scarlett O'Hara didn't dig men! She was a lesbian!

"I ask the questions, remember?"

"Okay, okay...I've been watching her at Roscoe's and I fell in love with her. But she keeps rejecting me," I lied. "Now I know why."

"Stupid man. I'm probably going to have to kill you, you realize. No one is supposed to know where Scarlett lives—especially any man."

Before she could say another word I swung around full-fisted and punched the gal flat to the ground. Her gun went flying. She was out cold. Yep, chivalry died right here. I picked up her .32 and dragged the gal's body into the dark shadows at the side of the building. Then I checked her for keys. If she had a key to Scarlett O'Hara's heart, she might have a key to her living quarters. I was in luck. I grabbed the keys and sure enough, one fit the big metal door Scarlett had entered through earlier. I carefully opened the door and closed it quietly behind me. There was a stairway to my immediate right. I stealthily climbed the stairs. The door to her apartment was open. It was a large room, quite cozy, actually. I could hear the shower running in a bathroom over to my left. I entered cautiously and seeing no one, began poking around. She wasn't all that tidy and clothing and underclothes were strewn here and there. There was a big poster on the wall from a Robert Mitchum-Jane Greer movie called *Out of the Past*. The babe on the left of the picture reminded me of Scarlett—pretty, just a little trashy. It was a new movie I hadn't seen. Being a detective, of course I began to question why this particular poster was in such a prominent place? I continued poking around. I heard a strange noise coming from behind a closet door. I got out my .38 and approached the closet. Slowly I opened it. I could hardly believe my eyes when I saw a young woman gagged and bound in only her slip. Her eyes brightened when they saw me. It was Maggie Loggins! Just then I heard the water turn off and I calmed Maggie by whispering to her everything would be alright as soon as I took care of Miss O'Hara. I closed the closet door.

Scarlett was in a robe with the front wide open. Quite revealing. She had a great body and fine tits with pink nipples. She got some water in a mug and went over to Maggie's closet and opened it. "Hey, bitch—thirsty?" Maggie's hands were bound, so she had to balance the cup between her two palms in order to drink. I was hidden behind a curtain at the entrance to Scarlett's bedroom. "I'll bet you miss your boyfriend just about now, huh? I've seen him come in to the club and drool over me—I'll bet you didn't know that, huh, little whore? You do fuck him, don't you? Why else would you risk your life to find where I live? And what do you know? Nothing!" She sniffed the air. "Did you piss your panties? I'll bet you did! A sissy-bitch, huh? Hell, I never pissed my panties when I was in the nut house—ha! I just pissed on the floor and let someone else clean it up!" She took Maggie's cup away. "I hate to tell you this, but I asked a friend of mine to come here tonight to get rid of you—permanently! I'd do it if I could, but I'm not the killer type. But *she* is." I was thinking about the babe I'd left out cold on the side of the building. Sooner or later she'd be coming to. I had to make a decision. While Scarlett went to the sink with the cup, I slipped out, went down the stairs and out to the side of the building. The homely dark-haired babe I'd knocked out was indeed coming to.

"Sorry!" I said as I conked her again and out she went. I had to consider my next move carefully. I took out a cigarette and lit it. I puffed away in the dark, thinking. How would I rescue Maggie? How could I do that and still find out what Scarlett O'Hara was really all about? I decided to rescue Maggie and take my chances with Scarlett. But things often work out contrary to one's plans. Scarlett appeared at the door, and darted off for the same car the other lesbian must've come in. She sped off and I jumped up the stairs, dragged Maggie out of the closet and unbound her. As soon as I had removed her gag she shouted, "Evelyn Gossman's! She's going to Evelyn Gossman's! Cable!" I held the sobbing Maggie Loggins in my arms.

"Why *Evelyn's*, Maggie?"

"Because dollars to donuts, Scarlett O'Hara is Evelyn Nesbitt's daughter! That's why the picture in the compact, the traits that are similar—the singing, the concealment of where one lives—so many of those traits—don't you see?"

"Yeah, maybe, but why would Scarlett go to her mother's when she doesn't know anything about her?"

"She *does* know—or at least suspects." Maggie complained that she'd peed in her pants. I told her to get a pair of Scarlett's and put some of her clothes on to look decent. "That's when Evelyn checked out Scarlett at her place of work, remember? She began to put two and two together."

"But what does Scarlett do over at Evelyn's?"

"That's easy—unbeknownst to Evelyn, *she's* the one who's been poisoning the husbands and tonight I'll bet you she's beginning to poison Mr. Factor's liquor supply! If we can catch her in the act..."

I grabbed Maggie by the hand and we flew down the stairs and I drove like a maniac to Evelyn Gossman's place in Beverly Hills. I took a flashlight from my glove compartment. Sure enough, we spotted Scarlett's car three streets away. I got under the hood and fixed the ignition wires so she couldn't start it up just in case we arrived late. We ran to the rear of the house and the back door was open. We sneaked in quietly. Barely visible in the darkness I spotted Scarlett at the bar fiddling with a vile of something. I clicked my flashlight on. She turned around to face the bright beam, surprised, frightened.

"Fancy meeting *you* here," I declared. "This is where it ends Miss O'Hara—or whoever you are." I drew my gun. "Drop what you're doing and put your hands up, now!" Maggie held onto my overcoat.

Scarlett was defiant. "And why *should* I?"

"Hands, up!" I demanded. Hesitantly she did so. "*Circumstantial Adhominem*," I declared. "The jig is up, Scarlett! Don't even attempt to escape. I've already called the cops, lady," I lied.

"You! How did you find me—and what the hell is '*Circumstantial Adhominem*'?" she asked in a harsh voice. "Besides, you can't prove a thing, mister!"

"Maybe, maybe not, if ya wanna know, Missy," I replied. "You see, simply put, it's all a fallacy—you, your pretenses, your diabolical plan to kill your Mother's husbands and then implicate her—but why? That's the part I don't get. You got something against her?"

"I hate her! Ever hear of getting back at someone? Well, that's what it is, buddy! And that little bitch you screw ratted on me, didn't she!?" she shouted at Maggie. "But how'd she know—?"

"—because every criminal messes up, lady..." I interjected.

Just then Evelyn Gossman, now known as Marla Felix Factor, entered the room dressed in a light

250

pink robe. Her new husband followed. The two women looked at each other. "You! Catherine! What are you doing *here*?—you've become so beautiful, Catherine," Evelyn said with a tear in her voice.

"No thanks to that nut house, mother dear!" Scarlett snapped.

"I think I can explain," Evelyn resumed, looking at Maggie and me. "I bore my daughter out of wedlock when I was much too young for motherhood. I wanted to raise her but Catherine's soul was malformed—she was evil from the beginning and was deemed insane when she was four years old. I had her committed, but I never told Theodore about her when we were married. I tried to make a success of the marriage, but it was no good. So I met Eddie Grant and we ran away together—"

"—until you discovered that being pretty and all, you could make money by marrying rich men much older than you until they kicked off. Sure, literature is filled with such plots because chances are those old guys are gonna die a lot sooner than you," Maggie said.

Scarlett began to run toward her mother, flailing her fists at her. The husband restrained her. "*But I found you*, mother, didn't I? And you never knew it— you never knew I was killing off your husbands and making you rich until I could frame you for murder! Mr. Theodore Gossman—who screwed me because he couldn't screw you—provided me with the poisonous chemicals from his counterfeit currency printing presses downstairs. We both wanted to bring a deadly end to your many sins!"

"Ah, so you killed Gossman because you had to make sure you had a foolproof plan and your mother would hang for killing all those nice old men that had made her rich," I put forth. "A perfect revenge murder plot, if I ever heard one, but you forgot something, Catherine Nesbitt."

"Yeah, and what's that?" Scarlett snarled.

"Gossman hated your mother as much as you did, albeit, for different reasons. He would've been your silent partner until your Mom got the death penalty. But you wanted no witnesses to your evil deeds-- and once you pushed ol' Theodore off the Golden Gate Bridge, I asked why would someone do that? Then I began to suspect other people. Credit Maggie with figuring out the details. At the time I didn't make the connection between you and your mother. A few clues here and there, but nothing binding. But...finding your mother's picture in your makeup compact began to clench it for me. You also had the same traits as your mother. I've heard a lotta singers in my time, lady, and you sing and act just like her. It was something you didn't want the world to find out, so you were secretive about how and where you lived. You sang because it was a love-hate relation-ship with her and without really knowing it, you wanted to *be* like her in spite of everything she—"

"—that's not true—I hated her! I just wanted her dead!" Scarlett cried and broke down onto the floor in tears. She clawed her hand into the air, bawling and reaching for her mother. But Evelyn didn't budge.

I picked up the phone and called the downtown Division and asked for Police Inspector Lt. Lester Keith. He was home asleep, they told me. I told them to get him out of bed and send him to Evelyn Gossman alias Marla Felix's house. A lotta confessions were going on. "Will I be held liable in any way, detective?" Evelyn asked.

"I don't know. Maybe. You're not complicit regarding the murders. I don't think there's a law about marrying for money. I don't know about money laundering. But if you are innocent, you owe it to Maggie Loggins here, a lowly librarian who maintained your innocence and got me on the right track eventually."

"Well, thank you, Miss Loggins. How did you know?"

"You're welcome. How did I know? Intuition, I guess. Plus it was all too open and shut. There had to be more."

"How did you determine that, if I may ask?" Evelyn inquired.

"I read a lot," Maggie replied.

Police car sirens wailed through the night. Scarlett O'Hara was still sprawled on the floor, sobbing. Then she got a glare in her eyes and went for the liquor cabinet, she grabbed a bottle and broke it on the bar counter. "Okay, I'm gettin' out of here and nobody's gonna stop me, hear?! You're all full of bullshit—everyone's full of bullshit! The only honest thing that's left in this world is *music*—and I'm gonna sing until I die—got it?!" With that she darted from the room and disappeared into the night.

"Why don't you catch her?!" Evelyn shrieked. "She'll kill me if she gets another chance!"

"Not to worry, Mrs. Factor," Maggie spoke up. "She's trapped and desperate—the police are coming...plus Cable fixed her car so it won't start, so she won't be going anywhere."

The sirens approached the house and the police cars screeched to a halt. Then we heard gunshots and when they stopped, I knew it was all over. We all ran out into the street. There fallen on the sidewalk with a police officer standing over her bleeding body, lay Scarlett O'Hara—real name, Catherine Nesbitt—real occupation, inmate in a nut house on a distant planet somewhere far removed from this one. Or was it?

### Epilogue

**It was Sunday morning, almost noon.** Last night's events weren't exactly new to me. I'd gazed on the faces of many corpses in my time. This was just one more. Except to say when someone young and attractive and should have their whole life ahead of them... lies there under a sheet in the County Morgue it makes one wonder—what's the whole damn thing all about? What for? Why do all these people die and in time are forgotten? I felt sad for Catherine Nesbitt, who until yesterday was known as an up and coming nightclub singer, Scarlett O'Hara, who at the same time, happened to be a revengeful killer. I felt for her the same way I felt for Sonata McCambridge, a lovely kinswoman whose ancestors raced across the stars to find planet earth in order to elevate its consciousness. So far it hadn't helped. Maybe someday it would. But Scarlett was dead and Sonata would die, too. What the hell was I saying? We all follow, just in a different pecking order.

I had driven down to the County Morgue with Lt. Lester Keith and he was mumbling about how so often suspected killers are never caught until the crimes have been committed and there ought to be a way to catch a criminal before all the shit comes about. But then again I reminded him he'd be out of a job if that was the case. "Some cases have so many layers, Lester," I was saying as he drove me back to pick up my car. "But sometimes we have help from another dimension or other unseen forces. You know how it goes."

"No, Denning, suppose you tell me how it goes," he snarled. I guess he was still in a bad mood from me waking him the night before when we'd solved the murders—which had yet to be verified by the coroner's office.

"I get a call from Gossman. On the surface it's just another routine case, finding the missing wife so he can divorce her, right? Then we find out about the dead husbands and their untimely demise. Then I discover Evelyn Gossman's strange traits, right? I *'incidentally'* check out a nightclub singer named Scarlett O'Hara who ends up being not only Evelyn Gossman's real-life daughter but the husband killer! How many hoops did I have to jump through to arrive at that?"

"You didn't—you told me that little librarian of yours figured it out first. Maybe you're not as smart as you think you are."

"Maybe not. But we found the killer—and it's more than you did."

"Except I have 30 such cases on my desk—you had *one*."

"Yeah, and how many of those do you solve in one year, Lester?"

"In time, Denning, everything in time. Now get outta here—scram back into your seedy little underworld of private detectives and broads, alcohol and cigarettes. I don't expect you'll live all that much longer, you know. You're starting to look old for your years."

"How old is a 47 year-old detective supposed to look these days?"

"You that old? Crap, where did the years go?"

"I don't know, Lester, but it ain't no fun."

"I suppose I should say thanks to you and that little librarian you've been screwing. You saved me some shoe leather and the tax payers some money."

"Yeah, sure, Lieutenant. Be seeing you..."

Lester Keith let me off at my car and I decided to drive by Maggie's place on the way home. The hallway was quiet as I made my way to her door. I knocked. "Who is it?" her pert little voice asked.

"An old friend come by to check up on you," I kidded her.

She opened the door, grabbed my hand and pulled me in. "Cable! Why didn't you call?"

"Oh, me and Lt. Keith just finished up some business downtown, so I drove here thinking I might catch you with a another guy."

She snickered. "Yep, that's about as likely as finding snow on top of my stove. Would you like a drink? I bought some of your favorite honeyed whiskey and I can boil some water."

"Yeah, that'd be swell," I answered her.

I sat on the edge of Maggie's Murphy bed. Soon she brought me my drink. "How did she look—dead, I mean?"

"Oh, dead...how else should she look?"

"Was she still pretty?"

"Yeah—just real pale."

"I've never seen a dead person before—except in a book."

"They look about the same, I guess...just the life's gone out of them."

Maggie had a cup of hot tea in her hand. "Now that it's over, I suppose you won't want to see me much anymore—isn't that what you do, Cable—attach your lovers to your cases and when it's over, so is your newest lover?"

"I guess something like that." I reached gently for her wrist. "Look, Maggie, I'm not for you. I'd only end up making you miserable. One of us is enough."

Her lips trembled as she held some tears back. "Oh? Sure...I guess you're right, Cable. That's the way it ought to be, huh? And that's the way I ought to be, too—rough, tough, just ol' 'walk-away Annie' here."

"I didn't mean it to sound cold, Maggie."

"Have you ever loved, Cable?"

I swallowed the rest of my hot booze down and looked over at a dresser where I could see us in the mirror. "You tell me...do you see us in your future? An old alcoholic gumshoe and a cute little librarian?"

"If you want it to be, Cable," she whimpered under her breath.

"Then for your sake, I don't want it to be." I got up from the edge of the bed and she stood with me. I wrapped my arms around her and kissed her gently on the lips. "This is best, kid, believe me. You're swell all the way 'round and don't let anybody ever tell you you're not."

"I asked you not to call me 'kid', mister. I'm a grown woman who was your lover until a few minutes ago, remember? I'll—I'll miss that, you know...even if you don't. I guess you were my first real love affair, huh?"

"Yeah, maybe...take it easy, Maggie...life is just beginning for you. Hell, just dress up a little, put a little makeup on and you'll have guys flocking around you, wanting to read your very own private book behind closed doors."

"Oh, sure...as if that's what I want. I'm not like you, Cable. I can't sleep around like you do. Sex has to have meaning, feeling, love behind it—like I feel for you, even if you don't. And besides, where will I find a suitable man in a library? You spoiled me— now I look for passion, excitement, adventure— most people who go to libraries are boring, including me until I met you."

"I don't know what else to say, Maggie. It's kinda like a movie. This is the part where I came in. I don't wanna see the same movie twice."

"You seemed to like me in bed more than once."

"That's different—I like you, we were on a case together, sort of—and I have to admit making love to you was wonderful. But I'll be dead soon—and you won't."

"Why do you always talk like that? We do control our own destinies, you know, at least to some extent. Even Shakespeare said it's not in the stars that hold our destinies, but within ourselves. Buddha said, *'No one saves us but ourselves. No one can and no one may. We ourselves must walk the path."*

"Then let's just say, our paths are different, Maggie. I'm sorry. You don't think it hurts me to leave things like this?"

"I don't know, does it? I'm sure hurting just about now!" she cried.

"Yeah, I'm sure it hurts—"

"—if you ever get lost, Cable, knock three times on my door and I'll help you find yourself again. Everyone gets lost, you know...even you..."

"Yeah, I guess you're right...thanks, Maggie." I said no more. I let  go and left her standing there by her bed, tears rolling down her cheeks, like a wet duck with nowhere to fly in the rain. I guess I loved Maggie Loggins in a way I can't quite explain to myself. But life is more often that way, than being able to solve all the puzzles that are presented us in a given lifetime.

## Wet Streets and Warm Music

That night I walked the streets of Hollywood. The sky hung low and dark and it sprinkled a warm rain from the south. I felt like an invisible force moving in a trench coat and fedora, a semi-conscious force that had forgotten most of what it once remembered. A sweet music filtered through my head, that old saxophone playing a familiar theme of years gone by, of lovely faces looking up at me from soft pillows, sensual memories of passionate nights and beautiful women, great music being sung at midnight in a club somewhere while men and women smoked and drank their lives away because the reality outside was too hard to bear.

I walked all the way to the *Neon Flamingo* like the rain had floated me on silent wings. Few people were about and the sounds of the traffic swished by like dark funeral coaches on their way to Perdition. That was a state of final spiritual ruin, the loss of the soul—the pointless emptiness most humans end up in. Death doesn't leave a forwarding address. And maybe they're not aware. Depression gnaws away at you like a dog on a bone, and bones don't have nerves, so you don't feel it when they reach the marrow and you don't exist anymore.

Maybe that's why I smiled when I walked into the nightclub, still hearing the sounds of Irving Berlin, Cole Porter, George and Ira Gershwin, Jerome Kern and a lineup of great composer/lyricists who knew how to capture a mood. But the club was half-full and people sat in darkened corners sipping their drinks and smoking cigarettes. If they had a partner, the idle chit-chat persisted throughout the singer's song. But the people who were alone, like me, were most likely to listen intently to the song being sung. After all, that lovely young woman up there was our spokesperson, she represented our moods and the idea of complete romantic love—and loss. But at least we had loved, she said—at least we had thrown ourselves into the middle of that marvelous abandon and lost ourselves in that mutual exchange of ideal rapture. And who knows, maybe those two people had met before in a previous lifetime? Now the romance was too hot to handle and it burned out, for another experience was yet to be dealt the hapless couple. But while the wick burned it was magic and the passion would never end, but flow like a happiness only dreamed of. The pretty young blonde in a white sparkling outfit sang the Rodgers and Hart 1937 hit song *Where or When*. *"It seems we stood and talked like this before, we looked at each other in the same way then, but I can't remember where...or when...some things that happen for the first time, seem to be happening again..."* so the lyrics went. Whether they had a date or not, anxious young men in the audience wanted to buy the whole package, just like me in the old days. They wanted the young babe up there along with some magic nights in white satin and memories that would never die.

But life is seldom like that. Too many people believe that movie scripts are the way life is. But in truth the brain is imperfect. Memories fade and so we tend to relive what we didn't even know we'd already lived. They say when you die and come back it's like that. You don't remember having been before for the most part, maybe bits and pieces. But every once in a while people do recall having met before and that déjà vu haunts them or they do reconnect and fulfill something left undone the time before.

For whatever reason, I couldn't stay long. So I walked back in the drizzle toward Franklin. I was thinking of Sonata McCambridge and suddenly I wanted to hold her in my arms and feel the kiss of a female *Sens Parafactor* once again. I could feel it in my gut they were gonna kill her. I think it was because we were at least half of the same species and we could tell things like that. I hoped she would sense it, too, and get herself out of the way of the dark and present danger I felt she was in. Why did she become one of "those" undercover people who must spend their lives in the shadows and perhaps no one will ever know who they are—or were? I wonder about all of them. The Sens Parafactors were benevolent beings. Why should they take the brunt of a twisted, sick element of humanity—and *non-humanity*—such as the reptilians and other evil bastards who'd snaked their way into the governments of the world? I knew they followed me. I also knew Cronus-Gor and his malevolent society and the *Oculus Pyramis Mandatum* haunted the midnight streets of this town. The illusion of streetlights and safe little neighborhoods with Christmas lights and churches singing *Silent Night* that "all is calm, all is well" made me laugh because I knew what I knew and had seen what I'd seen. I knew how thin that skin was. I hoped Sonata would get herself free and clear of the menace that now threatened her. I privately hoped she'd come running to me for protection and I could truly help her. Maybe I loved her. I don't know. Love's funny that way.

I started to open the street-level front door to my building, then I heard a voice behind me. "Sir, you got a quarter on you?" a gentle male voice spoke.

I turned to see a silver-haired man with twinkling blue eyes and an unshaven face. "Yeah, sure, " I said as I dug into my pocket. I had an extra buck, so I gave it to him. "Here..."

He looked at the paper dollar. "I don't mean to seem ungrateful, sir, but the quarter would have more value than the paper."

He handed it back to me and I dug again. This time I found a fifty-cent piece. "Maybe this'll do?" He smiled and accepted it. He was shivering. "You...you, uh, wanna come in outta the rain for a while?"

"You would do that for me? Bless you..."

He followed me up the stairs and I unlocked my office door. He said nothing about my living in these quarters as he looked around. I had an old coal oil heater in the corner. I lit it. Soon we stood around it to dry off. "All of this is so old-fashioned, you know."

"All of what?" I asked.

"Using petroleum, the blood of the earth, to run the outside world. All the energy the human race will ever need is in the air, contained within the sun's illumination."

"Oh, yeah? Says who?" I asked, smoothing the back of my damp trousers.

"Many men had perfected it in the 19th century—but the price of coal and the petroleum industries were owned by the rich and the automobile and likewise machinery would be coal-tar driven. But it is destructive to the environment and very backward in thought."

"I see," I said, seeing this guy actually made sense. "What's your name, buddy?"

"No names, sir. I'm just a visitor and do so appreciate your kindness on this dark and wet night."

"You're welcome. Okay, so I'm Cable Denning, I'm a private investigator and I've more or less bumped into people like you—I mean, people who have had hair-brained ideas that actually worked and then they were either bought out by the oil industry or everything disappeared, including the inventors. Are you one of those?"

"Could be, sir, I suppose...but no." Then a strange thing happened. He took a golden crystal out of his pocket and held it between his forefinger and thumb. "You have been weakened by the world, soul traveler. If you would take your left hand and do as I do on the other side of this stone, it can help restore you. You will also lose your desire to partake of tobacco and alcohol. You have something yet to do in this world, you realize."

I was surprised and delighted at the same time. It was no accident that this old man had followed me to my office. Without another word I took the crystal between the thumb and forefinger of my left hand.

Immediately something began to buzz through my body and I felt all of it was lighting up as the amazing golden crystal took on a life of its own. The whole crystal began to glow a glorious golden light and it entered me like a healing balm! "Wha—!" I exclaimed as my body began vibrating.

After about five minutes the golden light subsided, but my body continued to spasm. I fell onto my knees. "Your mind and heart will be clearer as well, sir. In fact in three days' time, you'll lose much of your past memory. It is memory that burdens us, you know."

"Thank—thank you," I ventured meekly. I made my legs lift me back up.

"You are welcome, sir—yours has not been an easy earth life. But you will finish as you were destined to do." He placed the golden crystal back into his pocket. "Now...I must take my leave, sir. Thank you for the coin—I have always liked the fifty-cent silver coin—it represents freedom walking toward the sunlight. One day she may reach it."

"Thanks again, Mr.—Mr.—"

"—Uh-uh, no name for me, sir. Just know I have visited you and gave you a little assistance along your way. Good-bye now." He turned and opened my office door and vanished down the stairway to the street below. Suddenly I felt fifty pounds lighter and my attitude was buoyant. I didn't even take my hat or trench coat off. It was late but I was compelled by some force to go do something. I ran downstairs and hopped into my little Dodge coupe and drove toward Edgemont Manor Apartments.

I got to her door and knocked three times. There in her simple little nightgown stood Maggie Loggins. "Cable!" she cried out. "You remembered—three knocks." Then she took a big breath and became sexy like a put-on actress. "Is it me you're looking for, big boy?" she taunted. But she knew. She saw in my eyes the eagerness, the new life that had taken me over, my desire for her and the closeness and companionship we shared. She walked over to the bed, took off her glasses, turned off the light and slipped her pretty white nightgown off. She lit a small candle by the bedside. "Did you—did you really come to—to be with me?" she asked in a hesitant, innocent tone.

"Yeah, Maggie Loggins, I came for you. We've—we've got some unfinished business to do."

She smiled in the darkness. "Oh? Does that include doing what I just did and what I think it might lead to?"

"You bet, lady, and that's only the first verse!" I came over to her and took her into my arms and kissed her strong so she'd know I was gonna be with her all night long—and maybe even part of tomorrow.

"You—you look so young, Cable—as if years had been shed from your face since yesterday. Did something wonderful happen?"

"Oh, yeah, something wonderful happened, Maggie. I feel twenty years younger and lighter."

"Well, you look it, lover boy. Dare I ask? Maybe now you'll remember me more often, huh?" She came up to me and pressed her young body against mine. "Was it me by any chance—I mean, thinking of me, desiring me? What are the chances?"

"Yeah, babe, it was you," I lied. "Oh, I think I'll remember you for at least a few days," I half-kidded, knowing that if the old man was right, I'd forget Maggie Loggins in time.

"Oh, you!" She took my hand and soon we lay on our backs in bed, holding hands. "Cable...? Before we make love, will you do one thing for me?"

"Yeah, sure, what?"

"Tell me you might love me?"

"Okay...I might love you, Maggie Loggins..."

"Damn, Cable Denning, you're so frustrating!"

All of a sudden a shock went through my body and I knew Sonata McCambridge was gone from this world. I knew she was dead. They'd gotten to her. I shuddered inside, but I knew life goes on for each of us the way it's supposed to until that guy with the scythe comes by to mow down a new crop of souls. One of these days I'd be one of 'em. But Sonata was so young, so beautiful, so intelligent—and a *Sens Parafactor.* "Frustrating? I guess I *can* be at that, can't I? Sorry, kid."

Her eyes reprimanded me, but she just said..."Can we make love and go to sleep?"

"Why?"

"Because I've gotta work tomorrow."

"Oh..." I heard that melancholy sax float through my head like a breath of sexy warm air. Yeah, tomorrow is already today, isn't it?

After Maggie and I made love I lay awake in the darkness, listening to her gentle breathing. I was thinking about Maria Voldt and one of my favorite poems of hers that she wrote to me, what seems like many years ago:

> *"All of life, all of breathing, all of loving*
> *It is but a poem, a little song sung in the dell*
> *And if you enter there, my love, I will be waiting...*
> *For we have begun and must end together."*

I hoped that were true. I would love to end my days in the arms of a gentle, rebel soul whose wisdom would cast a light on my pathway all the days of my life. Good night, sweet Maria! Then I thought about the magic phonograph Gossman had somehow willed to me. What could have been in his mind? What made me so exceptional that I should be so honored? What was the meaning of the fantastic journey I'd taken? What did I hear that most did not? I turned over and went to sleep, listening to Maggie's little alarm clock ticking away our lifetimes.

## *The End*

## Acknowledgements

## Cover Images:
Scarlett: ©Can Stock Photo/Vegas
Evelyn Nesbitt: ©Can Stock Photo/Nejron

## Original Cover Designs: Frances Walker-Moss

## Editing and Research Consultant:
Frances Walker-Moss